SAINT PETER'S

SOLDIERS

A James Acton Thriller

By J. Robert Kennedy

James Acton Thrillers

The Protocol
Brass Monkey
Broken Dove
The Templar's Relic
Flags of Sin
The Arab Fall
The Circle of Eight

The Venice Code
Pompeii's Ghosts
Amazon Burning
The Riddle
Blood Relics
Sins of the Titanic
Saint Peter's Soldiers

Special Agent Dylan Kane Thrillers

Rogue Operator
Containment Failure
Cold Warriors
Death to America

Delta Force Unleashed Thrillers

Payback
Infidels
The Lazarus Moment

Detective Shakespeare Mysteries

Depraved Difference
Tick Tock
The Redeemer

Zander Varga, Vampire Detective

The Turned

SAINT PETER'S

SOLDIERS

A James Acton Thriller

J. ROBERT KENNEDY

ISBN-10: 1517361281

ISBN-13: 978-1517361280

First Edition

10 9 8 7 6 5 4 3 2 1

In memory of Syrian archeologist Khaled al-Asaad, beheaded while protecting the archeological sites and antiquities to which he had dedicated his entire life.

SAINT PETER'S

SOLDIERS

A James Acton Thriller

"In the sweat of thy face shalt thou eat bread, till thou return unto the ground; for out of it wast thou taken: for dust thou art, and unto dust shalt thou return."

King James Version, Genesis 3:19

PREFACE

On April 11th, 2015, in the scientific journal Protein and Cell, a paper was published by Chinese scientists entitled "CRISPR/Cas9-Mediated Gene Editing in Human Tripronuclear Zygotes". The title is meaningless to most, but for those who understood its contents, it sent a chill through the entire community.

For the Chinese had broken the germ line, succeeding in manipulating DNA to change the human genome. This is not the act of fixing a genetic defect; this is changing what it means to be human.

Science fiction has become science fact.

There is a very good reason this research is illegal in most of the civilized world.

And this book describes one of those terrifying reasons.

Sapienza University, Rome, Italy
Present Day

"You realize how much this is worth? It's priceless!"

Inspector General Mario Giasson of the Corps of Gendarmerie of Vatican City State looked from Father Rinaldi to the archeologist the exclamation had been directed to. Professor James Acton stood back, his arms crossed, finger tapping on his elbow as he eagerly awaited his chance to peer through the microscope. His wife, Professor Laura Palmer, had just announced the unbelievable. The red chalk drawing, a self-portrait of Leonardo da Vinci himself, shown on a large screen in Sapienza University's art restoration department, was genuine.

Yet it couldn't be.

Or at least it shouldn't be.

What was thought to be the real drawing had been on display since 1998 at the Royal Library in Turin, Italy. Yet clearly there was more to the story than he and the world had been made aware.

Professor Acton glanced over at Father Rinaldi, who had begun pacing, continuing to mutter. "If this falls into the wrong hands, it could be worth millions, perhaps tens of millions. Especially if someone believes the legend."

Giasson turned toward Father Rinaldi. "What legend?"

"That if one stares into the eyes of the portrait, one is imbued with great power."

Giasson dismissed the comment with a flick of his wrist. "Ridiculous."

Their friend and Interpol Agent, Hugh Reading, snorted. "I find it impossible to accept that people would believe in such nonsense."

Acton stepped up to the scope as his wife finally relinquished her place, taking in the magnified view. Yes, it was shown on a separate monitor for everyone to see, but there was something special about looking through the lenses, manipulating things yourself. Giasson felt himself itching for his own chance.

A real da Vinci! Lost until yesterday!

And four people were already dead because of it.

Shouts on the other side of the door had Acton standing upright as they all spun toward the sound. Gunfire suddenly erupted and Giasson stepped toward the doors as Acton reached out, guiding his wife behind him. Reading moved from his position near the window to stand shoulder to shoulder with Giasson just as the doors burst open.

Giasson breathed a sigh of relief as he recognized the two Italian State Police officers entering the room. There were half a dozen outside, the value of the portrait, should it be genuine, demanding a protection detail. His sigh however turned to a gasp as they raised their weapons at them.

Footsteps clicked on the tile floor of the hallway, Giasson only getting a glimpse of several bodies past the doors, the police blocking most of his view. A man appeared in the doorway, tall, athletic, perhaps mid to late thirties, with blonde hair and striking blue eyes that took in the room, coming to rest on the display showing the portrait.

He pointed at the genuine article and snapped his fingers, the two officers rushing toward the table it was sitting on.

Giasson stepped in their way, holding out his arms. "This is the property of the people of Italy."

The blonde man stared at him for a moment, a slight smile suggested at the corners of his mouth before he pulled a weapon from a shoulder holster and fired, Giasson spinning away, crumpling to the floor with a cry.

"You are mistaken. It is the property of the Führer."

3

Casa del Conte Verde, Rivoli, Italy
July 4ᵗʰ, 1941

"But the Nazi's are on their way!"

Vincenzo Donati frowned at his young apprentice's outburst. He continued to stare through his magnifying glass at the rare 45 centesimi Lombardy stamp from 1850, a rare find if there ever was one. He never tired of gazing at it. It was a piece of history, and history was his business.

And with the war, *protecting* history was now his primary business.

The Nazi's were looting galleries across Europe, the only thing protecting his the fact Italy had aligned itself with Hitler and his armies. Though how long that would last was anyone's guess. Hitler had just broken his agreement with the Soviet Union. Could Italy be that far behind?

Plans were already underway for protecting collections across the country, yet it was a rumor that had reached his ears only this week that had him concerned. A colleague in Rome had told him of a special group in the SS, the Schutzstaffel or "protection squadron", that was searching the globe for religious artifacts. Anything that had ever had something magical or mystical attributed to it.

And his town now housed such a relic.

A self-portrait of Leonardo da Vinci in red chalk.

The legend was completely unfounded, he himself having tried to duplicate the claims unsuccessfully. But it was no matter. Once legend, rumor was nearly impossible to dispel.

The drawing had been stored at the Royal Library in Turin, its curator contacting him two days ago after hearing the same rumor of the SS group, and a plan had been set in motion, the drawing moved here, to his relatively insignificant institution, in the hopes the Nazis would pass them by.

"Sir!"

Donati sighed, putting down his magnifying glass and looking up at young Nicola. "I am fully aware of what is happening. And plans are already underway to protect the portrait."

Nicola approached Donati's desk and dropped into a rickety chair older than him. "But shouldn't we move it now, tonight? Your contact said they could be here tomorrow morning! If that's true, we have no time to waste."

"And we aren't wasting any—"

"But you're staring at stamps!" He leapt back to his feet, pacing the small room, the oil lamps casting dancing shadows on the stone walls, the fire in the corner barely taking the chill out of the cool night.

"I find it calms me and allows me to think clearly. You might try something similar."

Nicola spun, about to say something, then stopped. He took a deep breath and returned to his chair. "Sir, with all due respect, if there is even a remote chance that the legend is true surrounding the portrait, it mustn't fall into Hitler's hands. If it does, his armies could become unstoppable."

"Some Italians might think that a good thing."

Nicola's jaw dropped as he stared at the older man in shock. Then he smiled. "You're toying with me."

Donati smiled, leaning back in his chair. "It is sometimes too easy."

Nicola pinched the bridge of his nose, closing his eyes. "I'm tired."

"Then get your rest and be here at sunrise tomorrow morning. And bring your moped."

"Why?"

"Because tomorrow morning the portrait will forever be placed out of Hitler's reach. By you."

Casa del Conte Verde, Rivoli, Italy
July 5th, 1941

Nicola leaned his moped against the side of the museum, stepping out of the alleyway and walking toward the front entrance. The streets were still mostly empty, the roosters trumpeting their wakeup call only minutes ago. He knocked three times and within moments he heard footsteps then the door unlocking. It creaked open and Donati smiled at him.

"Come in, quickly!" hissed Donati, stepping aside and ushering him across the threshold. The door was immediately closed and bolted, the normal pleasantries ignored as Donati rushed toward the backroom. He pointed to a worktable, a small handcrafted wooden crate sitting on it, it the proper size to hold the small framed portrait. "The portrait is ready to go."

"How the hell am I supposed to get that out of here without anyone noticing?"

"Language!"

Nicola flushed. "I'm sorry, I didn't mean any disrespect."

"You disrespected the Lord, not me. Remember it at confession."

Nicola's head dropped to his chest. "I will. Sorry."

Donati stopped what he was doing and stepped over, squeezing the young man's shoulder. "I forgive you, as will He." He let go and glanced at his watch. "But plans have changed. My colleague in Rome is sending someone to retrieve the portrait. He should be here any moment."

Nicola frowned, a feeling of betrayal filling his stomach and gripping his chest. "But I thought *I* was going to take it?"

Donati shook his head. "No, it's too risky. Apparently these people have experience. They'll take it—"

A knock at the front door had Nicola's heart leaping into his throat, Donati's head darting toward the sound.

"Who could that be?" asked Nicola as his heart raced in his chest.

Donati looked at his watch. "It's them. Right on time."

Donati rushed toward the entrance, Nicola following. Donati peered through the small Judas hole then unlocked the door, pulling it open. A man stepped inside and the door was immediately closed.

"A-are you the one I'm expecting?"

Donati sounded terrified.

The man nodded.

"P-please pr-prove it."

The man undid the top several buttons of his shirt, revealing an intricate tattoo of a cross, two crossed keys intertwined with it.

"Th-thank you." Donati rushed to the back of the room and the man followed, Nicola letting them both pass, eyeballing the man, the new arrival doing the same.

He didn't trust him.

Whoever he was.

Donati pointed at the table. "This is it."

The man nodded. "That shouldn't be a problem." He pulled a piece of paper out of his pocket and handed it to Donati. "Should there be any questions, any problems, this is how to reach us. Memorize it then destroy it."

Donati's head jerked nervously up and down as he read the paper, his lips moving repeatedly.

Nicola assessed the man with a critical eye. He seemed to be in his late twenties or early thirties, an impressive moustache and slightly longish hair, his skin dark and healthy. If it weren't for the hair, he'd look smart and not out of place wearing a military uniform.

7

As would I. What makes him any more qualified than me to protect the portrait?

"How are you going to get that out of here without anyone noticing?"

The man glanced over at him, his eyes assessing him then appearing to dismiss what they saw. "That is none of your concern." He turned back to Donati. "Any special instructions?"

"No, but y-you said you had experience in these things."

"We do."

"Then do whatever it is you would normally do."

The man nodded.

"Wouldn't it be easier to just take it out of the frame and roll it up?"

Donati gasped at Nicola's suggestion. "Are you insane? Have I taught you nothing? It must be protected!"

"What's more important, it getting wrinkled or Hitler ruling the world?"

"I'm not willing to allow an extremely rare portrait by one of the greatest masters the world has ever known to be destroyed because of a ridiculous legend."

"It's a legend you obviously believe in, otherwise why are we doing this?"

Donati glared at him then his expression softened. "You're right, my son, you're right. When I think of what could be, I tremble with fear. And if there is something about this portrait that is special, then it must be kept out of the hands of that man. My belief is that if *he* believes, then he might think himself invincible and commit even more horrors upon God's creation. You are right, my boy. Hitler is evil, a scourge upon this Earth that if there is even the slightest chance that this portrait might further his goals, it must be hidden, which is why we are doing what we are doing today." He paused, stepping closer and placing a hand on Nicola's arm. "But I am still not willing to see it damaged, or worse, destroyed. You understand that, don't you?"

Nicola nodded, not entirely convinced the risk of it being found outweighed the risk of it being damaged.

Tires squealed on the cobblestone outside and Nicola rushed for the front, pushing aside the curtain slightly. He nearly pissed his pants. A German car had just pulled up, four men climbing out, one clearly SS, the uniform unmistakable.

God help us!

He sprinted to the backroom and past the tattooed man. "They're here!" He hissed.

"Who?" asked Donati, the question rendered redundant as the pounding on the front door began.

"The Nazis!"

Nicola grabbed the crate and tore off the top, tipping the drawing out and onto the worktable. He snapped the frame at the corner, yanking the four sides off.

"What are you doing?" cried Donati as he rushed toward him, the distraction from the shouts and heavy pounding at the door momentarily forgotten.

Nicola yanked the portrait off the mat, quickly rolling it up, much to Donati's horror, his eyes widening, his jaw dropping.

"Somebody has to save you from yourself!"

He snatched the piece of paper the tattooed man had given Donati out of his hand then bolted for the rear entrance and yanked open the door, stepping out into the morning light. He peered around the corner, finding it clear, his moped only feet away. Stuffing the portrait inside his jacket, he pulled his moped away from the wall and began to walk it out of the alleyway as casually as he could, turning away from the Germans.

He started the moped and climbed on.

Someone shouted.

He gunned the engine as bullets tore into the façade of Innocenti's bakery. He squeezed his brake and leaned hard, his rear tire skidding out on the damp cobblestone, the morning sun not yet having burned off the overnight moisture. Regaining his balance, he twisted the throttle, the bike leaping forward as the Germans quickly closed the gap. Racing through the market, the shopkeepers just starting to set up their stands leapt back, some shaking their fists at him then diving for cover as the Germans opened fire.

I have to get off the roads or someone is going to be killed.

It never occurred to him that that someone might be him. He was running on adrenaline now, the portrait, tucked into his zipped-up jacket seeming impossibly heavy. It was all in his head, the portrait barely a foot square, yet it was the weight of responsibility he was now painfully aware of. The Nazi's clearly wanted this drawing and didn't care who died to get it. That meant their experts believed the legend could be true, and wanted it for Hitler himself.

I'll destroy it before I let them have it.

He could almost hear Donati's voice screaming in his head at the very notion. It was a priceless, irreplaceable piece of history. To destroy it was unthinkable. But history would be meaningless if the world was lost to the likes of Adolf Hitler. Though his country was an ally in the war, he had never supported the fascists. Mussolini was a thug that ruled through fear and lies. Nicola was convinced the masses followed him because they were brainwashed after years of propaganda.

At least the trains always run on time.

Though that was bullshit propaganda too. They didn't actually run on time. His dad told him they were better than before, but only due to work done before Mussolini came to power.

And if Mussolini's claim to fame was a lie, how much more was?

Yet you didn't dare question.

Otherwise the OVRA secret police might show up on your doorstep one day and you'd never be seen again.

He careened into a tight alleyway, kicking out with his foot and pushing off the wall as his rear tire fishtailed its way deeper into the long passage. A quick glance over his shoulder had him breathing a sigh of relief.

The Germans were stopped at the end, unable to fit their car in the narrow gap.

He eased off the throttle slightly, finally having a moment to think.

Where am I going?

He couldn't stay in town; the Germans would have it sealed off within minutes with the help of the local authorities. He couldn't go to his house, he'd be putting his parents at risk.

Leo!

Yes, he'd go to his cousin's. He had a farm outside of the city and he'd know what to do. He was also anti-Mussolini, despising the man, especially after he had aligned the country with Nazi Germany.

He'll know what to do.

He emerged from the alley, crossing the road and cutting through another gap between the houses, thanking God for giving man the intellect to design the moped now saving his life.

In the distance, he heard the whistle of the morning train and chuckled.

It's on time today.

He slowed as he emerged from the alley, turning right and continuing down the hill that the town was built upon, heading toward the valley where his cousin's farm lay. The streets were filling now, the day underway, and his hammering heart was finally settling down. He ventured a wave at the butcher's daughter, Maria. She waved back with a smile, his hand easing off the throttle for a moment as he forgot what he was doing.

Tires screeching behind him smacked his libido back down and he gunned the engine, not bothering to look back as the gunfire confirmed who it was. He heard a girl scream and his heart leapt into his throat. He stole a glance and felt bile fill his mouth as he spotted Maria lying on the ground, her father rushing from the shop, crying out in horror.

You killed her.

His eyes filled with tears, the street ahead suddenly a blur. He wiped them clear with the back of his hands, the train whistle louder now. He could see the tracks ahead where they crossed the road he was on, heading toward the station in the center of town. Looking to his right as he rapidly approached them, he spotted the trail of steam puffing from the engine and made a decision.

A decision that would save him, or doom him.

He hit his brakes, skidding to a near halt then turned, gunning it down the railroad tracks, this part filled with cobblestones, keeping the ride relatively smooth, as he raced toward the bridge. He heard the Germans' brakes behind him as he cleared the edge of the town, his tires bouncing on the railroad ties, every bone in his body nearly jarred loose from the pounding. He could see the train coming around the bend, the whistle announcing its arrival, loud.

He leaned forward, urging his moped ahead as the engine raced toward him. Brakes squealed, the engineer apparently spotting him. Gunfire from behind him was barely heard over the screeching metal on metal, but something bit him hard in the arm and he cried out, nearly losing control of the bike as he grabbed for his shoulder. Both hands back on the bars, he twisted the throttle, the bike leaping forward, a game of chicken underway he had to win, his opponent having no way to turn. He was almost across, the massive black of the engine looming large in front of him, though not yet at the bridge.

I'm not going to make it!

He said a silent prayer as he glanced back, the Germans now stopped at the other end of the bridge, apparently content to let him die at the hands of Mussolini's efficient rail system, there now nowhere for him to go.

He was almost there, only feet left, the train just coming onto the bridge. He steered to the right slightly, pulling up on the handlebars to lift his front wheel off the ties and cleared the rail, racing on the edge of the ties, the river below appearing more vicious than he remembered.

The train was upon him.

And he steered hard to the side.

Sailing through the air, he hit the ground beside the track, the wind from the train whipping around him, its brakes still screaming in protest, nearly knocking him off the bike. He locked up his brakes, coming to a halt as he looked back and smiled.

At the Germans trapped on the other side as the train slowly came to a halt, blocking them from crossing.

He gave them a wave that was returned by a shaking first, then accelerated down the hill toward the road that would carry him to his cousin's farm.

Thanking God for answering his prayer.

Entrance to St. Peter's Square, Rome, Italy
Present Day
One day before the theft

Diego resisted the urge to check his watch. It would merely show it was one minute later than the last time he had looked. He scanned the crowds from his vantage point, a bench along the outer wall of Vatican City. The entrance to St. Peter's Square was to his right and hundreds if not thousands of tourists were pouring in and out constantly. He had been there countless times himself, of course, his order literally worshipping at the altar of the man himself.

St. Peter.

The founder of the Church, the man Jesus himself had tasked to continue his ministry after he was gone.

And I say also unto thee, That thou art Peter, and upon this rock I will build my church; and the gates of hell shall not prevail against it.

St. Peter had been a faithful disciple of the Lord, spreading his teachings until his death at the hands of the Romans, and in the end he had insisted he be crucified upside down, feeling himself unworthy to be put to death on an upright cross as the Lord had.

And from that moment forward, his symbol was the inverted cross.

It annoyed Diego to no end that ignorance among today's youth meant the holy symbol had been coopted by idiots who thought it was satanic, some sort of symbol representing evil, anti-church activists tattooing it on their flesh as a monument to their obliviousness. He felt like grabbing every one of them and smacking them up the side of their head and giving them a history lesson.

He sighed, absentmindedly rubbing the tattoo on his chest. It was impressive, an ornate inverted cross, paired with the keys to Heaven, given to him upon his admission into the Keepers of the One Truth. He bore it proudly, though it did at times limit him in today's liberal society. He could never take his shirt off in public, though that merely forced him to live modestly. Casual relations with a woman were precluded, the need to explain the tattoo to just any carnal desire not acceptable.

It forced him to lead a better life.

A moral life.

He had married eventually, explaining the tattoo to his wife as a youthful indiscretion. Only the first of many lies he had told her, she unable to know what he did with his life. She thought he had a government job that he couldn't talk about, with a workplace she wasn't allowed to know the location of.

And she was fine with that.

She loved him.

She trusted him.

And it tore him apart at first, until he realized that all of the men in the Keepers of the One Truth had the same problem and had learned to live with it, as had his own father. Only the sons of Keepers were invited to join, and in modern times, many refused, too often turning their back on the Church in exchange for instant gratification, instead of a life of service dedicated to protecting the Church in exchange for an eternity in Heaven.

He had embraced the group wholeheartedly, recognizing the evils of modern life that threatened to overwhelm those around him, and instead devoted himself to a life of servitude.

And lies to his loved ones.

It was a necessary evil that helped keep true evil at bay.

For the world was filled with evil, filled with enemies of the Church. It always had been, and it always would be.

And St. Peter had foreseen this.

And created an army.

The Keepers of the One Truth.

Their mission was to protect the Church from its enemies. All enemies. Of this earth and not. The evils of man were easy enough to protect against. They were predictable. It was those of Satan himself that were the challenge.

Thus the establishment of The Vault.

The Vault was a secret archive located under the grounds of the Vatican, its existence known to very few outside of the Keepers. Over two millennia the leaders of the Church had hidden away anything that challenged or threatened the faith, eventually establishing the Vault to secure these abominations so they could never be unleashed upon mankind.

Yet their mandate went beyond ensuring the integrity of the Vault and ensuring the current Pope performed his duty as handed down to him by St. Peter himself, it extended to protecting the Church and the Christian faith in general from outside threats, not the least of which had been the Nazis.

One of the few loose ends of that era tied up by the man he was meeting today.

He checked his watch.

Where is he?

In 1941, the Keepers had received word that the Nazis were attempting to acquire religious artifacts from around the world. And the Keepers had acted. They had immediately made contact with anyone who possessed something the Nazis may be interested in, and offered to take it into safekeeping. Few accepted the offer, the Keepers mere strangers, though once the threat became real, contact began to be made, including a small museum in the town of Rivoli.

With regard to a self-portrait of Leonardo da Vinci, drawn in red chalk.

He had never seen it beyond the photos. It had been preserved in one of the Keeper's archives, and once the world had been deemed safe again, it had been returned.

News of the return had spread like wildfire, the compelling story of how it had been returned anonymously after having been secreted away from the Nazis, quickly gaining attention.

He had been there the night it was returned, the very man he was waiting for the one who had placed it on the doorstep of the modest museum. Diego had been but an apprentice then, Saverio his master, but now he was a full-fledged Keeper, tasked with duties he could only have dreamed of in 1998 when the portrait had been returned.

And when he had received the call to meet Saverio here, at this hour, his heart had raced in anticipation and curiosity.

As it did now at the sight of the older man making his way toward him, a rather large satchel slung over his shoulder. Diego was about to rise when Saverio held out a hand, stopping him. He dropped onto the bench beside him and shook his hand. "How are you, my boy? It has been a long time."

"Over fifteen years." The years hadn't been kind to Saverio. He looked older than he should. In fact, he appeared unwell.

Saverio seemed to notice the concern. "Your eyes do not deceive you, my young friend. I am dying."

Diego felt his chest tighten as his eyes widened and his jaw dropped. "How? Why? I mean—" He stopped himself, casting his eyes at the ground. "I'm sorry."

Saverio patted Diego's shoulder. "I appreciate your concern, young one. It is cancer and I have little time left, which means I need to settle my affairs." He patted the large leather satchel beside him. "You remember the last time we met?"

"Of course."

"We returned a portrait to a small museum in Rivoli."

"Of course, I remember it as if it were yesterday."

"What if I told you it was all a lie?"

What Saverio told him next shocked him to his very core. Everything he remembered of that night, the pride he had felt in reading the news reports and knowing his small part, were shattered in the several minutes it took to impart the truth.

"But why?"

"It was necessary. After the war, we knew there would be many Nazis left remaining and it wouldn't be safe to return any of the artifacts put into our safekeeping. With the new millennium approaching, it was decided that enough time had passed that any Nazis still alive would be too old to be of any threat, and with the fascist dream dead, little chance they might actually bother trying anything. After all, the artifacts were hidden away because of rumors surrounding them." He flicked his wrist. "Like our portrait."

"You mean the legend that if you stared into da Vinci's eyes—"

"You'd get great power. Exactly. Nonsense, of course, but these were valuable artifacts that we didn't want to see stolen or destroyed due to dogma. But by the end of the millennium, with over fifty years past, it was decided it was time to start returning these items. It was a decision I didn't agree with."

"Why?"

"Because I had been hearing rumors."

"What rumors?"

"That the Nazis were still alive and well. I couldn't prove it, so I was forced to go along with the decision." He smiled. "But if you knew me like your father did, you would know I don't always play well with others."

Diego turned away slightly, not sure what to say.

Saverio patted the satchel. "Inside is the legacy of my decision. I hand it down to you, to do with as you see fit. Should you not share my concerns, then you know what you must do, but equally, if do you, then you must fulfill your duty as a Keeper." He turned slightly on the bench, facing Diego. "What I ask of you is a duty that cannot be taken lightly. You will be going against the leadership, though they are unaware of what truly happened all those years ago. Their lack of awareness will protect you." He peered into Diego's eyes. "Are you up to the task?"

Diego bit the inside of his cheek, looking from the man he had idolized after their single encounter so many years ago, then at the satchel that contained the shattered truth.

He nodded. "Yes."

Saverio smiled broadly, squeezing his shoulder. "Good boy, good boy! I knew I could count on you. You know I've been following your career since the moment you became an initiate. Your father and I were recruited at the same time, went through our training together. We kept in touch over the years. I was deeply saddened to hear of his passing."

Diego frowned, looking away, not trusting his emotions. His father had been killed several years ago in a car accident. A useless death, a meaningless death. Killed by a teenager who was texting. The only satisfaction he was able to get was from the knowledge the teen had died a horribly agonizing death.

And though he was a man of God, he felt no guilt in taking pleasure in that knowledge.

19

Saverio motioned toward the gates to the Vatican. "I never pass up an opportunity to pray when I am in the area. Would you care to join me? Together we'll say a prayer for your father?"

Diego smiled slightly, nodding. "It would be an honor."

Saverio rose and nodded toward the satchel. "This is yours, now."

Diego lifted the bag, slightly heavier than he was expecting, and slung it over his shoulder. They began to walk toward the gates, slowly, Diego now realizing why the man had been late. The crowds surged around them as the traffic whipped by on Largo del Collonato Street. They continued in silence and had arrived at the gates when the sound of squealing tires and screams behind them had Diego spinning to see what was the matter.

He gasped, a large SUV careening toward them, pedestrians bouncing off the large heavy-duty grill guard bumper, the driver giving no indication of slowing down.

Diego shoved Saverio out of the way, the frail man crying out as he hit the ground, staring back in horror as the SUV slammed into Diego. He could feel his bones break with the impact, but grabbed the grill guard as the vehicle continued forward, trying desperately to hang on while the agony of his crushed chest threatened to sap him of his remaining strength.

He was about to let go, to fall under the wheels, when the vehicle suddenly came to a screeching, immediate halt, sending him sailing through the air. He slammed into the ground, his head smacking hard on the stone, and his world began to fade. Saverio was limping toward him, his arm outstretched, when the doors of the SUV were thrown open and two men leapt out, guns firing. The crowds scattered in panic, Saverio crying out in pain as round after round embedded itself in his back. Diego struggled to stay conscious, to see his mentor's final moments, when he heard heavy boots hammering on the ground behind him, shots erupting from the new arrivals.

His head dropped to the cold stone, his eyes slowly closing as he gripped the satchel over his chest.

And prayed the Vatican Gendarmerie would protect its contents.

South of Turin, Italy
July 5th, 1941

"Keep quiet, there's a road block!"

Nicola's cousin Leo's hissed warning had him holding his breath until he thought better of it. Better to have steady, regular breaths than gasps. He had arrived at his cousin's farm without incident and told him what had happened.

What had happened next had shocked him.

His moped had been immediately taken and put into the root cellar under the barn then piled with hay, his cousin saying little except that they had to move fast. Leo had ordered the kids to prep the horse and wagon while his wife patched up Nicola's arm, the bullet just having grazed him. When she finished, he was left to run after Leo, begging for an explanation for the whirlwind of activity.

Leo had finally stopped for a moment and jabbed a finger in his chest.

"As long as you are here, you are a danger to my family."

Nicola had felt crestfallen. "I-I know. And I'm sorry. But I didn't know what else to do."

Leo took him by the shoulder. "You did the right thing, but we must move quickly." He pointed at the cart. "Get in the back and lift that panel."

Nicola jumped in the back, not sure to what panel Leo might be referring. His eyebrows popped as he spotted several boards in the center that seemed to be separate from the rest. He reached down and pried it up, revealing a small area underneath the floor that could barely fit a man.

"What's this?"

"We use it to smuggle people and supplies."

"We?"

"Not your concern. Just get in and stay quiet. I'm going to get you to a safe place."

Nicola crawled into the cramped space, his arms with barely an inch on either side to move, his head and toes pressed against the ends.

He wished he wasn't so tall.

Then thanked God he wasn't fat when the cover was placed back over him, it so close he was forced to turn his head to the side.

"You okay?"

He nodded then realized Leo couldn't see him. "Yes."

"Okay, watch yourself."

He felt the cart rock as his cousin jumped down, then the sound of hay being loaded into the back. He squeezed his eyes shut and struggled to get a hand up over his mouth and nose as the dust slowly covered him.

He sneezed.

And it wouldn't be the last.

He could hear his cousin urging the horse to slow as they approached the roadblock. They came to a halt and he heard the brake applied as his nose started to itch. He reached up and squeezed the bridge of it, trying to resist the urge, it meaning certain death if they were to be caught.

Though not before agonizing torture.

"Hey, Leo, you're early."

"Yeah, I lost a bet last night so now I have to deliver this load to Angelo. That bastard is too lucky. I think he cheats."

Whoever Leo was talking to roared with laughter. "I learned when we were kids to never play with him. I always lost my lunch to him."

"So what you're saying is I'll never learn."

More laughter. It was clear they knew each other, which was a tremendous relief, though even that wouldn't save them should he sneeze.

This guard or soldier or whatever, might be a friend, but he was probably loyal, so he would follow orders. Nicola considered himself a loyal Italian, though not loyal to the government. As far as he was concerned, they were two distinct things. He'd never betray his country so that harm may come to it, but he also couldn't support a government that would take part in such a brutal war that threatened to consume the world.

His exposure to the Germans had been minimal, their town spared for the most part, but the stories were horrendous, and whenever they had made an appearance, it was never good, people usually hauled away, some never seen again, those that were, never the same.

The Nazi's were murderous barbarians that would sack his country in a heartbeat if they felt there was a need.

Which was when he would truly show his loyalty.

By fighting back.

As probably would this guard just doing his job.

Somebody else spoke up from a distance, but Nicola couldn't hear what had been said.

"I know him, he's harmless."

He could hear footsteps approaching. "Nobody goes through without being searched. Orders of the Regional Commander."

"Okay, okay." The owner of the friendly voice stepped away and Nicola heard the distinctive sounds of pitchfork tines scraping on stone. "Sorry about this, Leo. It'll just take a minute."

The sound of the metal passing through the hay near the rear of the cart had Nicola finally holding his breath, his heart slamming hard, his ears pounding in a panic as the probing neared him. The sound of the pitchfork directly overhead had his bladder letting go slightly, his eyes squeezed tightly along with every other muscle in his body.

"Okay, you're clear. You can go."

24

"Thanks, Thomas, let's get together for a drink this weekend."

"Count on it! You're buying."

Nicola heard the brake release and the reigns flick as they jerked forward. "I might not be able to afford it!"

Laughter from the guard had Nicola breathe a sigh of relief.

Then he sneezed.

"Halt!"

It was the other voice that had his cousin pulling up on the reins.

Another sneeze erupted, this one from Leo. "What?" asked his cousin.

"Oh, sorry. Umm, nothing. Get moving."

The reins flicked again and they were moving, Nicola pinching his nose shut, his other hand clasped over his mouth as he struggled to keep control. As they gained a little speed, he heard his cousin hiss. "That was close!"

"Sorry."

"That almost got us killed, little man, but don't worry. It should be clear sailing now."

South of Turin, Italy
July 6th, 1941

Nicola pushed the plate away as he wiped his mouth with the back of his hand. "Thank you, Mrs. Feraldo. That was fantastic."

"You're welcome, Nicola. You have a big journey ahead of you. We can't have you leaving on an empty stomach."

Nicola grinned as he rose, patting the little ones on the head as they still worked on their breakfasts before heading for school. He had spent the night at Angelo Feraldo's farm, his cousin having delivered him just before noon the day before. The swiftness with which it had been done, and the lack of questions, had him thinking Angelo was not only a gambling buddy, but also part of whatever underground movement his cousin was involved with.

He just prayed his cousin got back home without incident.

The sound of a motorcycle pulling up out front had him grabbing the portrait and heading outside, eager to see what had been arranged. His moped was still at his cousins, though he had a feeling it would be moved in case the area was searched, and with the efficiency he had seen displayed so far, it may have already been done.

He smiled as he caught his first glimpse of the motorcycle that would carry him to Rome. A BMW R6. It was beautiful, at least compared to his simple moped. It was beat up, hardly any of the original paint left, so it wouldn't attract any attention. But it was bigger and more powerful than he was used to, and it would get him to his destination that much more quickly.

Angelo was already examining the motorcycle when he glanced up at Nicola. "All fed?"

"Yes, sir. Thank you, sir."

"Good. She's got a full tank of gas. You remember that address in Bologna I gave you?"

"Yes."

"He'll have gas for you and you can overnight there. That should be enough to get you into Rome."

"Thank you, sir."

"All I ask is that if they catch you, you tell them that you forced us to help you."

"I will. You have nothing to worry about."

Angelo frowned. "I'd agree if it weren't the Nazi's after you. If it was just the locals, I wouldn't care. I grew up with most of them and I know most just think of it as a job. There's a few zealots, but they've mostly moved to the big cities where there's problems. They leave us alone out here." He turned to the man who had delivered the motorcycle. "Which one?"

"Left."

Angelo motioned for Nicola to join him as he took a knee at the rear of the bike. "As we discussed." He unscrewed two bolts on the underside of the left exhaust then swung the outer half away. "They won't check this. At least they never have. We've used it to smuggle documents and other things too many times to count."

"Won't it get hot? Mr. Donati will kill me if anything happens to this," said Nicola, eyeing the opened exhaust as he held the rolled up drawing.

The other man shook his head. "No, the exhaust has been all routed to the right side. It cuts down on your horsepower, but you shouldn't notice it unless you get in a high-speed chase. And if you do, you're screwed anyway."

"I got away from them yesterday."

"That's only because there was one vehicle. Once you get near Rome, you'll have to outrun a radio, and that's not going to happen." The man stabbed the air with a finger. "Don't get cocky."

Nicola flushed then nodded. "Yes, sir." He handed over the drawing and Angelo gently placed it inside, securing the bolts. Nicola looked at the man. "Have you heard anything about Mr. Donati?"

The man nodded. "Yes, he's been arrested. Apparently he hasn't talked yet, but I don't know how long he'll last. The Nazi's are very good at torture. Does he know the plan?"

Nicola nodded. "Yeah, it's his plan, or at least I think it is."

"Then there isn't much time. He'll eventually tell them you took it, which will lead them to your cousin, and someone will remember he delivered a load of hay here yesterday." He reached behind his back and pulled out a gun, handing it to Nicola. "You had this all along, given to you by Donati. You used it to force your cousin to take you here, then used it to force me to give you my bike when I arrived here to visit my friend. Understood?"

Nicola trembled out an acknowledgement as he took the gun. He had never handled one before and the very feel of it terrified him. He looked at the two men, it clear they held no such fears.

Angelo took the gun from him. "I think I better show you how to use it."

Corpo della Gendarmeria Office
Palazzo del Governatorato, Vatican City
Present Day
One day before the theft

"Quiet day, today. I should be home on time. What's for dinner?"

"I thought I'd cook you something from your old country."

Mario Giasson smiled as his stomach rumbled in appreciation. His wife Marie-Claude was a fabulous cook, but she was Italian, though with a French father—hence the name—which meant mostly delicious traditional Mediterranean cuisine and pasta, mixed in with some rich French delicacies.

He was Swiss.

And he missed the food he had grown up on. Whenever he visited his home country he loaded up, usually leaving with his belt a notch looser—or was that tighter?—than when he arrived, and his wife had taken notice, secretly getting the recipes of some of his favorite dishes from his mother.

He had been thrilled the first time he had arrived home to the mouthwatering aromas of veal schnitzel and rösti. And been stunned that his mother had shared the family recipes. It had made him realize that Marie-Claude had been accepted into the family.

And it had warmed his heart to the point of tears when he had heard the news.

She was an amazing cook, and food of any culture she could master.

So tonight would be a treat.

"I can't wait!"

"Do you still want to know what we're having?"

"Umm, no. Surprise me."

"Thought you might say that. I wasn't going to tell you even if you begged me."

He chuckled then frowned as he saw a bustle of activity outside the windows of his office, the entire security room exploding with activity.

An alarm sounded.

"I've gotta go, sorry. Love you!"

He hung up and jumped from his chair, rushing out into the security office, his job as head of Vatican security taking over from that of husband and father. "Report!"

"Shots fired in St. Peter's Square!"

"Secure his holiness and the other senior staff, lock us down!"

"Yes, sir!"

His second-in-command, Gerard Boileau, ran into the room, a radio pressed to his ear. He handed it to Giasson. "Eastern guard post."

"Status report!" He pointed at Boileau and two others as he rushed out the front entrance to the security office and through the corridors of the massive complex, toward St. Peter's Square.

"A vehicle hit a pedestrian, it looks like intentionally. Two men then exited the vehicle and shot two civilians. My men responded and eliminated the two gunmen."

"Whose soil were they on?" He charged through the doors and into the huge square that had stood for over three hundred years and seen too much blood shed for a place so holy.

"Sir?"

"Were they on Italian soil or ours?"

"One civilian was on Italian soil, the other was thrown past the border by the impact."

"I don't care about the civilians. The gunmen! Did you shoot across the border?"

30

He was sprinting across the cobblestone, the thousands that would usually be filling it gone, many ringing the edges, warily looking at the crowd of guards near the entrance, a security perimeter of flesh blocking his view of the scene.

"They were on our soil when they were shot."

Thank God!

The last thing the Vatican needed was the negative press that shooting people on Italian soil would bring, and the paperwork would have been insane, especially if any innocents were harmed. He'd have to trust for the moment that any stray bullets hadn't hit anyone else.

Surely, someone would have mentioned it by now.

"Make a hole!" shouted Boileau, the guards parting to let them through. A man was lying on the ground, gripping a satchel, one of the Swiss Guard pressing down on a nasty wound, but the man looked done for. Another man was closer to the gates, a jacket already over his face, and two suspects, guns kicked out of reach, were dead just inside the bollards. He stared past into the street and saw nothing but curious onlookers.

And no other casualties.

Thank God for excellent training.

"Sir, he's trying to say something!"

Giasson turned then knelt down by the man as he struggled to reach up to him. Giasson took the man by the hand and leaned over to hear the barely whispered words.

"Save the—"

A gasped last breath, then a slow sigh as the final spark of life left his body, cutting off his dying wish. Giasson looked at the satchel, tightly clasped to the man's chest. If something needed saving, it had to be inside. He moved the arm and gently opened the clasp, peering inside.

What could that be?

31

It was a wooden crate. Small, like any other he had seen dozens if not hundreds of times over his career at the Vatican, used to ship artwork.

But if it was just a piece of art, how could it be worth four lives?

Outside of Orte, Italy
July 7th, 1941

"Halt!"

Nicola eased off on the throttle, slowly applying his brake as he rolled up to the second checkpoint of the day, and according to the contact in Bologna who had refueled him and put him up for the night, the final one. Once past this last hurdle, he'd be in Rome and hopefully it would be clear sailing to his contact point.

But this checkpoint was different from the rest.

A German Volkswagen command car sat parked to the side, a driver leaning against the door, smoking a cigarette, bored with the proceedings. Inside the guardhouse, a temporary affair reinforced with sandbags and cinderblock machinegun nests, was a German officer, the crisp black uniform of the SS obvious even from where Nicola sat.

The sight sent his pulse racing.

"Papers."

He produced his identification and prayed his name hadn't been discovered. When refueling, his contact had indicated his name had yet to make it onto the watch lists, which suggested poor Donati had yet to divulge it.

What a brave man!

He fought the lump that formed in his throat at the thought.

"What is your business in Rome?"

"My aunt is sick. My father sent me to look in on her." He sighed. "I'm to decide if he should leave the farm to pay his respects before she dies."

The guard's eyes narrowed slightly. "Is there some doubt?"

Nicola forced a chuckle. "Let's just say this isn't the first time she's claimed she's dying."

The best covers were always the ones closest to the truth, at least that's what his cousin Leo had explained to him. He did indeed have an aunt in Rome, and she did have a propensity to declare every illness her final one. He had her address with directions written down and because she had no phone, the story would be difficult to check.

And if they decided to invest the time, he was done for regardless.

"Pull over there." The guard pointed to the side where several vehicles were parked, the guards ripping them apart, clearly searching for something.

Probably the portrait.

He couldn't believe this one drawing could be worth so much trouble, but the Nazis were insane, and if they thought what he had hidden in one of his exhaust pipes could win them the war, they'd stop at nothing to possess it.

And here he was, a single man on a motorcycle.

An engine revved behind him and he glanced back, another man on a motorcycle pulling up.

Okay, maybe I don't stand out that much.

Motorcycles were a popular form of transport now that gas was being rationed. They got extremely good mileage, were easy to maintain, and easy to fix. Those that had them usually had them before the war, motorcycles not cheap anymore, and few people had the money to spare.

He was fortunate his moped had been a gift on his fourteenth birthday, just before Germany invaded Poland.

"I'll take this one," said one of the soldiers, striding over from his perch against a wall, flicking a cigarette at the concrete. The guard that had pulled him over handed the ID to the new arrival. He inspected them then handed them back to Nicola. "Please step away from the bike."

Nicola nodded, climbing off and stepping back as the man looked it over. He knelt down and began to search the saddlebags.

"Nice machine. Where'd you get it?"

"My uncle leant it to me for the trip."

Finished with one of the bags, he knocked on the gas tank, it ringing slightly hollow, it about half full. He touched the exhaust on the right side and winced, yanking his finger away and sticking it in his mouth. He searched the other saddlebag then touched the other pipe, his facial expression revealing nothing.

Nicola held his breath, wondering if the soldier would make the connection. The man rose, turning toward him, scratching at his chest, moving his shirt slightly to the side. Nicola's eyes flared momentarily and the man gave him a slight glare, as if warning him to control himself.

For there was little doubt, the partially revealed tattoo matched that of the man who had arrived in their small museum two days ago.

"You're good to go."

Nicola's head bobbed rapidly and he tried to calm himself as he climbed back on his bike, kick-starting the engine and slowly easing around the barriers. As he passed the German car, he felt sweat trickle down his back as the driver seemed to take an interest in him, his gaze following him the entire way through until Nicola was far enough along for the man to be out of his field of vision. Clear, he gently accelerated and didn't breathe easily until he had put a good distance behind him, the mighty city of Rome clearly visible ahead.

As he opened up the engine, gaining more speed, his mind reeled with what had just happened. This man had clearly been waiting for him, was clearly part of the group supposed to protect the portrait. If they knew who he was, then that suggested the other man had escaped as well. Or Donati had finally given up his name and they had somehow found out.

He shook his head, immediately dismissing that possibility.

You'll have to outrun a radio.

If Donati had talked, all of Italy would know his name by now.

He smiled slightly as he realized the implications.

You've got a guardian angel.

It didn't take long for him to reach his destination, and he was soon making his way down Via Dello Statuto, it thick with traffic and pedestrians, bicycles weaving in and out, he content to stay with the cars as he eyed the names of the businesses as he rode by. The paper he had grabbed from Donati's hand had the name of a bakery on this street with an odd phrase written on it he had memorized. It made no sense, and he had a feeling it was a mistake.

I would like exactly seven casareccio loaves like you advertised yesterday.

Now that he was here, the bustling market so crowded his small-town upbringing had him feeling almost claustrophobic, to the point he drove past the bakery without registering it. His mind caught up with his eyes and he glanced back.

Regoli's.

He smiled, his heart picking up a few beats as he realized his journey was almost over. He turned down an alleyway and parked his motorcycle away from the hustle and bustle, pretending to tie his shoe. Clear, he quickly undid the nuts underneath the modified exhaust pipe and removed the drawing, shoving it into his jacket, then reattaching the bolts. He stood and turned, nearly bumping into a man walking toward him.

"Excuse me," he said, stepping to the side to avoid the man. The man tipped his hat, saying something in German. Nicola felt the blood drain from his face but the man continued on, deeper into the alley, Nicola left shaking against the wall. He forced himself off the perceived safety of the stone and walked as calmly as he could manage out into the street, immediately caught up in the flow of pedestrian traffic, his shaking legs carrying him by instinct with the mass of humanity.

He could smell the bakery and it was divine, the fresh baked bread reminding him of home, his mother baking her own fresh almost every day. Gloom washed over him as he thought of them, praying nothing would happen to them for what he had done. His cousin Leo had reassured him they at most would be brought in for questioning, and Leo had already promised to coach them in what to say, a promise Nicola assumed had already been fulfilled.

Please, Lord, take care of them.

He stepped inside, his hand absentmindedly pressed against his jacket, pushing the portrait against his chest, it almost a source of comfort to him. He wasn't sure what to expect, and he definitely wasn't sure what to do now that he was here. There were two people behind the counter and several customers in line. Was he supposed to just go up and tell them who he was? That would be ridiculous.

He listened as the orders were placed. One of this, a dozen of that. Never anything between. And he flashed to the phrase.

"What can I get you today?"

He froze, his eyes wide as he stared at the man.

"Come on, there's people waiting."

"Umm…"

Then it hit him.

"I would like exactly seven casareccio loaves like you advertised yesterday."

The man shook his head. "No way. Talk to my wife, if she's in a generous mood, she might give it to you at that price." He pointed to a door in the back of the store. "Through there." He raised his voice. "Greta, a customer for you!"

A woman's voice shouted from the back in acknowledgement and Nicola tentatively walked toward the door. He pushed aside a wall of hanging beads and stepped into a dimly lit room, his eyes taking a moment to adjust.

And he gasped.

Two police officers were standing on either side of a woman. He turned to bolt but was blocked by another man who raised a finger to his lips then opened the top of his shirt.

Revealing the same tattoo that had followed him for the past two days.

"Who are you?" asked Nicola, his voice trembling as he in no way felt safe. He had no idea who these people were, and for all he knew, he was about to be betrayed and handed over to the two police officers standing behind him.

"Who we are is of no importance to you, the fact that we are here to help you is."

"It was your man at the roadblock."

"Yes."

"And at the museum."

"Yes."

"Is he okay? Did he get away?"

The man nodded.

Nicola's eyes narrowed. "How did your man know about the bike, I mean the modification."

The man smiled. "We have sources among the partisans." His face became serious. "Do you have something for us?"

Nicola nodded and unzipped his jacket, pulling out the portrait. The man's eyes flared slightly and he carefully took it from him. He unrolled it gently, frowning at the creases.

"I'm sorry, but there was no time. I had to take it out of the frame."

The man shook his head, dismissing the apology with a wave of his hand. "You had no choice, you did the right thing. We will fix it."

"You can?"

"We've been dealing with priceless art for longer than you can imagine. It will be safe, I can assure you."

"What now?"

"Now you go to your aunt's. You will be contacted with new identity papers."

"I don't understand."

The man looked at him, sympathy in his eyes. "My son, you can never go home. At least not until the Nazi scourge is condemned to Hell."

Carabinieri Comando Stazione, Rivoli, Italy

July 7th, 1941

"No! Please, no more!"

The man directing the unending pain held up his hand, the police officer delivering the blows immediately stopping. Donati's head slumped to his chest, his breathing labored, his eyes swollen to the point he could barely see. His nose throbbed and bled into his mouth, his fingers and toes screamed in pain, every bone broken.

He had held out for over two days.

Two long, excruciating days.

But he could take no more.

His body was finished.

His mind was broken.

He just wanted it to end.

He wanted it all to end.

Please, God, why won't you let me die?

"You have something to tell us? A name perhaps?"

"Nicola," sputtered Donati, a wave of shame flooding through the bloody pulp that was his body. "Nicola Santini."

"This is the boy who took the portrait?"

He tried to nod but didn't have the strength to raise his head from his chest. "Yes."

Tears burned in his eyes, rolling down his cheeks, the split skin crying out at the salty intrusion as the realization set in that he had betrayed a boy, a young man who had yet to know love, had yet to experience what true joy was, all to save himself further pain.

God, forgive me!

"And where does he live?"

"I know his family," said the man who had been delivering the blows, a man Donati had once thought of as a friend until he had given himself over to Mussolini's fascists. "I'll take you there."

"Please, kill me."

He was ready to die, wanted to die, had to die. He couldn't live with the shame of what he had just done, and if Nicola hadn't been caught yet, then there was every chance he had reached his destination where the men who had contacted him, presenting him with an offer he had at first refused, might be able to help him.

His only fear now was that should he die, the secret he held might die with him.

For Nicola had just been a pawn.

Yet another thing of which he was ashamed.

Hugh Reading Residence, Whitehall, London, England
Present Day
One day before theft

"Everything smells wonderful, Hugh."

"Agreed." Archeology Professor James Acton put his wine down before pulling out a chair for his wife. She sat, giving him a smile and he dropped into a chair opposite her, their host putting the last bowl of food onto the dining table.

Interpol Agent Hugh Reading sat at the head of the table, admiring his handiwork. "It does smell brilliant."

Acton leaned over in his chair, motioning toward the overflowing garbage can, Styrofoam takeout boxes poking out the top. "Cooked all day, I see?"

"Hey, if you wanted a home cooked meal, you should have stayed home."

Acton laughed and began to dig in, piling his plate with the various offerings of Westernized Chinese delicacies. "We're here to see you, not your cooking skills."

"Or lack thereof," interjected Acton's wife, Professor Laura Palmer. Their friend was a committed bachelor, the only romantic dalliance after the man's divorce years ago that Acton was aware of taking place over several days in the depths of the Amazon rainforest. It had been a tragic end that Reading had taken a long time to recover from, if he ever had. Acton and Laura both feared he would never risk putting his heart out there again.

It was sad to see.

The lack of a life lived was all around them. The apartment was sparse, few personal belongings, there only three photos in evidence. One of Reading with his son, only recently back in his life, one of the three of them together in Italy, and one of Reading with his former partner at Scotland Yard, Martin Chaney—a man none of them had heard from in well over a year.

A sore subject to be sure.

Which was why they tried to visit the man whenever they could. Laura was rich, very rich. Her late brother had left her a windfall after his death, he having sold his Internet company before the bubble had burst. When they had married, he had been shown the books and it was in the hundreds of millions.

They would never hurt for money.

They lived a modest lifestyle, neither of them into fancy cars or big houses, rather using her wealth to fund their first love—archeology. It was that love that had brought them all together several years ago. Acton had made an accidental discovery that had led to him being chased by the elite Delta Force across the globe, the Special Forces unit provided with false intel that he was the head of a domestic terrorist cell. He had fled to London, to the one expert who might tell him why what he had discovered might be so important.

And that expert was archeology professor Laura Palmer.

It hadn't been love at first sight, though she had taken his breath away, and it had turned out she was a fan of his for years. Yet that spark, forged under a hail of gunfire, had started something that had never faltered, never wavered, and had changed his life forever.

Despite Hugh Reading arresting her the first time he had met her.

Reading had been the Scotland Yard detective assigned to the case, and after the events of that week had sorted themselves out, they had all become friends.

Good friends.

And there was nothing like a meal, takeout or otherwise, with good friends.

He took his first bite and moaned. "This is good. Reminds me of that place you ordered from the first night we met."

Laura smiled, reaching across the table and giving his hand a squeeze. "You remember that?"

His eyes widened. "Of course I do! It was the most important night of my life."

She grinned. "Mine too. I meant the take out." She turned and glanced at the garbage can in the kitchen.

"Yes, yes, it's the same place," said Reading. "Every time I'd visit you for dinner when you were still living in London you'd order from them, so I took one of their menus. It's a bit of a drive but it's worth it."

"Definitely," agreed Acton as he filled a wrap with his favorite, moo shu pork. He poured a thick black bean sauce over it then rolled it up, savoring the first bite. "Soo good."

"But raw cow would taste good right now?"

Acton's eyes narrowed at Laura's comment then his eyebrows rose as he covered his mouth, remembering what he had thought that first night, it having been days since he had eaten a decent meal. "Ha! I forgot I told you about that!"

"And you say that was the most important night of your life."

He swallowed, taking a sip of his chardonnay. "Hey, considering how many attempts had been made on my life up to that point, I'd say my remembering anything beyond how gorgeous you were is a miracle."

"Good save."

Acton grinned at Reading. "Thanks, I thought so too."

Laura giggled. "Don't encourage him, Hugh."

Reading smiled, a slightly forlorn look on his face as he seemed to stare off into the distance for a moment, and it wasn't until Acton realized how much Laura's laugh had sounded like Kinti's that he knew why.

He exchanged a knowing glance with Laura, neither saying anything as Acton searched for a way to continue the conversation without letting their friend know he had been caught. Acton knew how he had felt the few times he thought Laura had been lost to him, and he had been devastated. To actually have the woman you loved, even if it had only lasted a few days, die in your arms was something he couldn't imagine having to live with.

Reading's phone vibrated next to his wine glass, saving Acton from having to come up with a clever witticism to break the melancholy. "Work?"

Reading shook his head as he picked up his phone. "No, it's Mario."

Acton and Laura glanced at each other, surprised. "Does he call you often?"

"More often than not when something's wrong. But you two are here, so what possible trouble could there be in the world that would warrant a call from the head of Vatican security?"

Acton gave him a look. "Hey, we don't *cause* the trouble, we just end up in the middle of it somehow."

"Yes, every—single—time." Reading swiped his thumb, putting the call on speaker. "Mario, how are you?"

"I'm well, my friend, and you?"

"I'm having dinner with Jim and Laura."

"Hi Mario!" called Laura, waving at the phone, one of the many cute things Acton loved about her.

"Hey Mario," he said, giving the phone a double thumb-shot à la Fonzie. Laura shook her head at him, half a smile betraying her true feelings.

"Thank God! I've been trying to reach you two. I've called your cellphones, your home, the University, the Smithsonian. I got nothing but voicemails."

Acton felt the outline of his phone in his pants pocket. "Sorry about that, I turned my phone off for dinner."

"I left mine in the hotel room by accident," said Laura. "What's the problem?"

"We've got a situation."

Acton put his fork down, leaning back as they all exchanged looks. When Giasson called, it was rarely good news. He was a great man, competent, loyal, and Acton trusted him with his life, even considering him a friend—though he'd never make a special visit to see the man at his home like they would Reading. They were comrades in arms, having been under fire together, saving each other's lives, but outside of that context, they had never socialized.

And he just knew they were about to get into the thick of it again.

Situation.

Not a project, a discovery, or anything benign sounding that still usually turned to pot, but a *situation*.

That never sounded good.

"Situation?" he asked, dreading the answer.

"There was a shooting today at the Vatican."

"Really? I haven't turned on the news all day and I've been out of the office," said Reading, Acton knew mentally cursing himself for being unaware. "What happened?"

46

"It looks like it was targeted. Two men ran down a civilian just outside the gates, then shot the man and his companion. Our guards shot the perpetrators—"

"On Vatican soil?"

"*Yes!* I'm glad to know I'm not the only one who was concerned about that."

"Shitload of paperwork if it wasn't."

"Agreed, though my men would have shot them either way, I'm sure. I've already told the Commandant that the instructions are to protect civilian life, even if off our territory."

"Of course."

Acton decided to steer the conversation back to how they might be about to become involved. "Why are you calling *us*?"

"Well, I'm actually calling you at the behest of Father Rinaldi. Do you know him?"

"Yes, of course," replied Laura. "We worked with him a couple of times in the past. He's the curator of the Vatican Secret Archives."

"Exactly. We made a curious discovery."

Acton leaned forward.

"The man who was hit by the vehicle had a satchel, and inside was a small crate."

"What was it?"

"A drawing. A drawing he shouldn't have had."

Laura's forehead furled. "Why shouldn't he have it? Was it stolen?"

"No, that's what we thought at first, but Father Rinaldi made some phone calls and confirmed that it hasn't been stolen."

"A forgery?"

"That's just it. It must be, but the Father's preliminary examination suggests it isn't."

"Why call us?" asked Acton. "Surely there're experts there who can confirm its authenticity."

"Two reasons." Giasson hesitated. "Do you remember what happened when his holiness was kidnapped?"

"Of course," they all echoed.

"The two men that were assassinated—for lack of a better word—both had the same tattoo we found on the bodies of his holiness' kidnappers."

Acton felt the hairs on the back of his neck stand up as a shiver rushed through his body. The Keepers of the One Truth had kidnapped him and the Pope, and by some miracle, they had managed to survive. And it had been his sincere hope he'd never hear from or see them again.

It appeared as if his luck, as usual, had run out.

"And the second reason?"

"Because, Professor Palmer, you were on the team that authenticated the original."

Testaccio, Rome, Italy
July 7th, 1941

"Oh, Zia, this is incredible!"

"Don't talk with your mouth full!" scolded his aunt with a wagged finger.

Nicola covered his mouth, mumbling an apology as he swallowed his mouthful of homemade spaghetti with olive oil. "I've missed your cooking."

"It looks like you've been missing eating! You're all skin and bones! Is your mother not feeding you?"

Nicola immediately leapt to his mother's defense. "Yes she is, lots, but I'm always out working so I burn it off. Besides, I have to look good for the ladies."

His aunt grunted from the other end of the table. "Do you have a special girl?"

He shook his head, flushing slightly as he twirled his fork against his spoon. "No, I, umm, like to keep my options open."

"Uh huh. I think your father needs to sit you down and explain what is what."

Nicola felt his ears burn, shoving a ball of spaghetti into his mouth, providing an excuse to not reply.

"You kids nowadays, always trying to have fun instead of thinking of your future. In my day, you'd have been married by now, already working on your second child. But today? No! You all want to run around kissing different girls and dancing and riding around on your bicycles." She jabbed the air with a slice of the loaf given to him at the bakery before he left. One,

49

not seven. "You need to settle down, get married and have babies before I die."

"You're not dying, Zia."

"Not today, but I won't be around forever."

"With this war, none of us might be."

"Oh, don't get me started on this war. We should have left for America, your father and I, when we had the chance. But he loved this country too much to leave it." She harrumphed. "I bet he's regretting that decision now."

Nicola shrugged. "If he had left he wouldn't have met Mom, and then I wouldn't have been born."

His aunt reached across the table, patting his hand. "I guess there are always good things to come from bad decisions."

He wasn't sure how to take that.

Someone hammered at the door.

And he nearly threw up his pasta, he immediately flashing back to the museum.

They found me!

He rose from his chair as his aunt threw her napkin on the table, anger on her face. "Who would dare knock in such a way, especially at dinner time!"

He placed himself between the door and his aunt, not sure what to do, wishing he hadn't handed the gun over when he had refueled. Suddenly the door burst off its hinges, two men in leather trench coats stepping inside, an SS officer behind them along with two Italian police officers.

"Are you Nicola Santini?"

He stood, frozen, not saying anything.

"How dare you break into my home!" shouted his aunt, pushing him aside as she rushed toward them, waving her fork at them. "You're going to fix that if I have anything to say about it!"

One of the men backhanded her in the face, hard, sending her spinning into the wall. Nicola cried out as he rushed to her side, cradling the now sobbing woman as blood trickled from her nose.

He turned toward them to find a gun pointed at his face.

"Don't make me ask again."

He hugged his aunt as he glared at the man, his shoulders finally slumping.

"Yes."

OVRA Headquarters, Rome, Italy

July 7th, 1941

Nicola hadn't lasted long. In fact, if it had been an hour he'd be surprised. He had never experienced pain before, not real pain. But it was when they threatened to do the same to his parents that he had given in. He couldn't imagine his mother or father being punched repeatedly, shouted at, smacked, threatened and insulted for hours on end.

And as the words poured from his mouth, he wondered if his confession would actually condemn those he was trying to protect. Would admitting his involvement condemn his family, or save them?

But it was too late, he had already sobbed out the admission.

"I took the portrait."

"Why?"

"I-I wasn't thinking. I heard you pounding on the door and I panicked. I took the drawing and ran."

"Why *that* drawing?"

"It was the only one I could carry. Everything else was framed."

He was impressed with how well he was lying, and he hoped that his interrogators would be as well. After all, even if what he was saying was a lie, it ultimately, at its most basic level, was the truth. He *had* panicked. He *had* taken the drawing. Denying it was of no use.

"You removed it from a packing crate and then removed it from its frame."

It was another voice this time, from the shadows behind him. He had known someone was standing there all along, though he hadn't seen a face. Whoever he was, he was a chain smoker, the only evidence he had been standing there the flare of matches and the scuffs of the toe of his shoe as he stamped out a spent cigarette.

Yet now he had revealed himself.

And his voice was chilling, his Italian excellent though thick with a German accent. Two clicks of leather boots on the stone floor and he was in sight, his crisp black uniform immediately sending a shiver up Nicola's spine.

SS!

He only knew them by reputation, and that reputation left little doubt they were the most vicious of soldiers. According to his friends—and how they would know was beyond him, everyone seeming to preface their statements with "I heard that…"—the SS hated everyone who wasn't SS themselves. And those who weren't SS gave them a wide berth lest they incur their wrath. He had never seen one this close, and never wanted to see one again.

He had a feeling that wasn't going to be a problem.

He nodded. "L-like I said, it was the smallest thing I thought I could save."

"Save from who? Aren't you a loyal Italian?"

"Of course."

"And isn't Italy an ally of Germany and the Führer?"

He nodded, not trusting his brain to deliver a firm enough answer.

"Then why would you try to save it from your ally?"

His mind raced for a reasonable reply, but came up with only one thing that he regretted before he had finished saying it.

"It belongs to Italy. If Germany wants it, she should ask politely."

He was rewarded with the back of a gloved hand, his left cheek stinging, his ears ringing as his mouth filled with a metallic taste.

"Insolence will not be tolerated."

He said nothing.

"Your motivation for taking it is no longer of any concern. Your employer, Mr. Donati, has given us a full confession."

Nicola's shoulders sagged as he thought of the man who had given him a job outside of the fields his allergies tortured him in. It wasn't much of a job, simply manual labor in and around the small museum, but it was work that paid enough to hire a hand at the farm with a little left over.

It was enough that he felt he was contributing.

Until he would be forced into the army.

"All I need to know from you is where you took the portrait."

Nicola looked up at the man, deciding whether or not to reassert his manhood, to reclaim his soul from his cowardly act of admission.

The man smiled at him. A smile devoid of any sense of pleasure or joy or friendliness. It was the opposite of what a smile should be. It was evil. "I sense defiance in you, boy." He pointed at the door. "Let me remind you, we have your aunt in the next room, and your parents back home, and your cousin, and his friend. All their lives depend on your next words. Do you understand me?"

Nicola nodded, closing his eyes.

"Where did you take the portrait?"

Tears burned his cheeks as he revealed the truth, condemning even more lives.

Via Dello Statuto, Rome, Italy
July 7th, 1941

Sturmbannführer Bernard Heidrich removed his hat as he entered the bakery, his nostrils filled with the aromas of fresh baked goods he missed so. He longed to return to the streets of his beloved Munich, yet it wasn't to be, not for some time at least. He had been tasked to collect a set of artifacts in Italy that Dr. Mengele himself had compiled. What the purpose for this was, he wasn't privy to, all he did know was that he had been given tremendous latitude in fulfilling his mission, the orders in his breast pocket impressively signed by the Führer himself.

It was a license to do anything.

*Any*thing.

Including torturing Italian farm boys who got in his way.

But he wasn't a monster. Far from it. He had parents whom he loved dearly, an older brother in the Wehrmacht that he was immensely proud of, a sister who was a file clerk in Berlin, and several nieces and nephews, all in the Hitler Youth and Young Girls' League. They were all proud Nazis, and loyal Germans. It didn't mean they were vicious animals without hearts. If you cooperated, you were left alone. If you didn't, then the law would be applied without mercy.

The young man had cooperated quite quickly.

And if he had told the truth, he just might survive the day.

But if he lied and wasted his time?

He would be shown no quarter.

"Are you the owner?" he asked, stepping ahead of the line of patrons, none daring to protest.

The man jerked out a quick nod, it clear he was terrified.

Good.

"Y-yes. Unless you ask my wife, then she's in charge."

Heidrich smiled slightly. This one was quick on his feet, even when scared. He held up a photo of the boy before he had been beaten. "Do you recognize this young man?"

The baker leaned over the counter and nodded. "Yeah, he was here earlier. Asked me for some expired offer and I sent him in the back to talk to my wife."

So he didn't lie.

"How long did he stay?"

"Maybe five minutes. He came back out and I gave him his bread."

"Did he pay?"

"Damn right he did." The man frowned. "But at the lower price." He shrugged. "My wife is a soft one with anyone but me."

"Where is she?"

"In the back." He turned toward a door and shouted. "Greta! A German officer here to see you!"

"Send him in!"

The man motioned with his chin and Heidrich bowed slightly, snapping his heels together with an impressive click, before walking toward the bead-covered opening. An Italian police officer with him sped ahead, holding the beads aside and Heidrich ducked slightly as he entered, his eyes adjusting to the dimly lit room. A woman sat at a desk covered in what appeared to be receipts.

She eyed him suspiciously, though with little fear.

He doubted any man actually scared her, and felt a moment of pity for the hard working baker outside.

He held out the photo. "I am led to believe you met with this man earlier today?"

She took a quick glance at the photo then shook her head. "No."

"No?" Heidrich frowned. "Your husband says you did."

"He's an idiot." She shouted an insult in Italian through the beads, it was greeted with a shouted, "Yes, dear, I know." She looked at Heidrich then shook her head. "He was here, but he didn't meet with *me*. There were two police officers here that were expecting him. I don't know their business, just that when the police ask me to do something, I'm smart enough to do it."

Heidrich had to admit this was a surprising development, and a quick glance at the two officers accompanying him suggested they felt the same, along with a bit of fear at how he might react. "Police officers?"

She nodded. "I've never seen them before, but then again I don't really pay the police any mind. They came here in the morning with another man, asked if they could wait here, said that a young man would be coming later asking for a deal on a ridiculous amount of some bread and I was to have my husband send him back here." She glared at the door and raised her voice. "I'm amazed the idiot didn't screw that up and send him away."

"I heard that!"

"Of course you heard that, you were meant to, you inbred alcoholic!"

A curse was returned that even Heidrich's excellent Italian couldn't fully comprehend. "Who was the other man?"

She shrugged. "No idea. He wasn't in uniform. Never seen him before."

"And what was said when he arrived?"

"Not much. He handed over a drawing of some sort, then was told to go to his aunt's. Then they all left."

"And that's all."

"Yes."

Heidrich frowned. "If you're lying to me—"

"Then you can shoot me." She waved a hand at the pile of receipts. "The way my husband gives away food, we'll be bankrupt and begging on the streets ourselves before long. Shoot me now and you'll save me that disgrace." She pointed out the door. "Shoot *him* and you'll be doing me a favor."

Heidrich stifled a chuckle. "Is there anything you can tell me about the three men that might help identify them?"

She shook her head. "Two were in uniform, like I said. I didn't see much beyond their guns. The third was dressed like a laborer, maybe your age." Her eyes widened and she raised a finger. "And he had a tattoo. It seemed to be of some significance. He showed some of it to the young man and it seemed to calm him down quite a bit, as if he were expecting it."

Heidrich's eyes narrowed. There was no doubt the woman was telling the truth and wasn't involved. Mentioning the tattoo could serve no purpose. She had helped these people out of a sense of duty or fear, which, it didn't matter. That in itself was enough to have her put in prison if he wanted, though he saw no need for it. He got the sense however that she had been told to cooperate fully, any information she might have of no use.

These three men were shadows, at least to people like her.

She'd never see them again.

"Could you draw the tattoo?"

"No need. It was the cross of Saint Peter."

His eyebrows rose. "Excuse me?"

"Upside down cross with two keys? The cross of Saint Peter?" She frowned. "You're not religious, are you?"

He didn't answer, he the one asking the questions. He glanced over at his liaison officer, Captain Luzzatto, and noticed he seemed nervous.

Interesting.

Heidrich bowed, clicking his heels. "Thank you for your time, signora."

He quickly exited the room, shoving the beads out of his way as he marched outside and into the early evening sunshine. Climbing into the back seat of his car, he turned to Luzzatto.

"Tell me everything you know."

Beads of sweat covered the man's brow and he wiped them away with a handkerchief. "A-about what?"

"That tattoo."

Luzzatto looked about then lowered his voice. "When I first started on the force, oh, almost twenty years ago, I worked on a case where we found the body of a man, badly beaten. He had a tattoo exactly as she described on his chest." He mapped it out with his finger, the tattoo large, stretching from the top of the ribcage to the solar plexus. "It was very detailed, very unusual, unlike anything I had ever seen before."

Heidrich sensed there was more, hesitation in the man's voice. "And?"

Luzzatto looked about again. "Well, the next day the body was gone from the morgue and the case reassigned. My notes were confiscated and my captain told me to never mention the case again or I'd go to prison."

Heidrich's eyes narrowed. "That seems odd."

"I've never encountered anything like it since."

"And where was this body found?"

"Outside the walls of the Vatican."

OVRA Headquarters, Rome, Italy
July 7th, 1941

"He had help, sir."

"You are certain?"

Heidrich nodded, the phone pressed against his ear. "Yes, sir. He was met in Rome by three people, two dressed as Italian police, a third in civilian attire with a Christian symbol tattooed on his chest."

"What symbol?"

"I'm told it is the cross of Saint Peter."

"Upside down with two keys?"

Heidrich's eyes widened in surprise. "Why, yes. You're familiar with it?"

"Of course I am. And you should be too. You're seeking out religious artifacts, familiarize yourself with the damned religions."

Heidrich felt his balls shrink. "Yes, sir! We're continuing to canvass the area, but I'm not optimistic. They were disguised as police so most people look away."

"They probably did that on purpose. But you assume they were disguised."

"Sir?"

"What if they actually were police? That is where I would start. And Sturmbannführer?"

"Yes?"

"Don't bother coming back to Berlin without it. The Führer wants that portrait. Failure is not an option."

Every muscle in Heidrich's body momentarily contracted. "Yes, sir."

"Heil Hitler!"

"Heil Hitler!"

The call ended and he hung up the receiver, noting his hand was trembling. Dr. Mengele was the most terrifying man he had ever met, and he had met the Führer himself. The Führer was a terrifying man to those who didn't devote their lives to him, and Heidrich had no doubt of his loyalty to the man. And it would never be the Führer that would kill him should he fail. It would be someone like Mengele who would be given the task.

And that was far more terrifying than the Führer's bark.

The question he had to now face was how he was going to find a small self-portrait hidden in a city of millions.

By a group of people who seemed well connected and well protected.

I guess we bring in the bakers.

"That's one of them."

Heidrich peered at the photo the baker's wife was pointing at. "Are you sure?"

She nodded. "Yes. He was the one in charge. He did all the talking, except for the one who wasn't police. Once the boy arrived, he did almost all the talking."

Heidrich turned to his liaison officer, Captain Luzzatto. "I want his file and photos of everyone he works with, now!"

Luzzatto nodded, taking the binder of police personnel files and leaving the room. Heidrich turned to the woman and pointed at the stack of binders. "Keep looking, there're two of them."

She gave him a glare that would have withered any other man, especially a husband, then returned to flipping through the pages. He stepped outside and headed for the office assigned to him while he was here. Sitting behind his desk, he propped his feet up on the corner as his secretary brought in a cup of espresso. It was a guilty pleasure he had developed a taste for while here, one he feared he'd never be able to continue when he returned home.

If you don't find that damned portrait, you won't need to worry about going home.

He wondered how long Dr. Mengele would tolerate failure. He doubted long. He couldn't expect to be simply exiled to Rome. Eventually he'd be called back to Berlin to explain himself, then probably sent to one of the good doctor's laboratories, to be experimented on.

He shivered, setting aside his cup.

He closed his eyes and there was a sudden knock on the door, startling him awake. He checked the clock to see how long he had been out.

Almost an hour.

He hadn't realized how exhausted he was, his chase after the portrait now in its third day with only a few hours sleep squeezed in while travelling. Luzzatto stood in the doorway, holding several file folders.

"I have what you asked for, sir."

Heidrich motioned for Luzzatto to hand the files over. He flipped the first one open as Luzzatto gave him a summary.

"Lt. Lupo. He's the one she identified. He's on duty now. I'm having him picked up. He should be here shortly."

Heidrich cursed. "You shouldn't have done that."

Luzzatto immediately paled. "Why?"

"We should be following him, to see where he goes. Picking him up means any chance of finding out who he's involved with is now impossible."

"I-I'll call it off." Luzzatto turned to leave when Heidrich waved off his departure with a flick of the wrist. "No point. It went out over the radio, I assume?"

Luzzatto nodded.

"Then he knows, or someone he's connected with knows."

"I-I'm sorry, sir."

A young officer poked his head inside the office. "Excuse me, sirs, but Lt. Lupo is here."

Heidrich rose, straightening his uniform before grabbing his hat. "Let's see what he has to say for himself."

He stepped out into the hallway to see the officer being led down the hallway, flanked by two of his colleagues. Lupo didn't seem nervous at all, there no fear in his eyes. He stared directly at Heidrich as he approached, a slight smile on his face.

We'll see if you're smiling after I'm done with you.

Three gunshots rang out from behind him. Heidrich stepped to the side, his head spinning toward the shooter as he reached for his own weapon. But it was too late. The man turned the gun on himself, tearing a hole through his own head before collapsing to the floor. Heidrich turned back to see Lupo on the ground, a large pool of blood oozing out on the tile floor, the same smile still on his face, as if he died contented.

Heidrich leaned over and tore open the Lupo's shirt, but found no tattoo.

He stood, cursing as he looked from one body to the other, realizing his case had just died with these two men.

Two men willing to die for their cause.

A cause he knew nothing about.

Except that it had just sealed his own death warrant.

Reich Air Ministry, Berlin, Nazi Germany
April 4th, 1945
One month before the official surrender of Nazi Germany

Heidrich resisted cringing as the Russian shells bombarded the city overhead. Germany had lost, yet the Führer held on, refusing to admit defeat.

And it was the people who were paying the price for it.

And Heidrich felt no sympathy.

If the people had been more committed to the war effort, had thrown themselves into the fight as he had, body and soul, Germany would have been victorious, of that he had no doubt.

She had to win, for she was the home of the Master Race.

A home overrun with vermin who had weakened her in her time of need.

They had exterminated over eleven million, displaced millions more, and if they had just had another few years, the final solution would have been successfully completed, and the world a better place for it.

And then phase two could have begun.

For the problem went far beyond the Jews and the Gypsies. They were merely the tip of the iceberg. Russians, Africans, Orientals, Muslims. They all needed to be eliminated to make room for the Aryan race.

Though that wouldn't be today.

Not now.

Now that they had been betrayed.

Now that they were defeated.

But this was a war, and what had been going on for the past six years was merely a battle.

Germany would win the war. The Third Reich may be about to fall, but the Fourth Reich would someday rule the world, the Swastika proudly fluttering over the capitals of every nation the new empire allowed into the fold, willingly or not.

And from what he had just heard, he had every confidence this new empire, this new plan, would work.

It would just take time.

Perhaps a very long time.

It was sad to think he probably wouldn't see it, though he was honored he had been chosen to take part. He had been officially executed yesterday for his failure in Rome, but instead of dying, he had been given whispered instructions as the blindfold had been put in place.

"Play dead."

And now he found himself in a room with young SS officers, much like him, fine examples of the Master Race, with the Führer himself at the head of the table, Dr. Mengele and other senior staff on either side.

He was fiercely proud.

"We have failed you, Mein Führer."

Hitler looked at Mengele and nodded. "Yes, you have, but we have been betrayed as well."

Mengele bowed slightly in his chair. "Yes, we have. But no matter what happens here in the coming days, the eugenics program must continue so Germany may one day rule the world as it should. The Master Race must continue, even if silently in the background so that one day she can fulfill her destiny." Mengele looked at those gathered then back at their Führer. "The Third Reich has failed, long live the Fourth Reich!"

"Heil Hitler! Heil Hitler! Heil Hitler!" cried those gathered, outstretched arms stabbing toward the heavens.

Mengele turned toward the Führer. "And you, Mein Führer, will be at its head."

The Führer nodded then rose, the entire room leaping to their feet. "Gentlemen."

"Heil Hitler!" shouted the enthusiastic group, the Führer returning his trademark version of the salute, bent at the elbow, before leaving the room. When the door closed, everyone returned to their seats, Dr. Mengele taking the seat at the head of the table. He turned to one of the senior scientists on his team.

"Your research?"

The man nodded. "We are limited by the times we live in, however I am one hundred percent confident we will succeed in time."

"How much time?"

"I cannot say. It could be years, decades even. It may not be we who succeed, but our children or our grandchildren. But eventually we will succeed, and the Fourth Reich will be born, an unstoppable army its sword."

Mengele's head bobbed slightly, as if pleased with the words. He looked at those gathered. "Germany is about to fall, but you will go on. Every one of you are loyal to the Führer, loyal to his dream, but none of you are known. You are all dead as far as the world is concerned, so you can continue the fight long after men like me are dust. It will be up to you to keep the fight alive, in the background.

"Provisions have already been made so you will have enough funding to last several lifetimes. All of our research has been copied and moved to secret locations that the files in front of you contain. You will be split into three units, each working independently, compartmentalized, so should any one unit be captured, the others will continue on." He looked about the room, his eyes coming to rest on Heidrich for a moment before continuing down the table. "Some of you have been gathering religious artifacts for some time. Those have mostly been moved to these locations, however the allies have intercepted some of these shipments. But it is of no matter. You will recover these artifacts when the time comes that they are needed."

Mengele rose, as did everyone else.

"Gentlemen, you are the Congress. Like a congress of ravens picking at the corpses littering a battlefield, you will take what is left of the Fatherland and ensure that the Germany we tried to create lives on. It is up to *you* to keep the dream alive. My generation has failed, but you, or your progeny, will succeed. Learn from our mistakes, and the Fourth Reich will not be just a dream, but a reality that will bring stability and order to the entire world. And with science and the will of the gods, the Führer will once again stand in the Reichstag, and the world will tremble at the might of the Fourth Reich! Long live the Congress! Long live the Führer!"

Shouts of Heil Hitler erupted, Mengele joining in before leaving with the senior staff. The exuberance among the young men still in the room continued for several minutes before they returned to their seats and opened the envelopes in front of them.

And what Heidrich read filled him at once with hope and awe, the might and superiority of the Third Reich clear.

And Operation Raven's Claw was proof.

Casa del Conte Verde, Rivoli, Italy
September 17th, 1998

Carmine Donati stared at the envelope, debating on whether to bother opening it. He had sorted through the day's mail long ago, setting anything aside he felt wasn't urgent. Now it was the end of the day and it was time to file most of the pile in front of him into the recycling bin.

Yet this wasn't some flyer, it was something different.

It was a high quality envelope, the stock not a discount store brand, though what had him curious was the fact the return address was the museum he was now sitting in, addressed to that same facility.

He sighed, his eyes closing slightly as the day caught up to him. It was always a struggle keeping a small museum going, especially in these times when people seemed to be losing interest in their history. He tried to keep the interest alive, urging the schools to come and visit their modest collection as often as possible, and he'd recount the story of how his grandfather had helped hide a portrait of Leonardo da Vinci himself from the Nazis.

And had died for it.

His father had instilled in him an interest in the arts and history, and though his father hadn't gone into the business, he had gone to university and eventually obtained his doctorate, returning to his hometown to work at the museum, and eventually run it, keeping his grandfather's memory alive as best he could.

And it troubled him every time one of the young children asked to see the portrait for which his grandfather had died.

For he couldn't.

It had never been returned.

Lost to history.

Lost to a war that had yet to give up all it had stolen.

He shoved the letter opener into the top of the envelope, slicing it open. Fishing out the single sheet of paper, he gasped, having to read it several times before he fully believed what he saw.

It is time for the portrait to be returned. Call when you are ready.

He looked at the number and reached for the phone, stopping just before gripping the receiver, his cynical mind taking over. He examined the letter again. A plain piece of heavy stock, the message typewritten with no identifying marks on it whatsoever. He held it up to the light, a watermark evident, but nothing that he recognized as important.

It must be a hoax.

But what if it isn't?

No one ever knew what had come of the portrait. His grandfather was dead, and the young man who had helped, Nicola Santini, had returned to the town after the war, refusing to talk of what had happened, living out his days on the family farm, almost a hermit, ashamed of something he had done.

His involvement had been forgotten by most.

He grabbed the phone and quickly dialed before he could change his mind.

"Hello?"

"Hi, I, um, received a letter?"

"Is this Doctor Donati?"

"Yes."

"Stay where you are."

The call ended and he stared at the receiver, not sure what to make of what had just happened, though the shivers racing up and down his spine suggested his subconscious was terrified of what it might be. He hung up the receiver and looked about, it suddenly feeling as if he were being watched.

Stay where you are.

That meant someone was coming.

But who?

And what was their motivation?

It suddenly occurred to him that they might think *he* had the portrait, and they wanted it returned. It wouldn't be the first time the idea had been floated that his grandfather had actually stolen the portrait and died before he could profit from his actions.

It was an accusation that enraged him every time it was suggested.

A knock on the front doors of the museum startled him and his heart leapt into his throat as he slowly rose. The museum was closed at this time, the hours clearly marked out front. It had to be them, but if it was, it meant they had been waiting nearby for his call.

He glanced at the postmark.

Two days ago. Rome.

So they could have been waiting all day today *and* yesterday.

They might be mad you didn't open it this morning.

He pushed his chair back, fear gripping him at the thought of upsetting them any further. He exited his office and strode through the small gallery, unlocking the front door. Holding his breath, he pulled open the heavy door and his eyes opened wide.

Nobody was there.

He leaned out and looked to the left and right. There were plenty of people on the street, though none seemed like they had just knocked, and none paid him any mind. He was about to close the door when something caught his attention.

A small box sat by the other half of the door.

And by its shape, he knew immediately what it was.

He eagerly grabbed it, looking again for whoever had left it, then stepped back inside, bolting the door and rushing toward the workshop in the back. Placing the box on a workbench, he sliced it open and pulled out a small crate, handcrafted some time ago by the looks of it, exactly the size he would expect the self-portrait to be.

Carefully prying it open, he lifted the contents out of the wood crate then gently removed the brown paper that wrapped it, brittle and dry, it so old he could picture his grandfather packaging it so long ago.

He fell into his chair, tears filling his eyes as he gazed upon what was revealed.

The red chalk drawing of the master himself.

He gazed up at the heavens, tears rolling down his cheeks, then down at the picture of his grandfather that hung on the wall nearby.

It's home, granddad. It's home!

Casa del Conte Verde, Rivoli, Italy
October 1st, 1998
Two weeks after the return

Laura Palmer peered through the microscope, her professor explaining what to look for. It was disappointing, yet exciting at the same time. She was only in her third year of university, and her Art History professor had invited several of the more promising students with her as part of a team to determine if a drawing recently discovered was indeed genuine.

And it wasn't.

It was actually a relief, the self-portrait, in red chalk, heavily degraded from years of neglect. If it had indeed been the genuine article, it would have been a travesty what had happened to it.

But it was unfortunate as well.

The drawing had a storied history, not the least of which was the fact the Nazis had tried to acquire it, legends apparently surrounding it that it could imbue great power to anyone who possessed it. Apparently, the curator of the museum had secreted it away, eventually dying after being brutally tortured for days.

She sighed at the thought this man's efforts would go unrecognized, the drawing still lost to history.

She rose and looked at the current curator, the grandson of the hero who had tried to save the genuine article.

"Are you certain?"

She nodded. "It's very good, but the paper is far too new. It's a near exact duplicate when you compare it to the photos you provided, but the paper is all wrong."

The man dropped into his chair, deflated. He pulled at his hair as he shook his head. "It's not fair! He died for nothing!"

Laura's heart went out to the man. His grandfather, whom he had obviously never met, had died a horrible death, and the fruits of his labor were still lost.

"You know some people still say he stole the portrait? That he got what he deserved?" He slammed his fist on the arm of his chair, startling Laura. He glanced up at her then at her professor. "It isn't fair."

Professor Cindy Osborne nodded. "No, it isn't. He was a hero. He protected the portrait from the Nazis. Eventually, one day, it will turn up, and he'll be recognized for what he has done."

Donati stared off into the distance, his eyes glassing over, then his eyes flared for a moment as if something had just occurred to him. He looked at Professor Osborne. "You are bound by the confidentiality agreement, correct?"

Osborne bristled, Laura getting the distinct impression she knew exactly what was about to be said.

"Yes." The word was drawn out, as if the answer was feared.

There was a knock at the door, interrupting them. Laura turned to see an old man standing there, a shaking cane in his right hand, his left gripping the doorframe.

Donati leapt from his chair. "Mr. Santini!" He rushed over to the old man, his mouth agape, then turned to the others before giving the man a chance to say anything. "This is the man who helped my grandfather, who took the portrait to Rome!"

"Is it true?" asked the man in English, his voice low yet still filled with vitality. He froze when he caught sight of the portrait on the worktable. "Is that it?" His voice was filled with wonder as he shuffled toward it, the excitement in his eyes clear.

And it crushed Laura to see his face when the curator responded.

"No. It's a forgery."

The old man leaned on the table, staring at the portrait then looking about. "Bring an old man a chair."

Laura leapt forward, dragging a chair toward him then helping him into it.

"Thank you, my dear." He looked up and smiled at her. "Aren't you a pretty one."

She blushed.

He patted her hand. "*You* can call me Nicola."

She smiled and squeezed his hand. "Laura."

He gave her hand a trembling kiss then pointed at the remains of the crate that the portrait had been shipped in. "Did he initial it?"

Donati's eyes narrowed. "What do you mean?"

"Did he initial it? Your grandfather always carved his initials in the bottom of any crate, that way he'd know if it had been repackaged." He looked at Donati. "He wasn't a very trusting man." His eyes narrowed. "Are you?"

Donati seemed unsure of what to say, but Laura was already examining the pieces of wood. She grinned, grabbing one of the pieces. "Here it is, VD, Vincenzo Donati!"

She handed the piece of wood over to Nicola who examined it himself then nodded, handing it back. "Interesting. Had it been opened before?"

Donati shook his head. "I don't think so, but it's hard to tell. I think Grandfather himself wrapped it."

"Wrapped a forgery." Nicola grunted, frowning, his knuckles turning white as they gripped the arms of his chair. "He tricked me, right from the beginning."

Laura knelt down beside him. "Do you have any idea where the genuine portrait is?"

"I'm not sure. I removed what I thought was the real drawing from its case so this"—he motioned toward the disassembled crate—"couldn't be from what I took." He sighed, his chin dropping to his chest. "This forgery was never part of the plan I knew about." Nicola looked up at her, tears filling his eyes. "I have no idea where the original is, but I have a feeling I never had it."

Casa del Conte Verde, Rivoli, Italy

July 3rd, 1941

The night before Nicola took the portrait

"He must think it's the genuine portrait."

Vincenzo Donati nodded, the pit in his stomach at deceiving the young man almost overwhelming. He wanted to throw up. He looked at the man whose name he had never been given. "What makes you think he'll take it?"

"The fact he wants to help tells me he is brave. His age tells me he is impulsive. If he thinks it is about to be taken by the Nazis, he *will* act."

"But if he doesn't?"

"Then I will place it in his hands and tell him to run. He won't think twice."

"I hope you're right." He stared at the forgery the man had brought. "It's really quite good."

The man glanced at the portrait and nodded. "We have experts available to us. They were able to recreate it based on the photo you provided. It won't stand up to scrutiny, but it will fool a teenage boy."

Donati shook his head, his head low. He looked at the packaged genuine portrait gripped in the man's hands. "You're sure it will be safe?"

"Absolutely. We'll take good care of it and return it when the time is right."

"When do you think that will be?"

"When every living Nazi is dead."

"Do you really think that will ever happen?"

The man nodded. "Evil will never triumph in the end, God will see to that."

76

Donati sighed. "I wish I had your faith." He checked the clock on the wall. "Okay, you must go now, before Nicola gets here. He must never know what we are doing."

The man shook Donati's hand, the top of an ornate tattoo revealed by a loose shirt button. "He won't, but we will help keep him safe for as long as we can."

"Please, you must. I feel guilty enough deceiving the poor boy. Should harm come to him…" Donati looked at the forgery. "He could die for nothing."

"If he dies protecting the forgery, then the Nazi's will be convinced it is genuine and never think to look for the real one."

"But if they discover it is a forgery?"

"Then you will claim it always was."

Donati reached out and touched the boxed portrait. "I feel as if I'm losing a part of me."

The man shook his head.

"No, you're protecting it for eternity."

Approaching Rome, Italy
Present Day
The morning of the theft

"So it was a fake."

Professor Laura Palmer nodded, not proud of what she had been forced to go along with so long ago. But she had been a student, bound by a confidentiality agreement she actually thought was important. Her professor seemed more concerned with the donation the curator had offered, and the unfettered access to the Turin Royal Library's impressive collection.

It had been so distasteful it had soured her view of the entire profession, and it was a meeting with the dean that had kept her in, despite her initial protestations.

"Why do you want to leave?"

"I can't say."

And it was immediately clear he knew exactly why. Which had soured her even more.

"I assume this is surrounding the events in Turin last week?"

She nodded.

"It's an ugly business, sometimes. Today too many museums are desperate for money, and money in cash-strapped times usually comes from donors and tourists. A da Vinci draws attention." He leaned forward. "Whether genuine or not."

She had opened her mouth to fire with both barrels at the man when he cut her off.

"The fact, Miss Palmer, that you are so offended by what happened, is exactly why you *must* stay on the path you have chosen for yourself. This profession needs people like you, desperately needs people like you, people who would never dream of agreeing to what your professor signed, then never sticking with it should what happened, happen."

"You mean I can violate the agreement?"

He shook his head. "No. *You* can't. Become a professor, with tenure, and you can do whatever you want."

Which was what she had done, *after* switching institutions.

But now her past had caught up with her.

"Yes, and we had all signed a non-disclosure agreement so we couldn't say anything."

"Doesn't sound like you."

She looked at her husband and smiled. He was the love of her life and her worst fear in all this was that he'd be disappointed in her, a feeling she never wanted to experience. "I'm sorry."

He put his arm over her shoulders, giving her a squeeze. "It's not your fault. You were barely in your twenties, what were you supposed to do? The important thing is you've never done anything like that again." He pushed away from her, turned in his chair and gave her a look. "You've never done anything like that since, right?"

She slapped his chest with the back of her hand. "Of course not!" He roared with laughter, dispelling her irrational fear that he had been serious. "Oh James, I feel bad enough as it is, don't toy with me like that!"

He gave her another squeeze as the pilot of their private jet announced their descent into Rome. Reading tapped an iPad he had been reading. "They really played this thing up, didn't they?"

She nodded. "It was horrible. They never actually claimed it was genuine, they just didn't say anything either way. But they did use it for major new funding to build a secure, climate-controlled vault to help preserve it, claiming heavy damage so it could never be properly examined.

When it was put on display, the story was inspiring. A secret operation to hide it from the Nazis, the legend surrounding it, the mysterious return over fifty years later. It's the stuff stories are written about."

"Quite often stories are based on fact."

Laura nodded. "And in this case it is."

"And you're certain it was a forgery?"

"Yes."

"How do you know it was ever real?" asked Reading.

It was a good question, one she had asked herself during the initial discovery that it was a forgery, but her professor had convinced her the genuine article did indeed exist.

"We know there were at least two versions of the drawing."

"How?" asked her husband, turning in his seat despite the seatbelt light being on.

"There were several photos of the drawing from back then. Three, in fact. Two were of it framed, one not. The one that hadn't been framed had da Vinci's signature in the bottom right, very near the edge."

"And the other two didn't." James nodded. "The frame covered it." He turned to Reading to explain. "Most likely it had been cut at some point, trimming the excess for some reason, leaving the signature too close to the edge."

"That was our guess as well," agreed Laura. "We believe—or rather my professor believed—that the forgers worked from a photo of the framed drawing, so didn't know the signature was supposed to be there. The museum knew, but claimed it had faded due to the degradation suffered from improper storage."

"Could it have?" Reading shrugged. "I mean, from what I just read it was in pretty rough shape."

"Absolutely, it was," agreed Laura. "But the paper was also from the wrong era, off by over a century."

"I've never understood that," said Reading as the wheels touched down. "How do they get away with that?"

James leaned forward, entering teaching mode. "Usually they take a painting or drawing from the same era and paint over it. Something much less valuable, obviously. You're not going to destroy one masterpiece to forge another."

"But this was a drawing."

"True. But there are thousands upon thousands of things from that era that have been collected over the years, quite often by unscrupulous people simply planning ahead. There's an entire black market for blank canvases and paper from all eras." James shook his head, frowning. "It's really quite the disgrace."

"What would the world be like without liars and thieves?" bemoaned Laura.

"Well, I'd be out of a job."

Laura smiled at Reading. "Well, we can't have that, now, can we?"

Reading grunted. "I'd give it up in a heartbeat if it were somehow possible, but there's just as much chance of me fitting into my bobby uniform tomorrow as that."

Laura laughed. "Well, I'll say this. If this turns out to be the genuine drawing, it will clear up a seventy year old mystery."

"And open up an entirely new one."

Laura and James looked at Reading.

"Meaning?"

"Why did two members of the Keepers of the One Truth have it, and who felt it was valuable enough to kill them for it?"

Approaching Sapienza University, Rome, Italy

Acton glanced behind them for the umpteenth time, Mario Giasson smiling at him. He had the distinct feeling the limousine the Vatican had sent to pick them up was being followed, but his eyes could find no evidence of what his intuition was telling him.

"Relax, Jim, no one knows you're coming."

Acton looked at Giasson. "Uh huh."

Laura squeezed his hand a little tighter as she too apparently was remembering the gut wrenching experiences they had been drawn into too often in what should be one of their favorite cities to visit. And with the Keepers of the One Truth involved, four dead bodies and a seventy year old conspiracy, he was going to feel uncomfortable, whether Giasson felt it was warranted or not.

Giasson seemed to sense his doubts. "Look, the portrait was moved by *my* men to the university only this morning, just a handful of people know what is being tested, and Italian State Police are providing security. Nothing will happen like last time."

Acton frowned. "*Which* last time?"

Giasson chuckled. "Good point." He started rhyming things off on his fingers. "You won't be kidnapped by the Keepers, protesters won't try to storm the university—"

"You say that now." Acton raised a hand, cutting off Mario's continued assurances. "Let's just get this over with and hopefully break the pattern."

"What pattern is that?" asked Giasson as the car rolled up in front of the university.

"The one where every time the Vatican calls, someone tries to grass my ass."

Giasson grinned, Reading stifling a laugh as Laura winked at Acton. "And such a nice ass it is."

"Indeed."

Acton gave Reading a look, the man shrugging. "I've been told I don't hand out enough compliments."

"I wouldn't be starting with my ass." Acton pointed at the open door. "You first, I wouldn't want to give you a show you'd feel compelled to praise."

Reading chuckled as he stepped out into the morning sunlight, Laura's private jet, part of a lease-sharing network, having got them to Rome in good time. They could have been here earlier, however Father Rinaldi had indicated the university laboratory wasn't available until regular hours. The elderly man was rushing down the steps, clearly invigorated by the excitement the discovery of a da Vinci merited.

"Professor Palmer, so good to see you again!" he gushed as he grabbed her by both shoulders, giving each cheek a kiss. He did the same with Acton, then moved on to Reading who caught the man's right hand with his own, placing his left hand on the art historian's shoulder, preventing the kissed greeting.

"Nice to meet you, Father."

"Come, come, you need to see this, it is incredible!"

He bolted up the stairs leaving the others to look on in wonder, Reading and Acton grinning at each other as Acton helped his wife up the steps. She had been shot outside of Paris several months ago and was still regaining her stamina. Stairs were one of her biggest challenges, and hours aboard a luxury jet might sound comfortable, though it wasn't compared to a pillow top mattress.

Reading looked at Acton then at Rinaldi as he disappeared through the doors ahead. "Good kisser?"

"Ooh, the best. If things don't work out with Laura and I, I might give the man a call."

Laura cleared the last step and took several gasping breaths, Acton fishing a handkerchief out of his pocket and dabbing her forehead dry. She smiled a thank you.

"You did good, hon. Two weeks ago I would have been carrying you up half that."

She nodded, pointing at the door. "Let's go before I have time to think about taking you up on that offer."

Reading went ahead and joined Giasson, already at the doors and talking to an Italian State Police officer, one of two at the doors. As they entered the building, Giasson joined them and they made their way to the lab, Rinaldi having already made it to the doors and back at least twice, urging them forward like a child desperate to get his mother to the ice cream truck before it pulled away.

Acton looked at Giasson, motioning toward the doors behind them and the two officers. "Problems?"

Giasson shook his head. "Not at all." He nodded to the doors ahead of them. "Four more. See, perfectly safe."

Acton looked to find four more State Police stationed outside the lab. One of them approached Giasson. "Inspector General, it is good to see you."

"Likewise. Where is Chief Inspector Riva?"

"He has been unavoidably detained and placed me in command. I assure you we are quite secure."

Mario nodded, smiling slightly as Rinaldi opened the doors. "I have no doubt. Carry on."

They entered the lab and Acton flashed back to the last time he had been at the university, examining what had been found in a Templar knight's sarcophagus. It had touched off worldwide chaos. He couldn't possibly imagine how this portrait could compare, however four were already dead because of it.

It simply made no sense.

"Oh my!" whispered Laura in awe as she pointed to one of the large displays showing an enlarged image of the drawing. It was a rather plain self-portrait by some standards, though the deftness of the chalk lines showed a steady, practiced hand at work, an artist who knew exactly what he wanted to put on paper, there nothing extraneous in his delivery, every line serving a purpose.

And the eyes.

The eyes were incredible. There was something about the way da Vinci did the eyes in his masterpieces that Acton could always feel at his core. Deep, pained, wise.

"Incredible."

Reading nodded as he stared at the monitor. "How old is it?"

"About five hundred years if it's genuine," replied Acton.

"I think it is."

Everyone turned to Laura, Rinaldi jumping up and down on his toes. "You see it, don't you?"

She nodded, pointing at the bottom right of the image. "It's his signature."

"Exactly! I read your email last night and checked for it, and sure enough, it was right where you said it should be."

"And right where it wasn't in the one I examined in 1998." She glanced at Rinaldi. "And the paper?"

"It appears genuine, however a sample has been taken for carbon dating. But I'm optimistic."

Laura nodded, peering through one of the scopes to get a closer look, one of the displays changing to show everyone else what she was seeing. She rose. "I agree."

Rinaldi looked at her, holding his breath, then turning away, as if he were afraid to ask the question he was about to ask. "Didn't you, I mean…"

"Didn't I authenticate the portrait in Turin as genuine?"

A burst of air escaped Rinaldi's mouth as he nodded. "Yes."

Laura glanced at Acton who shrugged. "I think it's safe to break your confidentiality agreement now."

She smiled. "I guess so." Turning to Father Rinaldi, Acton could see the relief sweep over his wife as she visibly relaxed, as if a weight she had been carrying for years had just been lifted. "Actually, *I* didn't. In fact, none of us did. We declared it a forgery almost immediately."

"Then why has it been publicized as genuine? I mean, they've spent millions preserving it!"

"I was just a student, but we had all signed non-disclosure agreements. When we discovered it was a fake we were sworn to secrecy otherwise we'd all be sued. Being young and naïve, I went along with what my professor dictated. Believe me, Father, it's something I've been ashamed of for most of my adult life."

"I don't doubt it." He pointed toward the drawing sitting under a high-resolution camera. "But now the truth can be told." He turned to Giasson. "You realize how much this is worth? It's priceless!" Father Rinaldi began to pace. "If this falls into the wrong hands, it could be worth millions, perhaps tens of millions. Especially if someone believes the legend."

Giasson's eyes narrowed. "What legend?"

"That if one stares into the eyes of the portrait, one is imbued with great power."

"Ridiculous."

Reading snorted. "I find it impossible to accept that people would believe in such nonsense."

Acton spun toward the door as shouts erupted from the other side. Gunfire shattered the calm of the university and he instinctively reached out and drew his wife behind him as he put himself between the woman he loved and the violence he knew was about to descend upon them. Reading leapt to his feet, positioning himself beside Giasson who was now standing between them and the doors.

They burst open and Acton closed his eyes, allowing a held breath to escape, two police officers entering.

Thank God!

Clearly, whatever had happened outside these walls had been thwarted, Giasson's precautions seeming prescient now that it was over. He had been right to be nervous all along. Four were dead already, so somebody felt this drawing was worth killing for, and with the Keepers of the One Truth involved, he knew these men were capable of anything.

The two police officers raised their weapons, pointing them at Giasson and Reading.

Laura drew in a quick breath behind him and he took a step back, feeling her body press against his.

Footsteps outside the doors echoed through the halls and into the lab, the pace slow and deliberate, as if the person had no concerns of being caught.

And why should they. The police are on their side!

A tall man appeared, quite tall to be seen over the imposing figure of Reading, Giasson himself no small man. The man appeared Scandinavian. Blonde, blue eyes, chiseled features.

With a slightly maniacal look in the eyes.

I wonder what da Vinci would make of him.

The new arrival pointed at the portrait on the lab table and snapped his fingers, one of the officers moving toward it. Giasson blocked him, holding out his arms. "This is the property of the people of Italy."

A slight smile broke out on the blonde man's face then he suddenly drew a weapon from a shoulder holster and shot Giasson. The Vatican Inspector General spun then collapsed to the tile floor with a cry, Laura moving to help him, Acton holding his arm out, keeping her in place.

"You are mistaken. It is the property of the Führer."

Führer!

Acton's mind reeled as Reading placed himself between the man and Giasson, who lay on his back, gripping his shoulder. "Take it, it's not worth dying for."

The man raised his weapon, conceding Reading's point with a slight bow. He flicked the weapon and the guard resumed his track for the portrait. This time Acton's feet carried him almost irresistibly forward, blocking the guard's path.

The gun was aimed at him.

"Another fool?"

Acton shook his head. "No, but it's priceless. At least let me package it properly. It will only take a minute."

The weapon was raised again and the man nodded, Acton hiding his sigh of relief as he and Laura rushed to the table. The paper it had been wrapped in was to the side, awaiting analysis. He grabbed it and wrapped it around the unframed portrait, using the creases that had lasted seventy years. Laura held up the crate as he carefully slid the portrait inside.

Then he did something that he couldn't believe.

With his back to their assailants, he fished his cellphone out of his front pocket and slid it into the crate, Laura's eyes bulging slightly before she caught herself. She handed him the top of the crate and he tacked it in place. He lifted the package and handed it to the police officer who immediately headed out the door.

The blonde man's heels clicked together and he bowed slightly.

Just like Acton would expect a good Nazi to do.

The man looked at each of them, his eyes finally coming to rest on Reading.

"I bid you good day. But should you follow us, more will die."

Outside Sapienza University, Rome, Italy

Obersturmbannführer Franz Hofmeister climbed calmly into the passenger seat of the awaiting Audi A8, the engine already revving as his driver waited for Hofmeister's boot to clear the pavement.

It did.

And the car leapt forward, the door shutting itself from the force. An SUV ahead of them with his two accomplices peeled right as his driver turned left. The sound of a siren had him peering in the side view mirror to see if they were being pursued when the driver spoke.

"Ahead of us."

Hofmeister looked to see a police car, lights flashing, careen onto the street ahead of them, racing toward them. He held his breath as his driver pulled over to the right along with the other traffic.

And the squad car blew past them.

They were safe.

He turned in his seat, looking at their passenger in the rear. "It was exactly as you said."

"I have never lied to you."

Hofmeister frowned. "But you *have* failed us."

The man shook his head. "No, *your* men failed. I told you exactly where and when the drawing would be and your men were late, then overreacted. All they had to do was wait for them to leave the Vatican grounds, then take them quietly as was the original plan. If they had, then we could have avoided all this nonsense and the involvement of the authorities. Idiocy! Incompetence!"

Hofmeister felt his blood begin to boil. "You forget your place."

"My place is at God's side, and his is more powerful than your Führer ever was."

"We will see."

"An abomination of science is still just a man, not a god. I serve our Lord and savior. The only reason I've agreed to help you in your own mission is your promise to me."

Hofmeister checked his emotions, the fire in the man's eyes clearly enough for both of them. "And it is a promise we will honor."

The man raised a finger, a finger Hofmeister would have broken off if it were anyone else. "You better, or you will face the wrath of our organization and the Church itself."

Hofmeister smiled. "Do not worry, my friend. When the Fourth Reich is established, the Catholic Church will stand by its side, the only permitted religion in the new world order."

"And St. Peter's soldiers will ensure you keep your word."

Sapienza University, Rome, Italy

Reading had already called 112, the Italian equivalent of 911, as Acton and Laura leapt to Giasson's side. Reading hung up the phone and stepped out into the hallway to check on the four officers down in the hallway. Acton was pretty sure the two who had betrayed them were the two stationed at the front entrance to the building. They had clearly ambushed the four at the door.

They never stood a chance.

"How do you feel?" asked Laura as she pressed Acton's handkerchief over the wound.

"I'll live." Giasson winced at the pressure.

Acton rolled up his jacket and placed it under Giasson's head. "This is starting to become a habit with you."

"Only when you two are around."

Acton laughed, as did Laura, Giasson starting to join in before he decided the pain wasn't worth it. Acton patted his shoulder. "Take it easy. No more comedy."

Sirens sounded outside and Reading returned, going to the window and peering outside. "Police are here."

Acton frowned. "They were here before and that didn't help us."

"We've been betrayed," said Giasson through clenched teeth.

Reading grunted. "Yes, but by who? Who knew?"

Giasson looked at Reading, shaking his head. "It's a short list, I assure you."

Footsteps pounding on the marble in the hallway had them all turning toward the sound, Father Rinaldi rising from saying prayers, as Acton was sure they all wondered whether these police were truly on their side.

Four men burst inside, guns drawn, orders shouted in Italian, the waving of guns the only translation anyone needed to get their asses on the ground and their hands up.

Another man entered, shouting at the officers who immediately raised their weapons. He snapped his fingers, directing two of them to Giasson's side.

"He needs an ambulance immediately," said Laura, still on her knees, hands clasped behind her head. Acton watched her, concerned, sweat beading on her upper lip, her entire body trembling.

"Yes, ma'am, one is arriving as we speak." The man in charge looked at Giasson. "Are you okay, my friend?"

Giasson stared at him, his eyes narrowed slightly, giving Acton the distinct impression he didn't trust the man. "What are *you* doing here? I thought you were 'unavoidably detained'."

"I'm here now. What happened?"

Paramedics rushed into the room, the police relinquishing their efforts to the trained personnel. The man in charge motioned for everyone to get to their feet. "You aren't under arrest. Please, stand." He turned to the paramedics. "How is he?"

"The bullet went straight through, just hit muscle. Lots of blood, but he'll be okay."

Acton squeezed Laura's hand in relief as Giasson was lifted onto a stretcher. He held up a hand. "Wait." He motioned for Reading to come closer, then whispered something in his ear before dropping back down on the stretcher. "Okay, let's go."

The officer in charge turned toward the others as his officers exited the room, kneeling beside their fallen comrades. "I'm Chief Inspector Riva. Who is Agent Reading?"

Reading stepped forward. "I am."

"Good, a fellow law enforcement officer. What happened here?"

Reading gave him a quick summary of the events.

"And they took the portrait?"

"Yes."

"And you have no idea who?"

Reading shook his head. "None."

"Nothing was said that might give us a clue where to start?"

"No."

Acton hid his surprise, the reference to Führer certainly enough to give the police a starting point. Reading wasn't cooperating, which was completely out of character for him. Which meant Giasson must have whispered something to him that had him doubting whether or not this man could be trusted.

"That's unfortunate." He slapped the side of his leg, shaking his head. "Well, I'll need statements from all of you, of course, but then you're free to return home."

Reading nodded. "Of course."

"Just as soon as we know Mario is okay," said Laura, her voice conveying the fact she was going nowhere unless she decided it was time.

The man didn't hide his displeasure very well.

"Of course."

Leaving Rome, Italy

Obersturmbannführer Franz Hofmeister sipped his schnapps as he waited for the call to connect, he now occupying the rear seat of the Audi A8, their guest dropped off earlier. Yesterday's operation had been an unmitigated disaster, yet today's had gone off perfectly.

"Hold for the Doctor."

Hofmeister put his drink in a cup holder and straightened himself out of habit.

"Obersturmbannführer, report."

The man's voice was curt, rather high pitched, and terrifying. It was a voice he had been hearing since he was a boy, since he had begun his indoctrination. He was the third generation, the Doctor the second, the adopted son of the great Mengele himself.

A man who attacked his work with the same zeal as one of Nazi Germany's greatest gifts to medical science.

If only we had had more time!

He often chuckled at the debate over killing civilians in war. Tens of millions had died in World War II, and to the Allies' credit, there was no shortage of victims at their hands. What people conveniently forgot so many years later was that this war was a race against time. The Allies couldn't wage a slow war, protecting every civilian. If they had taken just another six months to win, Germany's scientists would have won the ultimate race.

The race for the atomic bomb.

And the war would have ended just as quickly as it had in the Pacific.

The Allies couldn't risk losing the race, so innocent people had to die in order that the majority could live.

He respected them for that.

As did Mengele.

He had been privileged enough to have dinner with the man, and he outlined how he would deal with a modern threat like ISIS.

"Carpet bomb the entire area, killing every last man woman and child. The innocents that live there are dying anyway, the women are being raped, the children sold into slavery, the men forced to fight or die. These people would rather be dead than to live another day under that black flag. Kill them all, put them out of their misery, and in the process, eliminate the threat." Mengele had sliced off a particularly rare piece of his steak, blood dripping onto his plate as he stabbed the air with his fork. "And it will have the added benefit of warning anyone in the future how they will be dealt with should they defy us."

It had been an exceedingly enjoyable dinner. His excitement at being there had meant he barely appreciated the delicacies served. It wasn't the food that was the draw. It was the company. Mengele rarely granted audiences, he now quite old. It was his son that directed most of the day-to-day activities, he having followed his father into the biomedical field and was, by all accounts, a genius.

If only we had won, the world would be such a better place.

Men and women would be living in space, on the moon, on Mars even. The world would be at peace, Germania ruling it all.

"Sir, I have the portrait."

"Were there any complications?"

"No, we got away clean."

"Very well. Report to me when you arrive."

"Yes, sir."

"Heil Hitler."

"Heil Hitler!"

The call ended and he dropped back into his seat, not realizing he was sitting upright, as close to being at attention as one could be in the back of a car. His heart pounded in his chest as he replayed the conversation in his head.

He wants to see me. Me!

It was more than he could have ever hoped for, and would be the greatest honor of his life. He imagined it would be much like when his grandfather had met the Führer himself when he was younger, when the Congress had been established.

Sturmbannführer Bernard Heidrich.

He didn't share his name. None of them did. Everyone in the Congress had new identities, and their offspring shared them. As far as history was concerned, his grandfather had been executed in 1945 for failing to retrieve the very portrait that now sat beside him, not dead from a heart attack twenty years ago.

He would be so proud at how close we are to accomplishing Operation Raven's Claw.

He picked up his drink, taking another sip, closing his eyes. The carnage in the world today was heartbreaking, especially when the solutions were so simple. The problem was a complete lack of political will. When leaders are obsessed with reelection, they too often fail to do the right thing. Sometimes the right thing was bloody, sometimes it was unpopular, sometimes it was dirty.

Like Mengele's solution to the Middle East.

Eliminate it.

It was an elegant, clean solution. Conventional weapons could wipe out the population without having to go nuclear. If necessary, chemical or biological weapons could be used to ensure complete victory.

It would probably be cheaper too.

The world was crying out for order, order only a Führer could provide. The world needed a man who was answerable to no one, who wasn't concerned with voters or polls, who wasn't concerned with what the press thought of him.

Russian aggression, Chinese expansion, Japanese pacifism, Islamic fundamentalism, a black in the White House, Jews controlling the banks. The world needed order, and the Congress was the solution. Once they were successful in fulfilling the dream, the work would begin to reestablish what had been lost, and in time, the world would demand a leader capable of protecting them from themselves.

The Führer himself.

Leaving Rome, Italy

Acton rushed into the hotel room, pointing at his laptop computer sitting on the table. "Login, now!"

Laura nodded, immediately grabbing it and sitting down, flipping open the lid, the screen flashing to life. Acton and Reading quickly swept the two-bedroom suite, making sure they were alone. They had all given statements at the police station, and they all had told the complete truth, except for the mention of the Führer. Even Father Rinaldi had omitted that point apparently, Reading getting him aside and out of earshot of Chief Inspector Riva before they had been taken to the police station.

They hadn't been alone for hours, this the first opportunity the three of them had to talk since the arrival of the police.

Reading grabbed three bottles of water and handed them out, Laura passing the laptop over to Acton as he sat beside her. "What's going on?" asked Reading.

Acton quickly logged into the tracking website. "I dropped my phone in the crate. We should be able to track where they went."

Reading's eyebrows popped as he took a seat. "Are you kidding me?"

Acton shook his head. "No."

"You've got a pair, that's for sure."

Acton grunted. "I acted on instinct. It was stupid. Dangerous."

Reading took a long swig from his bottle before responding. "Correct on all accounts. If you had been caught, they might have killed you."

Acton twisted the cap off his bottle as the map drew itself on the screen, a red dot finally appearing as he took a sip. "There! They're heading north!"

Reading climbed from his seat and rounded the table, examining the path the phone had taken over the past several hours. "Good. Now who do we tell?"

Acton frowned, leaning back on the couch, putting his arm around his exhausted wife. "We can't trust the police."

"No," said Reading, shaking his head emphatically as he returned to his seat. "Before they took Mario away he said to trust no one. Clearly he had concerns about Chief Inspector Riva."

"That much was pretty obvious," agreed Laura, holding her bottle to her cheek.

Acton watched the map update, the dot moving a little bit farther north on the highway. He looked at Reading. "If we can't trust the police, can we trust Mario's men?"

Reading shrugged. "Maybe it wasn't the police at all."

"But we saw them—"

Reading held up a finger. "No, we saw two men in uniform. We don't know if they were actually police."

Acton blasted a breath out his nose.

"So what you're saying is we can't trust anybody."

Giasson Residence, Via Nicolò III, Rome, Italy

Mario Giasson closed his eyes, enjoying the sound of his children pounding through the house, the aromas of last night's leftovers being reheated in the kitchen reaching the bedroom in which he now rested. He had missed the special dinner last night, four people dying on the sovereign territory where you were responsible for security sometimes a reasonable excuse.

Marie-Claude didn't mind. She was more concerned about what had happened and whether or not he and their friends were safe. He had an amazing job. He was responsible for security in a state that had less than 500 citizens, where the most common crimes were pickpocketing and purse snatching.

And that was never done by his citizens.

Tens of thousands of people visited every day.

Including criminals.

His job was predictable, in that he would rarely not be home on schedule unless it was known well ahead of time. The Pope was an important man, with millions who wanted him dead for the mere fact he was Christian. They were constantly vigilant, and when there were special events, he would quite often work late hours.

But on what were supposed to be normal days like yesterday and today? His arrival home was usually like clockwork.

His shoulder throbbed then a shot of pain pierced his body.

He gasped, it quickly receding.

It was just a flesh wound, tearing away part of his arm. It would need to be packed for a few weeks until the skin grew back in. That meant no stitches, no heavy bleeding, and hopefully, no scar.

And it also meant he wasn't about to be cooped up in a hospital room when there was a perfectly comfortable bed at home with his name on it.

One of the advantages of his senior position at the Vatican was that he had access to all the city-state had to offer, including its medical staff. He had already had his second-in-command, Gerard Boileau, arrange for a visit every two hours to assuage the concerns of the doctors at the hospital, and he had been officially transferred to their care.

Two of his men were stationed outside his home, and the State Police had a car on the street out front. He didn't know who he could trust, so at the moment, having both parties guarding his house he felt was the most prudent move.

They would keep a wary eye on each other.

The doorbell rang and the race was on as his daughters rushed to see who could answer it first. His wife yelled, halting them in their tracks as she ordered them back to their bedroom. He heard the alarm chime as the front door opened and he checked himself to make sure he was decent, as the real reason he had insisted on being taken home, arrived. He could hear the mumbled voices out front as pleasantries were exchanged, two of his guests having met his wife once before during even more unpleasant circumstances.

"Sweetheart, your guests are here!" Footsteps on the hardwood floors foretold their approach and moments later his wife entered the bedroom, the Actons and Reading entering.

"How are you doing?" asked Laura, stepping forward and taking his hand. "Shouldn't you be in the hospital?"

"That's what *I* said." Marie-Claude raised her hands, palms upward. "But will he listen to me? No!"

Acton and Reading shook his hand then he motioned for them to sit in the three chairs his wife had brought in earlier. "There was no way I was going to sit in a hospital when there's work to be done."

"You've got over one hundred people working for you. You should learn to delegate."

"I delegate you to get our guests something to drink."

Everyone shook their heads, not wanting to get in the middle of it. He smiled.

"I'll bring some iced tea."

"That would be lovely," said Laura. "Can I help?"

Marie-Claude waved her off. "No, no, you relax. You're our guests." She winked at her husband. "Besides, I think you'll need all your energy dealing with that one."

"Love you too, dear."

She winked at him then turned to leave.

"Close the door, would you, hon?"

"Anything for my wounded warrior."

She closed the door and he rolled his eyes.

"Laura, if he rolled his eyes after me you give him a slap!"

Everyone laughed, Giasson wincing and grabbing for his shoulder.

"Consider it done!" said Laura loud enough to be heard through the door. She looked at Giasson. "She clearly loves you."

"Thank God. If she didn't, I'm afraid what she'd do to me." He shifted slightly then looked at his guests. "First, thank you for coming. You are the only three people I trust in this matter." He patted the wound. "This is far less bad than it looks, or that anyone knows. I'm on some painkillers and antibiotics, but that's it. You're the only people who know this besides the doctor at the hospital, and I told him that little tidbit isn't to be shared. Assuming he honors doctor-patient confidentiality, we should be good."

"I assume you have plans?" asked Reading, a man Giasson knew would do exactly the same if the roles were reversed.

"We need to catch those responsible, but we've got a problem."

Reading pursed his lips. "We don't know who we can trust."

"Exactly. We need to figure out who talked. I've narrowed down the possibilities from my end. Did any of you tell anyone where you were going or why?"

Acton shook his head but Laura leaned forward. "I told my service where we were going, but not why. I had to arrange the flight."

"And I had to tell work I was taking a couple of personal days," said Reading. "No mention of the portrait of course."

Giasson nodded, pleased. "Good, I figured that would be the case. Which means the leak came at this end. We have Father Rinaldi, who identified the portrait and arranged the lab time at the university. He was supposed to tell no one, but could have. You know how scientists are."

Reading grunted, jerking a thumb at his friends. "Do I!"

Acton chuckled, elbowing his friend in the shoulder.

"There's Professor Salvay at the university who Father Rinaldi called. He too would have been told to keep it quiet."

"He wasn't there, was he?" observed Laura. "Isn't that a little strange?"

Giasson shook his head. "He had told Father Rinaldi he wouldn't be. He's apparently in Florence visiting family."

"Who else?" asked Acton, leaning forward.

"My second-in-command, Gerard Boileau, of course knew and I gave him explicit instructions to tell no one. And then there's Chief Inspector Riva."

"I get the distinct impression you think he's our man."

Giasson pushed his lips out as he nodded at Reading. "He was supposed to be there, wasn't. Arrived just after the shooting, which means he was in the area, and it was men dressed in State Police uniforms that did the shooting. If they weren't police, their uniforms had to come from somewhere."

Reading nodded. "He's definitely the most likely suspect, but I don't think we can rule anyone out. And all that being said, someone could have let something slip completely innocently. And if that's the case, the suspect pool could grow exponentially very quickly."

Laura leaned forward. "Let's see if we can eliminate anyone. If Professor Salvay is out of town, I can't see him being able to organize something like this on such short notice. As well, we have to assume this is linked to the shooting yesterday, which would mean he would have had to be involved in that. Do you think that's possible?"

Giasson shook his head, impressed at her reasoning. "No, I don't see it at all."

"Neither do I," agreed Acton. "I've worked with him before. He's a good man."

"And then there's Father Rinaldi," continued Laura. "We've both worked with him in the past. If he wanted to steal the portrait, why would he identify it and bring us in? He would have had many opportunities over the past twenty-four hours to switch it out with something else."

Giasson jabbed the air with a finger. "This is true. He's the one who identified it then figured out who to call in."

Reading rose, pacing in front of the door. "And if either of them mentioned it casually to anyone, it wouldn't matter. We know it has to be someone that was involved prior to the shooting yesterday."

"So that leaves two possibilities."

Giasson looked at Laura. "Chief Inspector Riva."

"Or your man."

Giasson nodded at Laura's conclusion. "I'm afraid you're right."

"How do you plan to figure it out?" asked Acton.

"Good old fashioned police work." He turned to Reading. "Care to help?"

Reading grinned. "Bloody right I would!"

Rocca d'Angera Castle, Angera, Italy

Hofmeister caught a glimpse of himself in a tall mirror to his right, his jet black SS uniform freshly pressed, not a thread loose, not a piece of lint in sight. He was perfect in every sense of the word. A fine specimen of humanity's future. Through selective breeding, the Congress was managing to turn out better stock with each generation, and soon, with the scientific advances being made here and around the world, they'd be able to manipulate the genome, changing the species for the better.

He kept abreast of the latest developments in genetics, and the recent announcement by the Chinese that they had successfully—and illegally—modified the germ line, had sent chills through the entire scientific community and the public who could understand it.

Here it had been a moment to rejoice.

It meant their work had made a major leap forward.

For they had two tasks here that needed completion before they could bring order.

Create the Master Race.

And perfect human cloning.

The latter task had a dual purpose, and with he being young and healthy, he fully expected to see all of their tasks accomplished within his lifetime.

Two soldiers snapped to attention at the end of the corridor, opening the large doors to the conference room. He entered, his chin held high, his chest thrust out, his shoulders back, and snapped a smart salute.

"Heil Hitler!"

The table of the executive returned his hail, though a little more subdued than he would have expected.

They're mostly old men. Maybe it's time for fresh blood.

He caught his breath as Dr. Josef Mengele Jr. himself entered the room. Everyone leapt to their feet.

"Heil Hitler! Heil Mengele!"

The salute was returned in typical Führer style as the head of the table was vacated, one side shifting down as their leader took his place. He looked at Hofmeister.

"You have something for us?"

"Yes, sir!" Hofmeister snapped his fingers and one of his men rushed in, carrying the crate containing the da Vinci portrait. He took it and placed it on the table, keeping his expression neutral though he felt a tremendous amount of excitement to be in the great man's presence. "We have the portrait."

"Excellent work. Show us."

Hofmeister held out his open hand and a small hammer was slapped into it with the crisp precision of a nurse handing a surgeon his scalpel. He pried off the top and placed it to the side, tipping the crate up slightly so the portrait would slide out. His fingers felt the edge of the portrait and he gently squeezed, pulling it free.

Something clattered onto the tabletop.

His eyes widened in shock, his stoic exterior broken.

"What is that?"

His wide eyes stared up at Mengele. "A cellphone!"

If rage could kill, he'd be dead already, Mengele's eyes conveying the anger and hatred his and his father's reputation were notorious for. "How did it get there?"

"It must be that damned professor. He asked to package it properly so it wouldn't be damaged."

"And you agreed?"

"At the time I didn't see the harm." His shoulders slumped, his chest deflated. "He tricked me."

"A clever man. Too clever for you, apparently." Mengele glanced at the others. "Perhaps we should recruit *him* instead."

Nervous laughter from those gathered suggested a history of doubt as to when their leader was joking.

Hofmeister drew a quick breath, forcing himself back into the pose of a proud German. "Sir, I will take care of this."

"How?"

Hofmeister picked up the phone. "With this. He slipped it in during a moment of bravado. It will still contain all of the contact information for his friends and family. I already know from our contact that an American and a British professor were being brought in. I'm guessing he's the American, so he'll be easy to find. And with a bookworm like that, we simply need to apply the right pressure. He won't be a problem."

"He better not be," said Mengele, raising a boney finger and jabbing the air with it. "Or you will become mine."

Giasson Residence, Via Nicolò III, Rome, Italy

"It looks like they've arrived at wherever they were going." Acton flipped the laptop around so Giasson could see it. "According to this it hasn't moved in almost half an hour."

Laura leaned over and looked. "They could just be stopped for a break."

"Let me see." Acton zoomed in on the map, his eyebrows jumping when he saw the pixelated image coalesce into a clearer picture. "What do you make of that?"

Everyone gathered closer.

"Is it a castle?" Laura's voice was tentative, as if she couldn't quite believe it herself.

Acton nodded, it appearing to him to be exactly that. "It looks like a castle at the edge of a mountain town in northern Italy." He glanced at Giasson. "Is that possible?"

Giasson nodded. "Yes. You Americans don't seem to realize how many castles there are in Europe. There're thousands of them and a lot of them are privately owned, usually in preservation deals. The governments can't afford to preserve them all, so most go to ruin, but there are private non-profit groups, and individuals, who will buy them and restore them as museums or even residences."

Acton peered at the picture then pointed. "It looks like there's at least half a dozen cars in the courtyard. This thing is definitely occupied."

"We'll need to find out who lives there," said Laura, returning to her chair and taking a sip of the iced tea Marie-Claude had brought earlier.

"Shouldn't be too difficult." Reading sat back down. "I'll use my Interpol access and see what I can find out."

Acton glanced at Giasson to see if he still wanted to look at the laptop. The man shook his head, waving his hand slightly and Acton sat back down. "Should we go there?"

"Absolutely not." Acton looked at Reading. "There's no reason to risk our lives over a drawing."

"But they're thieves and murderers! And who knows how long they'll stay there. If we're going to catch them, we have to act now."

"*We* don't have to do any such thing. We need to figure out who we can trust, and until then, sit tight."

Giasson yawned and Acton looked at him, the man beginning a battle to keep his eyes open. Acton stood. "We'll let you get your rest. We'll be at our hotel room, trying to find out as much as we can. Call us if you need anything."

"I'm sorry, my friends, it would appear that getting shot does indeed take a lot out of you."

Laura smiled and patted his foot under the covers. "Having been shot recently, I can attest to that."

Giasson smiled then his face became serious.

"Remember, trust no one. Whoever they are, they have killed six people, including four police officers. They won't hesitate to kill you should they think you're a threat."

Acton felt his body tense as Giasson's words sank in. He felt Laura's hand slide into his, squeezing hard.

"Don't worry. We will."

Rocca d'Angera Castle, Angera, Italy

"So, Karl, who is he?"

Hofmeister leaned into the screen as their lead tech's fingers flew over the keyboard, the iPhone in a shielded box so it could no longer transmit its location, giving up all its secrets as the contacts were pulled and cross referenced against the law enforcement databases the Congress had access to.

"His name is Professor James Acton. I requested his file for this morning's mission. It's quite extensive." Karl handed him a file folder. "He's apparently very well connected and his wife is extremely rich."

"How rich?"

"From what I can tell, approaching half a billion Euros."

Hofmeister whistled as he flipped through the file, his eyes narrowing as he read the little bit known about the professors, and their propensity for getting into trouble. What never seemed clear was how they got out of it.

Karl motioned toward the file. "He might not be the easy target you thought."

Hofmeister frowned, glaring at Karl. "You forget your place."

Fear flashed over Karl's face as he paled. "Sorry, sir. I meant no disrespect."

Hofmeister felt a rush of pleasure at the man's obvious fear. It was something he'd never tire of. "Of course you didn't. You are not a fool." He flipped the file shut. "You've read this?"

"Yes, Obersturmbannführer."

"Then what are his vulnerabilities."

"He has a wife but no children. His parents are still alive and he is an only child. There's no intel on friends yet, but we'll gather that from the contacts on his phone."

Hofmeister pursed his lips as he thought of how best to apply leverage. The man was married, but it could be a failing marriage for all he knew. Kidnap her and Acton might simply rejoice. He had no children or siblings, and friends were sometimes difficult to assess as to how willing you were to compromise your ideals for them.

But parents?

"Where are the parents?"

"They've recently moved to Germantown, Maryland."

"Have a team pick them up, immediately."

"Yes, Obersturmbannführer!"

Ellsworth and Dorothy Acton Residence, Germantown, Maryland

"I can't believe we're watching this."

Ellsworth Acton stared at the television screen, shaking his head. He'd rather nothing on than most of what was available today. Yet he found he couldn't pull himself away from the screen. It was strange, something he noticed even in public. If there was a screen, everyone's eyes were inevitably drawn to it. At a bar, a restaurant, the airport, the barber. Everywhere there was a screen, even if you couldn't hear what was happening, your eyes were drawn to it.

It was a sickness.

And now his son had given him an eReader, yet another screen to stare at.

"No, Dad, it's an eReader, not a tablet. It's a dedicated device with a special display that doesn't strain the eyes. You read it just like a book."

He had been skeptical but had given it a shot, unwilling to let good money go to waste.

And had become hooked.

His son was right. It was just like reading a book, only better. He hated staring at computer screens and trying to read anything for any reasonable amount of time. But the eReader? It was fantastic.

He glanced down at it, sitting in his lap, even it unable to compete with the insanity on the screen.

"What was that dear?"

He looked over at his beloved Dorothy, sitting in her recliner to his right, finally picking up on the fact he had said something. "I said I can't believe we're watching this. This isn't a talent show, this is America's Got Too Much Time On Its Hands."

"Oh, live a little, it's fun. Some of these acts are amazing."

"Right. You've got a Canadian, a Brit and a German telling America who's got talent."

"Yeah, that is a bit ironic, isn't it?"

"To no end." He shook his head.

Dorothy muted the television as a commercial started, still not embracing the full power of the Digital Video Recorder. "It's what the kids are watching today."

"I fear for my country."

"It's a new generation."

"That will drive us into the ground." He glanced over at Dorothy. "I shudder to think what will happen when these kids become the leaders of our country."

"They'll do fine. Look at Jim."

"It's not Jim I'm worried about, it's his students. When they get in the White House in thirty years, we're doomed."

Dorothy smiled, reaching over and patting his hand. "You have to think positively, dear, you'll be dead by then."

Ellsworth laughed, nodding his head. "If I'm lucky. Then it will be Jim who has to worry about it."

"But not his kids."

Ellsworth immediately sensed the gloom sweep over his wife. He felt his own chest tighten slightly. His son and his new wife had only recently learned they'd never be able to have children, complications from a gunshot wound Laura had received several months before. It had been devastating news. He couldn't care less if he had grandchildren, it was the pain in his son and daughter-in-law's eyes that had hurt. And it was the final straw for his wife, the house sold in Stowe and one closer to their son, bought.

He pointed at a lawn care commercial on the television, trying to change the subject. "Lenny said yesterday he was going to shoot anyone who tried to enforce the pesticide ban."

"If he ever followed through on these threats half the town would be dead."

"He's right though. It's junk science. I haven't been able to find a single study that shows proper use outdoors has harmed anyone. And now some jurisdictions that have banned them are seeing asthma rates go through the roof, emergency room visits are skyrocketing with respiratory problems, their cities look like overrun weed farms, and their parks and sports fields are unusable." He shook his head, rage building in his stomach. "It's bullshit like that that pisses me off to no end. These environutbars get something in their head then run with it to the exclusion of all else. How many people have died to save not a single life lost to pesticides. If you want *me* to not use it, fine, but let me hire a professional to spray my lawn."

"Remember what your doctor said, you need to watch your blood pressure."

Ellsworth growled. "Don't get me started on him."

The doorbell rang and Dorothy jumped from her chair. "Thank God!"

He grinned. "Saved by the bell?"

"Are you expecting anyone?" she asked.

"If I were, you'd know."

"Ha ha."

She disappeared down the hallway and he heard the alarm chime then a cry. He leapt from his chair, a little slower than he would have liked, and rushed toward the hall. As he rounded the corner, he charged as two blonde men stepped into the house, one with a black gloved hand pressed over his wife's mouth, her head pressed against the wall.

A rage built within him as he surged forward, hatred in his eyes.

You don't touch my family!

A gun appeared, pointed at his chest.

He kept charging.

Then it pointed at his wife.

He eased up, coming to a stop only feet away.

"Get your hands off my wife!"

The man holding her stared at him. "Don't be a hero, Mr. Acton. You'll just get your wife killed." He removed the hand from Dorothy and Ellsworth reached out, pulling her toward him.

"What do you want?" he asked, glaring at the intruders.

"It's not *you* we want. It's your son."

Ambasciatori Palace Hotel, Rome, Italy

Acton lay on the bed, his eyes closed, as Reading worked his phone in the other room, trying to find out anything he could on the castle Acton's phone had ended up in. Acton had decided the best approach right now was to let the system do its job—and Reading and Giasson were that system—while he got some rest. Laura lay beside him, gently snoring, exhausted from the ordeal, her stamina still a work in progress.

Her phone vibrated on the nightstand.

She moaned.

"I'll get it, you sleep."

"Who is it?" mumbled Laura.

"Blocked number."

He swiped his thumb over the display as he sat on the edge of the bed. "Hello?"

"Professor James Acton?"

"Yes?"

"Professor Acton, we have your parents, Ellsworth and Dorothy."

Acton leapt to his feet, yanking open the bedroom door and rushing into the living area where Reading was. He snapped his fingers and pointed at the phone, Reading immediately nodding and ending his call, dialing another number to start a trace.

"What do you mean? Are they okay?" he asked, not sure what to say, his mind racing with dozens of horrible scenarios.

"If you contact the police, they will die."

He glanced at Reading who was rolling his hand, indicating he needed more time. He decided not to stop him.

"What have you told the authorities about the theft?"

Laura entered the room, her brow furled with curiosity. He shook his head, holding a finger to his lips, silencing her unspoken question.

"Nothing."

"I find that hard to believe, Professor Acton. We found your phone. Clever. I assume you have traced its location?"

He said nothing, terrified the admission might seal his parents' fate.

"Professor, don't make me hurt your mother. These are simple questions. Answer truthfully and I won't be forced to apply pressure." There was a pause. "I will ask you once again. Have you traced your phone's location?"

Acton drew in a slow breath, closing his eyes. "Yes."

"So you know where the portrait is."

It was a statement, not a question. Acton decided to try a different tact, it clear this was of concern to the man. "I know where the *phone* was several hours ago. I assume you could have continued to another location, leaving the phone behind."

The man chuckled. "Yes, Professor, that is possible. Have you told the authorities where the phone is?"

"No."

"The truth, Professor."

"I haven't. I swear."

"Why not?"

Acton decided this was one instance where following the man's instructions might actually prove useful. "Frankly, I don't know who to trust. Very few people knew we would be there and it was police that were with the man who took the portrait. Telling them isn't exactly high on my priority list."

"And just what is high on your priority list now?"

119

Acton frowned. "It's changed."

"I should think so. Your focus now should be the wellbeing of your parents, and nothing more."

"Agreed. What do you want from me?"

"Your silence."

"You have it."

"Good."

Acton sat in a chair, squeezing his temples as he tried to control his exasperation. "What now?"

"Now we will wait to see if you keep your word."

Acton froze then sat up. "For how long?"

"That depends on whether or not I feel you are to be trusted. Right now, I am inclined to not believe so, after the stunt you pulled."

"I'm sorry about that. Please don't take what I did out on my parents. They're innocent in this."

"Which is exactly why you will do as you are told."

"You have my word."

"I trust I do. To that end, we will be keeping your parents for a little while, just to make sure you truly are a man of your word."

"How—?"

"How long? Perhaps a few days, perhaps a few weeks. I really can't say. I *will* say that as long as you maintain your silence, they will be kept alive. You will find, Professor Acton, that we think in the long term. The *extreme* long term. Your silence must be permanent."

"It will be. My only concern is my parents."

"They will be safe. Do not break your word, Professor, or I will begin releasing your parents. One body part at a time."

CIA Headquarters, Langley, Virginia

National Clandestine Service Chief Leif Morrison checked his watch and groaned. He closed his eyes, dropping his elbows on his desk and giving his scalp a massage. He was exhausted.

Time to go home.

It had been a quiet day. At least for his job. There had been over a dozen terrorist attacks around the world, though none high profile, none involving America or its allies. Just a typical day when Islamic fundamentalists were so well funded by supposed allies.

Today had been a good day, but with his wife visiting her sister, it had been a chance to catch up on paperwork. And it was now past midnight.

Definitely time to go home.

The phone demanded his attention and he sighed. He hit the intercom button. "Yes?"

"Sonya Tong, urgent."

"Put her through." Sonya was one of Chris Leroux's team. Leroux was one of the best analysts he had, and was turning into one hell of a team lead now that he had his sea legs under him. And for one of Leroux's analysts to be calling directly, something major had to be happening.

The phone beeped and he picked up the receiver. "This is Morrison."

"Chief, I'm sorry to disturb you, but, umm, I wasn't sure what to do."

Morrison frowned, the young woman clearly flustered, so whatever she had stumbled upon must be very serious. "Why don't you just tell me what has you so concerned."

"Umm, well, you know how we've been monitoring law enforcement reports for anything to do with certain, umm, *key* personnel?"

Morrison smiled slightly, the CIA monitoring for thousands of people. "You'll have to narrow that down a bit for me."

Sonya's voice dropped to barely a whisper. "I mean Chris and the others, you know, involved with the Assembly."

Morrison immediately bolted up in his chair, Sonya finally having his full attention. The Assembly had been a thorn in their side for several years, an ultra-secret organization that had apparently existed for decades if not centuries, with their fingers in so many pies it was impossible to get a bead on them.

Until just a few weeks ago when they had caught a lucky break.

Up to that point his prize analyst Leroux had been under constant watch by a protective detail, Morrison fearing the Assembly might try to take him out due to his investigation.

But they had gained leverage, leverage that appeared to have worked, the Assembly threat gone to ground as far as they could tell.

Yet he wasn't a fool.

So he had ordered the monitoring to continue, watching for any reports that might suggest the Assembly was moving on their problems, not the least of which was Leroux. Though it wasn't limited to Leroux. It included one of his prize agents and an archeology professor, James Acton, along with his friends and family.

"Continue."

"I just monitored a report that says Professor Acton's parents might have been abducted."

"What?"

"A neighbor reported seeing two men forcing them into a vehicle less than an hour ago."

"Jesus Christ! Wait right there!" He hit the *Hold* button then dialed another number.

"Dispatch."

"Team Sierra-Foxtrot-Four-One, have them secure their targets, now!"

Leroux and White Residence, Fairfax Towers, Falls Church, Virginia

Chris Leroux collapsed on top of his girlfriend and best thing ever to happen to him, Sherrie White. It had been a marathon session of lovemaking, touching upon more surfaces of their small apartment than he could have previously imagined. He *loved* it when she came back from assignment, her job as a CIA agent taking her away too frequently. He hated that she'd have to leave, but the rewards when she returned were worth it.

He tried to catch his breath as her own lungs heaved under his weight. He moved to get off her when she reached behind her and grabbed his waist. "No, I want to feel you on top of me."

He smiled, pressing his cheek against her back, closing his eyes. He loved the feel of her skin on his, their sweat dripping off their bodies, the mix of endorphins and pheromones exciting him in ways he had never known possible before he met the love of his life.

It had been a couple of years now since they met, she a CIA agent sent to test his loyalties with the ultimate temptation.

Her.

But she had failed, or he had succeeded. The perspective was a glass half-full or half-empty thing. She had developed feelings for him and requested reassignment, a request that had been denied, it too late to insert someone else to test him. She had been forced to go through with the deception, and he had resisted her. But the betrayal, once discovered, had cut deep and he had returned to his apartment, broken.

But his high school buddy and CIA Special Agent had forced the two of them back together, and they had never looked back, their relationship still strong, their sex lives even more incredible now that the security detail had been lifted, the Assembly no longer a threat.

It meant freedom to do whatever they wanted, whenever they wanted, without worrying about some security detail seeing something, or worse, barging in.

"You were an animal."

He smiled at Sherrie's gasped words. "You bring out the animal in me?"

"Wasn't that from a song?"

He shrugged. "Dunno. Probably. I'm not very original."

She pushed herself up, and turned around, her bum on the back of the couch, wrapping her legs around his shoulders as she stared down at him. "A few of those moves were pretty original."

He looked away, embarrassed. "Saw that last one in a movie."

"Disney, I'm sure."

He chuckled. "Oh, of course."

She grinned. "Now I know what you do when I'm away on assignment."

"Porn and video games. I am the modern male."

"Well, you're doing something right, baby."

Somebody hammered at the door, startling Sherrie. She yelped, falling backward and landing on the floor, her arms slamming down in a martial arts move designed to take away some of the force.

But it was loud.

The door burst open and Leroux whipped around, Mr. Happy swinging in the breeze, still at half-mast as his former security detail rushed in, the team lead coming to a halt, raising his hand to block the sight.

"Are you two okay? We heard somebody yell."

Sherrie stood up, not bothering to cover herself, any modesty hammered out of her as an agent. "That was me. You scared the shit out of me."

"Out of us," said Leroux, slapping his hands over his withering region. "Umm, what are you doing here?"

Sherrie tossed him a cushion and he let it drop to the floor in front of him, catching it meaning he'd have to expose himself again. And that assumed he actually caught it, his athletic skills never quite up to par.

Always last picked for the team.

Though not anymore.

He led a team of nine of the most talented analysts at the CIA, was respected by his supervisors and his staff, had an incredibly gorgeous girlfriend, and had been under fire without shitting his pants.

That was a life turnaround if there ever was one.

Sherrie slapped a pillow over his crotch.

"Director Morrison has ordered us to take you to a secure location."

"Why?" asked Sherrie as she put on a robe, loosely tying it in front.

The agent frowned. "We believe the Assembly might be making their move."

Kane Family Residence, Albany, New York

"And what do you think I found?"

Dylan Kane shoveled a forkful of scrambled eggs in his mouth while those gathered around the table shouted out guesses, all wrong. To his family he was Dylan Kane, Insurance Investigator for Shaw's of London, his job one of jetting around the globe, busting insurance scams and fraud attempts.

Of course, it was all bullshit.

And he hated having to lie to them.

Especially his father, who had a serious hate on for the insurance industry.

"Horses?"

He looked at his Aunt Ida. "Umm, no. Cars. Every single car he had reported lost at sea."

"How did he think he'd get away with it?" asked his mother. "I mean, didn't he think someone would look in his own garage?"

Kane shook his head. "You wouldn't believe the idiocy I come across. In this case, he was in some heavy debt to some loan sharks in Macao—gambling—so he decided to pretend to ship his cars to London, paid a ship captain to steer into a storm and have the cargo containers dumped overboard so he could claim the insurance. Then he'd sell the actual cars to settle the debt. Only problem was he didn't know how to unload the cars, and his creditors would only take cash. I arrived before he had a chance to move them."

"Fascinating," said his mother, taking a sip of her orange juice. "It must feel so good to catch these people."

127

"It does. Especially the bad ones. Sometimes they're just desperate people, but I don't deal with the little guys." His watch sent an electrical pulse into this wrist, discretely signaling a message from his employer. He ignored it. "Those are quite often the hard luck cases. I usually deal with the multimillion dollar policies. These people sometimes are desperate, but they never face the gutter." He wiped the corners of his mouth. "Excuse me, I need to use the bathroom."

He stood up, dropping his napkin on his chair, then headed for the bathroom. Entering a coded sequence into his watch by pressing the edges in a certain order, a message scrolled.

He cursed.

He couldn't remember the last time he had been able to visit his folks, his real job having him gallivanting all over the world, though like his cover career, this one demanded he drop everything at a moment's notice. He headed back to the table and sat down. "I'm afraid I'm going to have to leave soon. Emergency at work."

His father grunted his displeasure. "Emergency? In the insurance business?"

Kane shrugged as he shoveled each delicious mouthful of his mother's breakfast into his face, not sure when he'd get to enjoy it again. "Well, Dad, we don't schedule natural disasters or criminal activity."

"What is it this time, dear?" asked his mother as she leaned over and dropped another load of eggs and bacon on his plate. He grinned through filled cheeks.

"Oh, nothing serious."

"Then it can wait." His father's voice was gruff as usual when it came to him running off. He wasn't really mad, at least he hoped he wasn't. Kane was sure the man was just disappointed his son had to run off, especially for a job he didn't respect. "It's not like you're out there saving the world, you're trying to save some multibillion dollar company from paying out money on a policy some poor SOB paid into his entire life."

Kane felt his chest tighten at the words, it truly hurtful that his father disrespected his line of work so much that he'd say things like that. It wasn't the first time, though he had never been so blunt before. He just wished he could tell him the truth about what he did.

He'd be so proud.

His mother swatted his father, noticing the gloom clouding her son's face. "Take it easy on him, dear, what he does is important. If everybody was allowed to cheat the insurance company, just imagine how high our premiums would be. Dylan does an important job. Not everybody can be James Bond, saving the world."

Kane smiled.

If only you knew.

"Thanks, Mom."

He cleared his plate then rose, giving his parents and aunt hugs.

"I'll try to get back soon."

"We know you will, dear."

Kane left the home he had grown up in, his heart heavy as it always was. He missed his folks, especially knowing he might never see them again, his line of work not the safest in the career aptitude test.

He started the engine of his rental and pulled out of the driveway, waving to his folks who were standing on the porch, his father appearing particularly sad.

I knew he was just disappointed.

As he pulled out of sight, he hoped that someday he'd be able to reveal what he truly did for a living, and see the pride in his father's eyes he so desperately craved.

He turned toward the airport, a plane already waiting for him.

Time to save the world.

He chuckled as he switched from Dylan Kane, Shaw's of London Insurance Investigator, to Dylan Kane, CIA Special Agent.

I guess it was James Bond's night off.

Ambasciatori Palace Hotel, Rome, Italy

"It's all my fault."

Acton sat on the couch in the living area of the two-bedroom suite, Laura perched behind him, massaging his neck and shoulders, trying to ease his tension.

It wasn't working.

"It's not your fault, dear, you know that."

Acton patted his wife's hand and leaned back into her, ending the massage and giving her hands a rest. "If I had left well enough alone and not put that damned phone in with the portrait, none of this would be happening."

"And if criminals hadn't murdered six people and stolen it, none of this would be happening either." Reading placed his phone down on the table between them. "It's not *your* fault, it's theirs." He pointed at the phone. "They traced the call."

"Let me guess, the castle?"

Reading nodded. "They don't seem to be concerned that we know where they are."

"They don't need to be. They have my parents." Acton shook his head. "And it sounds like they intend to keep them."

"How long?" asked Laura.

"I got the distinct impression he was talking weeks or months, maybe even longer. I think he intends to keep them to keep me silent."

Laura laid her chin on his shoulder, squeezing him around the chest. "I'm so sorry." She extricated herself, sitting beside him. "I think we need to involve the police, FBI, someone."

Acton shook his head. "We can't. We don't know who we can trust, and if we tell the wrong person, and they find out, they could—" He stopped himself, not trusting the words to come out whole as he felt the overwhelming urge to cry. He leaned forward, his elbows on his knees, his head drooping low as he battled for control. "He said...he'd send them to me...one body...part...at a...time."

The tears escaped, rolling down his cheeks and dripping onto the carpet, though he controlled the sobs, determined not to let these bastards get control of his emotions. He had to remain strong, clearheaded, if his parents had any chance. Laura held him tightly from the side, her hand gently stroking his back, as Reading said nothing, the man uncomfortable with displays of emotions.

Acton wiped his cheeks dry and sat up. "Sorry, I guess I needed that."

"Never apologize for being human," said Reading.

Guess he's getting soft in his old age.

Laura turned to face him, bending her leg up under her on the couch. "So what are we going to do?"

Acton looked at her then Reading.

"We need outside help."

Laura smiled slightly. "A little Kraft Dinner?"

He nodded.

"I don't think we have a choice."

Operations Center 3, CIA Headquarters, Langley, Virginia

Leroux sat in a chair at the back of the Operations Center, his team working their magic as he orchestrated their moves. Police reports had confirmed that Professor James Acton's parents were missing, there signs they had left the house abruptly, their television still on, an evening snack half eaten.

Not to mention the reports that a neighbor had seen them getting into a black SUV with two men they didn't recognize, and apparently not dressed like they normally would to go out.

Apparently an overly observant neighbor.

He liked the anonymity of living in an apartment. He barely knew any of his neighbors beyond nodding to them or saying good morning or evening. Few even bothered with that, some turning the opposite direction, his security detail essentially creating a shield around him, both physical and social.

And he had no problem with that.

They liked Sherrie though, especially the guys. They never seemed to avoid her, and a few even expressed surprise when they'd be talking to her at the mailboxes and he'd arrive, she giving him a kiss.

At first he had felt jealousy at it, then pride.

Yeah, asshole, she's mine. Suck it!

He was a loner, a chronic loner, with one real friend—Dylan Kane, a high school buddy he had helped tutor. Kane was the jock, cool, every girl wanted him, every guy wanted to be him. But rather than be an asshole like so many of the other jocks, Kane had been a true friend, sticking up for him over the short time they knew each other, and never ashamed to admit to that friendship. They had lost track of each other when Kane had left for college, but a chance encounter in the cafeteria at Langley had rekindled the friendship, Leroux shocked to learn Kane was an agent.

A secret he had kept to this day, it the secret Sherrie had been tasked to test him with.

His passing had meant his boss, Leif Morrison, had invited him into his inner circle of agents and analysts he trusted.

It was a small circle and the rewards were few beyond respect.

Which was really all he had ever wanted. He had received none in high school except from Kane, and his adult life, until he had met Sherrie, had been one of long hours hunched over a keyboard. Few dates, almost no second dates, no girlfriends to speak of, and no friends.

When the pizza guy is the highlight of your Friday night, you know you've got a problem.

But Sherrie had changed all that. Passing the test had meant he had been given more responsibility, the tougher assignments and eventually a team—something he had been horrified at when he was first informed. His painfully shy and awkward ways did not lend themselves to a leadership role, but with Sherrie's help and Morrison's confidence and encouragement, he had proven himself up to the task, even the analysts twice his age respecting him.

He actually felt pride in himself now, something he had never felt before.

I love my life.

And it could be a much shorter life if the Assembly had decided it was time to eliminate the thorns in their side.

A large array of flat screens that arced around the front of the room showed various traffic cameras along with private security cameras in the area of the abduction, license plate recognition software grabbing the plates and comparing them to the DMV registries for vehicle type, anything that matched the description of a dark colored SUV flagged for review by a human.

His team was good, his team was efficient. He had no doubt they'd narrow down the thousands of vehicles to just a few, but eventually they'd need a more hands on approach.

A buzzer sounded and the door opened, National Clandestine Service Chief Leif Morrison entering. Leroux leapt to his feet. "Sir."

Morrison waved him off. "Sit, Chris, it's not the army."

"Sorry, sir." Leroux remained standing as Morrison came up beside him. "Status?"

"We're hitting every camera in the area, narrowing the list of possibles down, but we're going to need some boots on the ground to run down leads."

"The FBI is already taking over the case. If you find anything, send it their way, but we need to figure out if this has anything to do with the Assembly."

"Yes, sir."

"The FBI has no idea who or what they are, and the détente we have with the Assembly means we need to keep it that way."

"That limits the possibilities of whose boots are available."

"It does."

Leroux smiled. "Anyone in mind?"

Morrison nodded. "Oh, I've already got someone on the way."

Acton Residence, Germantown, Maryland

CIA Special Agent Dylan Kane rolled up on the scene, half a dozen emergency vehicles peppering the street, it now a full-blown investigation. He climbed out and flashed his fake Homeland Security ID to one of the officers who led him to the Agent in Charge.

"Special Agent Kane, Homeland."

The FBI agent in charge of the scene glanced at the badge. "McKinnon. What's Homeland doing here?"

"Their son has a rather high security clearance so I was called in. You've still got the lead, I'm just here as a liaison."

McKinnon grunted, apparently satisfied with the line of bullshit. He motioned toward the house. "Feel free to look around. We're running down vehicles now through traffic cameras. We'll find something."

"Let's hope so. Any signs of violence?"

McKinnon shook his head. "No. I've got a forensics team on its way, but nothing obvious. If we're lucky we'll get some prints off the door."

Kane nodded, doubting anyone hired by the Assembly would be so clumsy. "Have you notified the son?"

"No, we haven't been able to reach him. It keeps going to voicemail."

"Not the kind of news you want to leave in a message."

McKinnon grunted. "Nope. I'm sure we'll hear back soon."

"I'm sure." He tilted his head toward the house. "I'm going to take a look around."

McKinnon nodded, already turning away, indicating to Kane who the man perceived to be the alpha dog. Kane ignored it, used to being treated with disrespect by men far more dangerous and powerful than McKinnon.

136

The difference was he usually ended up killing them.

He walked up the front steps and into the home his former archeology professor had grown up in. Kane hadn't tried to call Acton yet, though things were in motion, the man too influential in his life to leave him hanging. It had been Professor James Acton that he had turned to after 9/11 for guidance. He had wanted to serve, to fight the terrorists that had attacked his country, but hadn't yet finished his education. It was Acton that had urged him to follow his heart, and he had ended up enlisting that week.

His father had been proud and annoyed.

He had distinguished himself, eventually becoming a Ranger then joining Delta. He was quickly approached by the CIA and leapt at the chance.

And left the army to become an insurance investigator with Shaw's of London.

That was the end of any pride his father had displayed.

If only you knew.

If Acton hadn't encouraged him, he might very well have toughed it out, perhaps become an officer at the end of it all, and never had the chance to fight in the trenches, to join Delta, to become a spy. He owed Acton a lot, and he trusted the man, he one of the few people outside of the CIA that knew what he truly did.

And helping him out now wouldn't be the first time.

Acton knew how to reach him, so the fact he hadn't heard from him meant Acton most likely didn't know about his parents yet, or if he did, he was dealing with it in his own way. Either way, Kane couldn't reach out. Not yet. He needed to determine if the Assembly truly was involved, because if they were, they'd most likely be monitoring Acton's communications. And if it weren't, whoever had kidnapped Acton's parents could still be monitoring him, and if a CIA agent reached out, it could sign their death warrants. He needed more intel.

He entered the house, quickly doing a cursory once over, nothing beyond the half-eaten bacon sandwich on a side table suggesting anything untoward.

And a television left on that had since been turned off.

He pulled out his phone, plugging an attachment into the bottom, an app automatically launching after he pressed his thumb on the sensor. It immediately began detecting signals all through the house, the software quickly eliminating identifiable ones. He stepped into the bedroom, scanning with the device and frowned as a strong signal was detected. It increased in strength as he approached an old phone sitting on a nightstand.

We've got a bug.

He found no more on the second floor, returning to the main floor, putting an earbud in as he pretended to be listening to voicemails. Two more phones had bugs though it wasn't until he found the one in the living room, behind a large painting of a winter scene, an old cabin perched at the edge of a frozen river, that he had his answer.

There was some dust on the bug.

Which meant it had been there for some time, though not too long, the Actons having only moved recently.

He frowned.

If these bugs had been here that long, it meant it was most likely the Assembly that had planted them, there no one else he could possibly think of that might have reason to monitor Acton's parents.

Kane froze, rage building in his stomach.

If they're watching his parents, then they're probably watching mine. And Chris'.

He unplugged the device from his phone, slipping it into his pocket as he exited the house, returning to his car. If they were monitoring the parents, then there was a definite possibility they were monitoring him, which severely restricted his options.

I need someone they don't know about.

He thought for a moment then smiled.

Lee Fang Residence, Philadelphia, Pennsylvania

Lee Fang pressed the sensor, making sure her pulse rate was where she wanted it, she at a full sprint on her treadmill, approaching the one-hour mark. She was dripping with sweat, the endorphins rampaging through her system giving her a natural high she thrived on. Her iPhone, strapped to her upper arm, blared a retro eighties mix, Erasure's A Little Respect thumping in her ears, she discovering decades of music she had never known existed until she arrived in the United States.

Against her will.

She had been a member of the Beijing Military Region Special Forces Unit. Tough, disciplined, and loyal. Loyal to a fault, as it would turn out. She had stumbled upon some information she shouldn't have, information that she felt threatened her country, even though some of its top generals were involved.

And when one of those generals tried to rape her, she had killed him.

And her flight had begun.

Reaching out to the only American she knew that she thought she could trust, a member of their Delta Force that she had met on assignment in Africa, she had been put together with a CIA agent named Kane. Kane had saved her ass and got her out of China, and as a thank you for her providing the United States with valuable intel that ended up saving them from a coup, she was given a new identity and a generous pension, despite still being in her twenties.

She was just now starting to get used to her new life, or perhaps she had just resigned herself to the fact she could never go home. She was a traitor and a murderer, at least in her government's eyes. She found it frustrating, the injustice of it all sometimes causing her to break down in tears, an uncharacteristic reaction for her if there ever was one. She loved her country, she loved her people, she loved her job. She had been the best of the best, and now she lived in a small apartment in Philadelphia, living out her days exercising and watching American television, surfing the Internet and trying to figure out what she could do with her life that would have zero chance of her being discovered.

She had no friends.

And was lonely.

Painfully lonely.

The treadmill beeped, her sixty minutes up and she began her cool down, reducing her speed gradually as her perfectly timed mix slowed its beat.

Waay too much time on your hands.

She knew she was lucky. Many people would be thrilled to have a government pension, guaranteed for life, with no need to work. But not her. She had to feel useful, she had to feel like her life had a purpose. And right now, it had none, and she could see no future that would make her happy.

You can never go home.

And in her new homeland, she couldn't put her skills to use. She couldn't join the military, the police, paramedics, or anything. Any job that might involve security was off limits as per her agreement with the American government.

On some of the dark nights, curled up on her couch, tears in her eyes, she had eyed the balcony, contemplating how easy it would be to end the pain, to end the torture of her new reality.

But she couldn't do it.

It would be the ultimate failure.

And she was no failure.

She had to look at this new existence as a challenge. If she couldn't work, then she needed a hobby. Something she could channel her energies into that would be satisfying.

You could always become an assassin.

She smiled as she hit the big red button, stopping the treadmill. Unhooking the safety key, she grabbed a towel and wiped down her face before taking a large swig from her water bottle. She stared at herself in the mirror and flexed. She had been told she had an amazing body, though looks had never been important to her. She turned to the side, checking out her bum.

Not bad.

She knew most women would kill to have her physique, she naturally blessed with a slim body. Her workouts however were intense, which is what gave her the six-pack abs and sculpted arms and legs. When she went out jogging, she received a lot of looks from men, Yellow Fever apparently an affliction among many American men. She hadn't known what it meant until she looked it up on the web.

It had caused her to wear loose fitting clothing when she went out, adopting a more tomboyish look.

A boyfriend was out of the question. She couldn't put anyone at risk like that, and she couldn't stand having to lie to them about her past.

She headed for the shower and stripped naked, activating the Bluetooth shower speaker, her tunes immediately piping out of the tiny speaker. Climbing into the shower, she closed her eyes and let the hot water run over her, relaxing her tasked muscles, her mind drifting to thoughts she fought to control, her sexual needs unmet in so long. It wasn't in her nature to have a one-night stand, and having ruled out a boyfriend, she was limited to her own methods of release.

She pictured her desire, her mind a blur of images that eventually coalesced into the smiling face of a man that surprised her.

Dylan?

He was extremely fit, good looking for a Caucasian, though she had never found white men really attractive.

Maybe living among them for so long has changed your opinion.

She wasn't sure about that. She watched a lot of television and never found herself admiring the men Hollywood presented to her hour after hour.

Maybe it's because he's the only possibility.

She reached down, realizing that he was probably the only man she *could* have some sort of relationship with. He knew her past, he led a life where commitment wasn't an option, and from the obvious interest in her he had displayed, he'd be willing.

She moaned.

"Dylan."

The doorbell rang, followed by three hard knocks on the door, shattering the moment. She turned off the water and stepped out, wrapping a towel around her and grabbing her Glock. She peered through the peephole and saw no one.

Her eyes narrowed.

Odd.

She opened the door, leaving the chain in place, and spotted a small box sitting in front of her door. She closed the door, undid the chain, and opened it again, leaning out. Looking down both ends of the hallway, she saw no one. She knelt down and examined the package. It was wrapped in a plain brown paper with no markings.

Not a delivery.

So it wasn't a mistake, and it wasn't anything normal.

Her radar immediately went up.

She did a quick visual inspection then picked up the package, stepping back inside and locking the door. The package vibrated and she threw it into the kitchen, behind the counter, and dove in front of the couch, covering her head.

Nothing.

She rose, the towel catching on her foot and falling to the floor.

It went unnoticed.

She tentatively stepped into the kitchen, the box on the floor, tilted against the cupboards, still vibrating.

It has to be a phone.

She grabbed the package, excitement rushing through her like a muscle memory of her former life. She tore off the paper, revealing a cardboard box with no markings. Opening it carefully, the vibrations louder now, her eyes widened as her suspicions were confirmed.

She pulled out the Blackberry and pressed the button to take the call.

"Hello?"

"Hi Fang, it's me, Dylan. Busy?"

Ambasciatori Palace Hotel, Rome, Italy

Acton stared at the phone sitting on the table. They had decided that since he had no phone, his parents' kidnappers had Laura's number, and Reading's phone might be compromised if there was a leak in Giasson's office, they needed a new one. Reading had gone out and purchased a burner, and they had used that phone to send a message to Kraft Dinner, they're own code name for Acton's former student, Dylan Kane. His secret contact number wasn't a phone that would ring and his former student would answer, it was a phone number connected to the web somehow that would contact Kane if a special coded sequence was sent to it.

A coded sequence unique to them.

Acton wondered how many people had this method of communication open to them, but given Kane's job, he doubted it was many. It had proven useful to them on too many occasions, and he hoped that it would prove useful once again.

But it had been hours, and they had heard nothing.

Acton sat back in frustration. "For all we know he's in the middle of a desert somewhere with no way of receiving our message."

Reading nodded, Laura in the bedroom sleeping. "Definitely possible. The way our luck is sometimes, most likely."

Acton half-smiled. "One pessimist is enough, thank you very much."

Reading motioned toward the window, the impressive view of the ancient city breathtaking. "You haven't slept all night. You should try to get at least a few hours."

Acton shook his head. "I can't. Not with my parents out there somewhere."

"You're not going to be much use to them if you're dead on your feet."

Acton frowned. "You're right, of course, but I know I'll just lie there and disturb Laura. I'll crash hard at some point, but it's not going to be now."

Laura's familiar morning stretch groan had him turning in his chair to see his wife stepping out of the bedroom, hands extending above her, eyes closed with a contented smile. She gave Acton a kiss then dropped on the couch, curling her legs up under her. "Any news?"

Acton shook his head. "Nothing. We're taking bets on what part of the world with zero cellphone coverage he's in."

Laura leaned over and took a sip from Acton's coffee cup. "Eww. How old is this?"

Acton shrugged. "I don't know, when did you make the last pot?"

"Men!" She rose and headed for the coffeemaker in the kitchenette. "You do realize his system is satellite based."

"Huh?"

"Dylan's comm system. It's not cellular, so it must be satellite."

"And how would you know that?" asked Reading, turning in his chair, an eyebrow cocked.

"Easy. Half the planet, and most of where he deals with, has no coverage. So his system can't be cellular, otherwise the CIA would never be able to communicate with him. And he told us once the method he gave us piggybacks off their system. So it has to be satellite."

Reading smiled, looking at Acton. "She's a hell of a lot sharper than us."

"I don't know what I'd do without her," replied Acton, smiling in appreciation at his wife.

The pot going, she returned to her seat, giving him a peck. "You'd be dead, dear." She winked at Reading. "Or he'd have you in prison."

Acton laughed, Reading joining in as they were reminded of the events surrounding how they all met.

Reading's new phone vibrated and Acton leapt at it.

"It's a text," he said, bringing up the message. He immediately put a finger to his mouth.

Room possibly bugged. If you rented hotel room before theft, leave immediately. Don't take anything except what you were wearing. Leave all phones and electronics. Take cab to St. Peter's Square. Exit north gate. Green Fiat will be waiting. Good luck. DK.

He handed the phone to Laura whose eyes bulged as she read it before handing it over to Reading. Acton rose, emptying his pockets of anything he didn't have on him at all times, Laura heading for the bedroom to get dressed. Reading rose, pointing at the new phone, Acton guessing he was asking if he should leave it as well.

He nodded, pointing at the pile of electronics on the table.

Kane clearly thought there was a significant risk of electronic surveillance, and the suggestion had him replaying the conversations that had taken place over the course of the night.

We talked about everything! Even Dylan!

Laura stepped out of the bedroom and nodded. They headed out into the hallway, saying nothing, the ride down in the elevator silent. Acton eyed everyone with suspicion, from the staff to the tourists, every innocent glance triggering his paranoia to the point he doubted whether or not they should trust the cab hailed by the porter.

His decision was made for him when Reading practically pushed him in. He slid over to the driver side of the back seat and Laura pushed up against him, Reading stuffing his large frame into the room remaining.

147

Acton was about to give their destination when Laura beat him to it. "Vatican, St. Peter's Square, please."

"Yes, signora."

They weren't far from Vatican City and they were between rush hours so the traffic was reasonable, at least by Rome standards. Acton paid the cabbie and they headed into the walled city, past the Egyptian obelisk and around the Apostolic Palace. Acton was keeping a brisk pace for the first few minutes until Laura pulled on his arm.

"Slow down a bit, you're going to kill me."

Acton immediately stopped, looking at his wife whose chest was heaving slightly. "Sorry, babe, are you okay?"

She nodded. "Yes, just not ready for a power walk across the city."

"Sorry. I forgot."

She hooked her arm in his and started them forward at a more comfortable pace. "No need to apologize, you've got other things on your mind."

"It's not far. I have a feeling Dylan selected our pickup location based upon your condition."

"Wouldn't surprise me. That boy thinks of everything."

Reading grunted. "Probably wanted to force anyone following us to abandon their vehicle."

Acton immediately glanced behind them, finding dozens of people walking in all directions, some following their path.

Of course they are. You're on a path!

"Just keep moving," said Reading, apparently noticing his constant backward gaze.

Acton frowned but looked ahead. "There it is." The gate that Kane had sent them toward was now in sight, the city street visible on the other side.

As they cleared the gates and reentered Italy, Reading elbowed Acton, his chin jutting to the left.

Acton smiled, their troubles forgotten if only for a brief moment.

A Jaguar with what appeared to be at least a dozen parking tickets tucked under the windshield wipers was being loaded onto the back of a tow truck.

"Fifty quid says he abandoned it."

Acton laughed. "Or he parked it near the Vatican, hoping for a miracle."

"There."

They both looked toward where Laura was pointing, a green car with a Fiat badge on the back, idling at the curb. They approached and the front passenger door was thrown open.

"Get in, quickly!"

Acton said nothing, hauling open the rear door, helping Laura inside then climbing in himself as Reading slammed the front door shut. The driver launched them from the curb the moment his ass hit the seat.

"Professor Acton?"

Acton nodded. "Yes."

"I'm Mr. Verde." He handed a cellphone between the seats. "Here, someone wants to talk to you."

Approaching Albany, New York

Lee Fang peered out the window of the Cessna Citation CJ4 that had been waiting for her. Kane had arranged everything, the package delivery, the cellphone call, the car waiting downstairs for her, the private plane at the airport.

He was good.

Damned good.

It reminded her of the old days. Military precision. She missed it. She missed it all. She had been stunned to receive a phone call from Kane, and even more so when he had asked for her help. It was like a dream come true, her prayers, if she believed in that sort of thing, answered.

Action!

It's what she had been craving for so long.

Purpose!

She had been desperate to slay the idleness that had taken over so much of her life. There was only so much exercise she could do without that in itself driving her crazy. Yet now here she was, winging into an airport on a private plane to meet up with a CIA agent who needed her help.

Maybe they'll give me a job.

She doubted it. Her agreement with the Americans specifically stated no jobs with any level of government, and she had specifically made them agree that they could never force her to betray her country in order for them to continue to honor the deal.

Her country may think of her as a traitor, but she wasn't.

The men I named were the traitors.

Who was guilty of what were semantics when it came to the Chinese government. They had been embarrassed, they had been caught, and the fact they had let America effectively flatten a major research facility buried in the side of a mountain, without so much as a peep, meant they realized they were in the wrong, and were just thankful that was the limit of the retaliation.

Nothing had made the news, the Americans had said nothing of the Chinese involvement publicly, and all was forgiven.

Or so it would appear. She having zero access to any type of intel meant she was as in the dark as any other citizen of her adopted country.

The plane touched down with a chirp of the wheels, the pilot having said nothing to her the entire trip, it clear he was not civilian by his demeanor.

It was just as well, small talk never her strong suit.

She sat quietly as the plane taxied off the runway, soon coming to a stop. The pilot turned to her and pointed at a black SUV sitting nearby. "Keys are in the ignition, details are on a phone on the passenger seat. Password is your birth year."

She smiled.

Time for some fun!

Outside St. Peter's Square, Rome, Italy

Luca Abbadelli sat in his nondescript pale blue Alfa Romeo Giulietta, watching his adversary change a flat tire, a tire Abbadelli had punctured only a few minutes ago. It was essential that Acton and his entourage had time to get away cleanly, and delaying their tail by ten minutes would almost guarantee that.

Kane had contacted him not even an hour ago for some help, help he was only too happy to provide, Kane having saved his ass in Syria just last year. And that was the nature of this business. You helped each other when you could, usually no questions asked, nothing expected in return, because you never knew when it would be your ass on the line, needing that same help.

He reached over for his phone, his target getting his own call. The man climbed into his car and shut the door, Abbadelli shaking his head as he watched the jack move slightly at the shift in weight, then smiled as the engine roared to life, the Bluetooth he had noted earlier coming to life, his adversary having foolishly paired the phone.

Allowing the bug Abbadelli had placed to pick up *both* sides of the conversation.

"Status?" They were speaking German, a language Abbadelli was fortunately fluent in. And not much of a surprise after reading Kane's briefing notes.

"I lost them."

"You idiot! How the hell could you possibly lose them? They're in a hotel room!"

"They took a cab to the Vatican then exited a different gate. I followed them on foot and spotted them getting into a vehicle. I think it was waiting for them."

There was a pause. "It sounds like they have somebody helping them."

"Yes, sir, it would appear so."

"Police?"

"I don't think so, I never saw any police and the car was definitely not police. Just a plain old Fiat, nothing even their undercover people would be caught dead in."

"Your plan to reacquire them?"

"They had no luggage, so they'll have to return to the hotel at some point. I'll pick them up there."

"Can you track their phones?"

"Negative. It looks like they left them all behind, at least that's what the computer is saying."

"That would seem to confirm that they're up to something."

"I agree. I have a flat tire that I'm changing. I'll be back at the hotel in about twenty minutes. Hopefully we'll get lucky."

"You better hope you do, otherwise the Doctor will want a word with you."

Abbadelli's eyes narrowed slightly. *Doctor?* Whoever the man was, his mention clearly had an impact on the man.

"Y-yes, sir."

There was a pause. "Professor Acton seems to have not followed my instructions. He has obviously contacted someone. It may be time to kill the mother, to assure him we are serious."

"Umm, sir, how would you tell him?"

"Excuse me?"

"Well, they left their phones. There's no way to tell him that his mother is dead. I'll get back to the hotel and put the word out on that car that picked him up. We should be able to trace it eventually."

"If you haven't found them in the next sixty minutes, his mother loses a finger, one every hour he is missing. We'll contact Inspector General Giasson to let him know. Surely he has some way of contacting him."

"Yes, sir, I'm sure he does."

Abbadelli started his car, pulling out into traffic, it essential he reach the hotel before his adversary did.

For he knew something they didn't.

Mario Giasson had no way to contact Acton, and Mrs. Acton losing fingers wasn't part of the plan.

Leaving Vatican City, Rome, Italy

"Hello?"

"Hey, Doc, it's me, Dylan. You guys secure?"

Acton smiled, mouthing 'Dylan' to the others, the tension of the past few minutes easing slightly knowing his former student was now involved. It didn't mean his parents were safe, but it at least meant there was now hope.

"We're in the car you sent for us. Not sure if that counts as secure."

Kane chuckled. "True. You can trust Mr. Verde, he's one of my go-to guys. He's going to take you to a safe house and we'll talk more."

"Dylan, they've got my parents."

"I know, I've already been called in on that case. Unofficially of course. The phone calls you've received were traced to a castle in northern Italy, same place your phone was apparently sitting until it was deactivated."

"That sounds about right."

"It appears to be their base of operations."

"Any idea who they are?"

"Not yet. I found several bugs in your parents' house so I'm having my own parents' house checked as well."

Acton felt his stomach flip as he listened. To think that his parents' conversations had been listened to, that their most intimate moments were recorded, was both sickening and outrageous.

And terrifying.

How long could they have been planning this?

It made no sense. The portrait hadn't been known to exist until two days ago. He hadn't even become involved until late the first night with

Giasson's phone call. How could they have possibly known to put bugs in his parents' house?

"That doesn't make sense. How could they have had time to do this?"

"They couldn't. I don't think the bugs have anything to do with the current situation. I noticed dust on one of the bugs in your parents' house which means it had been there some time, long before this situation."

Acton could feel a slow burn form in his stomach as his pulse quickened, the thoughts of someone listening in for weeks or months to his mom and dad's conversations, enraging.

"Then who?"

"The Assembly would be my guess."

Acton's old shoulder wound throbbed at the mere mention of the organization that had kidnapped him and Laura, along with two of his students. Acton had been shot, one of the students severely injured, and they had all been traumatized by the incident.

But it was supposed to be over.

His rage turned to fear. "I thought they were out of our lives."

"So did I, but I'm not going to lie to you, Doc, that can always change. In this case, however, I think the bugs are unrelated."

"Did you remove them?"

"No, just in case they are related, I didn't want them to know we were onto them. Once the current crisis is handled I'll have all our houses swept, along with anyone else close to us, and make sure everything is removed and monitors put in place to notify us of any new signals."

"So you think these bugs were in there since the Titanic incident."

"Yes."

"Somebody needs to put an end to those people."

"All in good time, Doc. All in good time. But for now the primary objective is retrieving your parents."

Acton nodded, pulling on his hair as he tried to calm himself. "Any idea where they are?"

"Not yet, but we're working on it. The only real lead we have at the moment is that castle. We're going to have to infiltrate it and gather intel."

"We'll do whatever it takes."

Kane laughed. "Doc, I have no doubt you would, and no doubt you'd succeed. You guys sit tight, I'm arranging for some specialists to join you. I'll be in touch."

The call ended and Acton handed the phone back, frustrated at the notion of sitting idly by while his parents were possibly tortured or worse.

Who could the specialists be?

Near Kane Family Residence, Albany, New York

Lee Fang pulled up to the designated coordinates, impressed, the scene exactly as she had been told to expect. In fact, she was impressed with the entire operation. Her government always touted the American stereotype of being fat and lazy, disorganized and weak, all symptoms of their love for inefficient and undesirable democracy and unbridled capitalism.

But if Dylan Kane were any indication of those that defended America from its enemies, she would have to advise her government that their official message was woefully inaccurate.

Kane had arranged everything perfectly, the delivery, the phone, the plane, the car, the supplies in its trunk.

Everything.

With none of his network comprised.

The only person she had seen was the pilot, and even then, she barely saw the man. He had a ball cap and shades, and had sat in the front with her in the back, directly behind his seat. If she had to describe him, she'd be able to give the sketch artist a detailed account of his right ear and cheek.

She climbed out of the SUV, surveying the area, several city vehicles, gas company, their orange lights flashing, parked in front of the address she had been given, emergency tape cordoning off the street.

Kane's instructions indicated the neighborhood would be evacuated for a fictitious gas leak, the strong odor of rotten eggs greeting her suggesting the ruse went beyond a phone call. She headed down a street around the corner from Kane's parents' house and looked to make sure she was alone. She reached up and grabbed the top of the fence, jumping then swinging her legs over, dropping silently on the other side.

A dog barked in the distance.

She repeated her efforts twice more before she was in the backyard of the Kane residence, still undetected. Climbing the steps to the rear deck, she tried the patio door.

Locked.

She pulled up on the door, the entire frame lifting out of its track, a basic security flaw of too many older doors. She stepped inside, the alarm system instantly wailing in protest as she sprinted for the front entrance, quickly entering the code Kane had provided.

The alarm stopped.

Five seconds?

Less than.

She listened, there no sound from the street suggesting anyone had taken notice.

But she couldn't take the chance someone had called it in, or the security company following up the alarm with a challenge call. She pulled out the phone and device Kane had left for her and activated it, quickly finding a listening device, oddly pleased to find what he had suspected was there.

It meant she had been useful.

The house phone rang.

She checked her watch.

Less than one minute.

Kudos to the security company.

She reset the alarm, leaving the same way she came as the system beeped its countdown, the phone still ringing. Performing her acrobatics again, she was soon back in the safety of her vehicle, starting the engine immediately, her training dictating being prepared for a fast getaway always prudent.

She dialed the number for Kane.

159

"Hello?"

"It's me."

"Hey, Fang. What did you find?"

"Exactly as you suspected. I found a bug in the phone and left immediately as you instructed. Did you want me to go back in and do a full sweep and remove them?"

"Negative. I don't want them to know we're onto them."

"Who set them?"

"I can't say, all I do know is that this pretty much confirms it has nothing to do with what I'm currently working on."

She had to admit she felt disappointed. If this was unrelated, it probably meant he didn't need her anymore.

And she so desperately wanted to be needed.

"Is that good?"

Kane chuckled. "I'm not sure."

"Do you need any more help?" She hoped her voice didn't betray her desperation too much.

"Yes."

She grinned, catching herself in the mirror, wiping the excitement from her face.

"Get yourself to Germantown then call me. The plane is still waiting for you and a car will be here when you arrive."

"Okay, I'm on my way."

The call ended and she put the car in gear, pulling away from the curb, her heart racing with the excitement of being back in the game.

I missed this!

Giasson Residence, Via Nicolò III, Rome, Italy

"How are you feeling, my friend?"

Giasson put a hand on his shoulder, wincing, overplaying his injury, not wanting Chief Inspector Riva to think he was fully on his game. "Weak, in pain, but I'll live."

"You shouldn't be here, you should be in the hospital."

Giasson smiled weakly. "I hate hospitals. With a passion. I'd rather be in my own bed with my wife's cooking and God at my side."

Riva frowned from his chair at the foot of Giasson's bed. "Just remember that God put doctors on this earth for a reason. Denying them is like denying His help."

Giasson chuckled then winced for real. "Too true. But don't ever mention that to a doctor, they have enough of a God complex as it is."

Riva laughed heartily, reminding Giasson of one of the many reasons he genuinely liked the man. He found it completely disheartening that he had to suspect his good friend of being the traitor in their midst, though if he examined the evidence, he was the prime suspect. The man knew about the portrait, knew where it would be and when, and it was men dressed as his police officers that had carried out the theft.

It has to be him.

The alternative was even more horrible to contemplate.

He nodded toward a stack of files on Riva's lap. "What can you tell me?"

Riva waved the files. "Very interesting stuff. The security footage from the university gave us clear images of all the thieves. We've run the photos through our database and confirmed they were *not* police officers."

161

"That's a relief."

"Indeed."

"And the leader?"

"Nothing yet. I've sent all their photos to Interpol, maybe they'll come up with something."

Everything Giasson was hearing was exactly as he would expect to hear from an honest police officer doing his job. It had him seriously reconsidering his doubts about the man. So much so, the internal debate on whether or not to share the information about Acton's phone and the castle it had been traced to, began to rage.

Prudence won out.

"Any idea how they knew where the portrait would be?"

Riva shook his head. "No, I told no one. I merely sent the detail. I was supposed to be there but I received a call where my presence was demanded."

"Seems to be quite the coincidence."

Riva nodded. "I agree. And it was no coincidence, at least I don't think it was. They should have called Tumicelli—I think you've met him"—Giasson nodded—"but his car had been vandalized the night before and he was still at home dealing with that."

"So you were kept away." Giasson frowned. "Why do you think they'd want that?"

"I know every man under my command and picked four of my best to be there that I knew I could trust. If I had arrived and found two more men who I didn't recognize, I would have aborted the entire operation." Riva shook his head. "Like I said, I picked the four men, sent them there with no idea why they were going except to provide security. I have no idea how anyone could have found out." He frowned, his eyes looking away, drifting to the floor. "I hate to say this, my friend, but I think the leak could be at your end."

Giasson drew in a slow breath, fearing Riva may actually be right.

And the very idea sickened him.

Maggie Harris Residence, Lake in the Pines Apartments, Fayetteville, North Carolina

Command Sergeant Major Burt "Big Dog" Dawson made sure his fiancée's legs were clear then shut the passenger door of his prized 1964½ Mustang convertible in original Poppy Red. He ran a finger along the hood as he rounded the front of the car, not a blemish revealed to his delicate touch.

He loved that car almost as much as he loved Maggie Harris.

Though he'd never tell her that.

She'd probably take it the wrong way.

The car had been his father's, left to him after the man died, and he had babied it like any other man who loved cars would. His father had rarely taken the car out, instead trying to preserve the engine, and Dawson knew it was one of the man's great regrets.

There had been only one stipulation in the will.

Drive it. Enjoy it.

So he did. He had put almost as many miles on it in the past few years as his father had in forty, though he was never tempted to go on any truly long trips with it. Yes, he'd drive it, but he also wanted to enjoy it, and the constant worry of some idiot doing something stupid on the interstate kept him tooling around town, enjoying the wind in his hair.

He looked at Maggie as he climbed into the driver's seat. "Top up or down?"

"Down. I haven't felt the sun in ages."

He smiled.

Definite progress.

His beautiful fiancée had been shot in Paris not long ago, a head wound that had left her near death. She had made a full recovery from the wound's perspective, it was her hair that was the stumbling block. They had been forced to shave half her head, and she had been left with a severe scar. His best friend's wife had clipped the remaining hair much shorter and maintained it that way as the shaved side started to grow back. It was only this week that Maggie had been able to look in the mirror and agree that the terrible days of mismatched hemispheres was over.

It would be years before her long locks returned completely, but at a casual glance, you'd never know she had been shot, her hair now long enough to cover the scar tissue.

Which meant she was public ready.

Everyone in the Unit was dying to see her, dying to see them together. The news of the engagement had spread like wildfire, as he had expected it to, and everyone was eager to congratulate them, though they also knew what she was going through so had respected their privacy.

But the Unit was tight.

Incredibly tight.

As members of America's elite Delta Force, officially the 1st Special Forces Operational Detachment—Delta, they were like family. Their jobs were classified, even their families didn't know what they did, except for their wives. Parents, siblings, girlfriends—all out of the loop.

And should one of them fall, it was never in combat.

Not officially.

He loved his job, loved it more than anything until recently. It wasn't until he had fully committed to Maggie that he realized he would be willing to give up his career if she asked him to, he loving her so much.

But one of the reasons he loved her is because she would never ask him to. Being his boss' personal assistant, she knew from the get-go what his job was and what she was getting herself into. She had an advantage none of the other girlfriends had. When an operator met someone, and decided to get married, his future wife would be read in, sworn to secrecy.

And more than a few ran.

Though most didn't. Military wives were a different breed. You didn't marry a serving member if you wanted the simple life in one spot for the rest of your life. You were marrying into a family that spread across the country and around the world, never knowing where you might be posted next. You either loved it or hated it, but you could never be surprised by it.

The wives of the Unit were phenomenal, all supportive of each other when their husbands were deployed, and every one of them from his team, Bravo Team, had stepped up to the plate to take care of Maggie during her recovery.

And they were both eager to thank them all, publicly.

So when he had called his best friend and second-in-command, Master Sergeant Mike "Red" Belme, to tell him that Maggie was ready for a public appearance, the word had gone out and a barbeque behind the Unit was organized that very day, everyone to a man apparently confirming their attendance.

He couldn't wait.

The comradery of the Unit was one of the greatest things about military life. Everyone who served had their own Unit. A group of men and women that knew what they were going through, that worked hard, every day, at each other's side. People you knew had your back, that you trusted like no other.

And a combat vet's Unit was quite often tighter than family.

The bond forged under fire was something no civilian could truly appreciate, and thanks to people like the men under his command, most civilians would never be forced to experience it.

It was a privilege reserved for the proud few who volunteered to protect the way of life they loved so dear, loved enough to be willing to die to preserve it.

As they drove through the main gate at Fort Bragg, clearing the heightened security that seemed always to be in place, he held Maggie's hand, enjoying the feeling of the sun beating down on them, the gentle breeze ruffling his outrageous Hawaiian shirt that had been closet bound for so long.

Life was getting back to normal. Sure, tomorrow—even tonight—he might be called away to some hellhole, but right here, right now, this was bliss. Driving with the only girl he had ever loved to meet the best friends a guy could ever have, to eat good old American barbequed food followed by a game of softball with the families, was his idea of a perfect day.

He pulled into the parking lot, smiling, giving a double-honk of the horn to announce their arrival.

"Everyone's already here," said Maggie, drawing in a loud breath.

He looked at her, taking her hand. "You sure you're up for this?"

She turned to him and smiled, giving a curt nod. "Absolutely."

He grinned and climbed out, rushing around to open her door and help her.

"Hey, you two, long time no see!"

Dawson smiled at his best friend Red, as he and his wife Shirley walked over, everyone else crowding around. Handshakes and hugs were exchanged, congratulations offered, the whirlwind of activity he could see quickly tiring Maggie. He steered her through the crowd and placed her in a lawn chair, pointing at a beech umbrella lying across a picnic table.

Sergeant Leon "Atlas" James grabbed it and tossed it over, Dawson catching it easily and jamming it into the ground behind Maggie.

"Ice tea?"

She nodded.

Shirley came over with a glass and Dawson took it, handing the ice-cold beverage to his fiancée. "Can I get you anything else?"

Maggie shook her head. "I'm perfect, thanks."

"You've got a keeper, there," said Shirley.

"Yup, he's going to make one hell of a wife," laughed Sergeant Carl "Niner" Sung, one of the funniest men Dawson knew, and probably the best sniper on the team, though in Delta that didn't mean much. If Niner was a 10, everyone else was a 9.5. The others joined in the good-natured ribbing, as he had fully expected.

They *were* family, after all.

"So, BD, will you be wearing white?" asked Sergeant Will "Spock" Lightman.

Dawson laughed, taking a beer handed to him by Niner. "No, but I'm looking forward to seeing you guys in your bridesmaid's dresses." He checked out Niner's legs. "You're going to look absolutely fabulous."

Niner did a dainty curtsy. "Always a bridesmaid, never a bride."

Atlas put an arm over Niner, the massive man making Niner seem like a plaything. "You remember our deal. If we're both single when we're forty, you can be my wife."

Niner wriggled his way free. "No, the deal was you're *my* wife."

Spock cocked an eyebrow, tilting his head down. "Umm, wouldn't that be like a Chihuahua trying to hump a Great Dane?"

Dawson spit his beer, Maggie giggling. "Ugh, that's one hell of a visual."

Sergeant Jerry "Jimmy Olsen" Hudson walked over, lighter fluid in hand. "Grill Master Sergeant, care to do the honors?"

Dawson grinned, taking the special Unit blend probably illegal anywhere outside of Texas. He soaked the coals, already prepared by one of the men, then struck a match.

"Fire in the hole!"

He tossed the match on the barbeque and a mini explosion tore skyward, a roar from those gathered as the barbecue was officially underway. The show over, the kids were back on the baseball diamond, tossing balls and Frisbees as the adults mingled, beer flowing, hamburger patties being readied.

Dawson winked at Maggie, talking to Shirley and Sergeant Zack "Wings" Hauser's wife Robyn. She flashed him a smile, she clearly enjoying herself. He was immensely proud of her. What she had been through had been harrowing, yet the bravery she had shown in fighting back, in regaining her health without losing her spirit, was inspiring.

His phone vibrated in his pocket and he fished it out, expertly tossing patties onto the grill. Glancing at the call display, he frowned, it a blocked number.

He swiped his thumb.

"Hello?"

"Hey, it's me."

Dawson immediately recognized Dylan Kane's voice. Kane had been a member of Bravo Team before joining the CIA, and had helped them out on more than one occasion, his own team able to return the favor from time to time.

He was a friend.

A trusted friend.

But also a friend he almost never heard from unless something was wrong.

"What up?"

"I've got a situation and need your help."

Dawson shook his head, a slight smile breaking out that quickly disappeared when he turned and saw Maggie laughing.

I think your vacation just ended.

"I've got three days until I have to report back."

"Let's hope it doesn't take any longer."

Uh oh. This could be serious.

"What's going on?"

"The doc's parents have been kidnapped."

Dawson froze, hamburger patty balanced on a spatula. Professor James Acton was one of the few civilians he actually trusted with his life, and one of the few he would drop almost anything to help out. Their introduction had been ignominious, his team having been given false intel indicating Acton was the head of a terrorist domestic cell, and that he and his followers were on the President's Termination List.

It had turned out to be all lies.

And had cost too many innocent lives.

Not a man involved in those infamous events had ever been able to live down the regret of those days, the shame at what they had done, or the anger at having been used. He had sworn he'd kill the man responsible, but someone had beaten him to it.

Which was probably a good thing, he liking life on this side of the prison bars.

But Acton had been an innocent victim, and over the years he and his men had been given numerous opportunities to help Acton and his now wife, Laura Palmer, and these two exceptional human beings had become friends, even returning the favor on more than one occasion, Laura Palmer incredibly rich, her open wallet saving his men only just recently.

And if Acton's parents had been kidnapped, and Kane was involved, then something big was going on.

"Do we know who did it?"

170

"We're not sure, but it all seems to link back to some group holed up in a castle."

Dawson's eyes narrowed, starting to wonder if Kane was pulling a gag on him. He glanced at Niner, but the man wasn't looking in his direction. If there were someone in the Unit who would be in on a gag, it would be him.

"Castle?"

"I sense your doubt. Trust me, I'm serious."

"Where?"

"Northern Italy."

"Jesus. What do you need?"

"A team to infiltrate it."

Dawson frowned, motioning for Spock to take over the grill. "Why not the locals?"

"It was an inside job. You remember Inspector General Giasson?"

"Head of Vatican security? Yeah. He's involved?"

"Yeah. Apparently four people were killed on Vatican soil and one of them had a da Vinci painting or something. They called the professors in to authenticate it, and a team hit the university dressed as police officers. They killed four police and shot Giasson."

"Is he okay?"

"Apparently just a flesh wound."

"How do you know about the castle?"

Kane chuckled. "Well, you know our doc. He slipped his cellphone into the crate then traced it."

Dawson shook his head, chuckling. "That bastard's crazy."

"Monster balls, that's for sure."

"So I'm guessing they discovered the phone and took his parents as leverage?"

"That's the working theory."

"Okay, so somebody talked and Giasson doesn't know who, hence the need for an outside team."

"Exactly. We need to infiltrate that castle to find out where Acton's parents are being held."

Dawson nodded. "Okay, let me talk to the Colonel, make sure it's okay with him that I leave the country."

Kane laughed. "Oh, that's been done. He said he didn't give a shit what you did on your vacation. He just doesn't want to see it on the news."

Dawson chuckled, it exactly what he would expect Colonel Clancy to say. Clancy was a soldier's soldier. He always had the back of his men, even when the brass wanted them hung out to dry. He was probably the only officer he had encountered that he trusted completely.

He was a good man.

"Okay, send me all the intel and I'll look it over."

"Already done. It's on your secure account. Laura's given us access to funds and I've arranged a private jet for you, it's ready when you are. You'll be met in Rome by one of my contacts."

"Will you be there?"

"Negative, I think his parents are still stateside, so I'll be working this end."

Dawson nodded. "Okay, I'll be in touch."

He ended the call and waved Red over.

"What's up, BD?"

"We've got a situation."

Red's eyebrows rose and he stole a quick glance back at the festivities. "What?"

"That was Dylan. The doc's parents have been kidnapped. We're needed in Italy."

Red shook his head, a smile breaking out. "Those two are the unluckiest bastards I have ever met."

"True. Canvas the guys, see who's willing to go on a volunteer mission. I'm going to go review the intel and figure out what we'll need."

"Will do."

Red jogged back to the group as Dawson headed over to Maggie's perch, kneeling down beside her. "Something's come up."

"What?"

"Professor Acton's parents have been kidnapped."

Her eyes widened and she gasped, her hand darting to her chest. "Oh my God, that's terrible! Are they okay?"

"We don't know yet, but they've asked for our help."

"Then give it to them."

His love for her just ticked up another notch. "I don't want to leave you alone."

She smiled. "Bullshit. You're itching to go help, I can see it in your face."

He grinned. "You know me too well."

She pulled his head to hers and gave him a kiss.

"Now go do what you do best."

CIA Safe House, Rome, Italy

"Your help should be arriving by the morning."

"Who?"

"Friends. You'll know them when you see them."

Acton grinned at the others, the phone on speaker. Kane hadn't said who he was sending, though if they were friends, and he'd recognize them, it had to be Bravo Team. The first time he had met these proud warriors they had done everything they could to kill him.

Until the end, when Dawson had let them live, realizing his orders had been illegal.

And over the years, they had become friends of a sort.

Definitely men he no longer feared, knew he could trust, and knew always had his back.

Kane had requested Laura free up some money to help with the operation, and she had, a special account already set up for these situations being unlocked with a phone call.

Kane could now fund whatever he needed to help save Acton's parents.

"I think I know who you mean," said Acton, putting an arm around Laura.

"I thought you might. They'll infiltrate the castle and get the intel on where your parents might be."

Acton sighed. "If only I hadn't planted that cellphone." Laura pressed herself into him.

"It was pretty ballsy."

"I wasn't really thinking."

Kane laughed. "No, Doc, you were definitely thinking. You were thinking that some painting was more valuable than your life."

Acton frowned, a wave of guilt sweeping through him. "You're right. I was stupid. My parents should be safe in their home, instead, because I put some artifact ahead of their safety, they may die."

"Bullshit, Doc. Pardon my French, but you did what you always do, the right thing. In this case, it backfired, but that's no reason to second-guess your nature. We don't know anything about these people. For all we know they might have kidnapped your parents anyway. You saw their leader, perhaps that wasn't part of the plan. They might have wanted this leverage over you regardless of what you did."

Acton grunted. "I think you're stretching it a little, just to make me feel good."

"Did it work?"

Acton chuckled. "No. Continue."

Kane laughed and Reading joined in. "Listen, as far as you were concerned it was art thieves, not some group with ties across the Atlantic and some ancient castle hideout à la James Bond supervillain."

"Any idea who they are?"

"Not yet, but we're working on it. Langley's cloning Laura's phone. We'll trace the activity and monitor it. For now, sit tight until the cavalry arrives and don't contact anyone."

"What about Mario?"

"Especially him. He's almost definitely being watched."

"Should we warn him?"

"No, then they'll know we're onto them."

"Won't they already know now that we gave them the slip?"

"Not necessarily. That loose end was taken care of."

"How?"

"The less you know, the better. Let's just say that right now, you're exactly where you're supposed to be."

Ambasciatori Palace Hotel, Rome, Italy

Abbadelli listened to the recording, smiling. He loved his job. The shit that Langley could pull together on such short notice was jaw dropping at times, and this was no exception. No, the tech was nothing spectacular, at least not in this day and age, it was the fact that someone had come up with the idea, executed it and got it into his hands to implement it, all in a matter of hours, from the other side of the planet, was phenomenal.

He had returned to Acton's hotel room and with his spare phone—for he always had one—played the recording Langley had sent him, instructions appearing on the screen as to what he was supposed to do.

Press play, open door.

He had entered the room.

Close door.

He had. A conversation between Acton, his wife, and their Interpol friend then played from the speaker of his phone, all three voice actors employed at Langley, their voices then altered by computer to sound as close as possible to the real thing.

Enough to fool anyone not expecting deception.

The end result were Acton and his wife heading into the bedroom to sleep, Reading on the couch, his snores now playing from the phone Abbadelli had been instructed to leave on the couch where Reading's head would be. A sweep by another agent before he had arrived had determined there was a single bug in the suite, placed under the table in the living area, nothing in the bedrooms.

If the deception worked, anyone listening would assume the three friends had returned to their hotel room after a quick meeting with

Giasson's man, who they had apparently told nothing to about the kidnapping, then decided to get some sleep since they had none the night before.

It would hopefully be enough to fool their adversaries for at least several hours, perhaps more.

He carefully opened the door and stepped out into the hallway, gently closing the door, cringing at the click.

Let's hope they didn't hear that.

1st Special Forces Operational Detachment-Delta HQ, Fort Bragg, North Carolina
A.k.a. "The Unit"

"Sir!"

Dawson hailed Colonel Thomas Clancy as his Commanding Officer exited one of the Operations Centers, an op obviously underway. Dawson had just finished reviewing the briefing notes sent by Kane and had transferred all the data to his secure phone. He hadn't expected to run into the Colonel, though he wasn't going to avoid the man.

"Do you have a minute?"

Clancy continued to walk away from him, though did deign him with a glance over his shoulder. "No, you're on vacation. And I don't want to hear from you, or *of* you, until you get back."

Dawson grinned.

Blessing received.

"Yes, sir!"

Clancy disappeared into another office and Dawson headed for his car as he formulated a plan. If they were to infiltrate the castle, it would have to be a covert operation. He had a dozen men on Bravo Team, but he wouldn't need that many. Half a dozen would be more than enough for any contingency.

And if shit truly went bad, it would leave six men to ride in and save their asses should it become necessary.

As he returned to the park behind the Unit, he thought of how he hated to leave Maggie, though it wouldn't be the first time he had left her, his job demanding it, though it would be the first time he had volunteered to leave, out on an off-the-books mission for a friend.

Then give it to them.

He smiled at her words.

She's amazing!

He loved his job and she seemed to love it just as much. They couldn't really talk about it, though just the fact he didn't have to lie to her about what he did for a living was such a relief. He had avoided relationships his entire career, not wanting to become attached to someone he may one-day leave as a widow. He had even spurned Maggie's advances, but conspiring wives had encouraged her to keep at it, and he had eventually folded.

Best damn surrender ever.

He arrived at the park and strode toward his team, everyone eating, Maggie now at one of the picnic tables. Red rose and served him up a burger, handing him a Diet Coke. Dawson noted the beers had all been stowed, sodas and water the orders of the day.

"What's the word?" asked Red as the other members of the team joined them.

Dawson took a bite and chewed for a moment before swallowing. He nodded at Spock. "Almost as good as mine."

"Grill Master Corporal?" suggested Niner.

Spock cocked an eyebrow at Niner. "You can cook next time."

"I don't eat meat."

"What's that in your hand?"

"Sorry, I don't eat meat I cook. You remember that one time I barbequed."

Atlas rumbled a chuckle. "You redefined charbroiled."

"Exactly. In Korea you never know if the meat is good, so you cook the shit out of it."

Jimmy groaned. "You're American. Your parents were *South* Korean."

Niner stared at him in surprise. "I didn't know you knew my folks so well."

"Just your momma."

A chorus of "Oooh"s erupted, Niner snapping a kick at Jimmy's head, it stopping at inch from his chin.

Jimmy didn't flinch.

"I knew you wouldn't make contact. Otherwise I'd have to tell your momma."

Dawson laughed, swallowing the last bite of his burger then taking a swig. "Okay, here's the deal. Professor Acton's parents were kidnapped last night and he needs our help. It could be dangerous."

"What else is new?" interjected Jimmy.

Dawson grinned. "Exactly. I guess that was redundant. Six man team heading for Europe in less than an hour. Volunteers?"

Every single one of the team stepped forward in unison. It made him proud, though he had never doubted they would. It was what they were meant to do, to fight for those who couldn't fight for themselves, though the doc would probably beg to differ on not being able to. There were only two civilians he had encountered in all his years in this business that he could count on in a firefight, and they were James Acton and his wife, Laura Palmer. With her wealth, she had hired a former British Special Forces colonel to head her security team while on dig sites, and after they began having some problems, expanded his duties to train them on how to use pretty much every type of weapon, as well as basic self-defense and other survival skills that had saved their lives more than once.

They were solid, reliable partners, but after what he had read, there was no way he was going to let them go up against that castle and its occupants, even with Bravo Team. It was one thing to use the skills you had as a civilian to get your ass *out* of trouble, but you didn't go rushing into it when there were trained professionals willing to do it for you.

These two professors had fought at their side before, even saved some of their lives, so every single one of his team owed them.

And they were eager to repay them.

"Okay, Niner, Jimmy, Spock, Atlas and Jagger, you're with me. Red, I want you to remain behind with the rest of the guys on standby. There might be need for a team here."

"No problem."

Niner slugged Jimmy in the shoulder. "That's from my momma."

"She does like the rough stuff."

Atlas high-fived Jimmy. "Good one, brother."

Niner mock-glared at Jimmy then turned to Dawson. "So, where in Europe is this shindig?"

"Italy."

"Ooh, I've always wanted to see Italy."

Jimmy slugged him in the shoulder. "You've seen Italy. More than once."

"Really, I'm terrible with math."

"Don't you mean geography?"

Niner gave Jimmy a look. "Okay, professor, geography. It obviously wasn't very memorable."

"You got shot at."

"Huh. Maybe if I *didn't* get shot at, it would stick out in my mind."

Jimmy laughed. "Now *that's* probably true."

Dawson slapped his hands together. "Okay, say your goodbyes, pack your gear and we'll meet at Fayetteville Regional in one hour. Expect to be gone three days so pack enough undies, Atlas, last time I had to lend you a pair and I never got them back."

"That's because your size medium barely fit over my calf, let alone my ass."

Niner smacked Atlas' ass. "I like big butts and I cannot lie, you other brothers can't deny. That when a girl walks in with an itty bitty waist, and a round thing in your face…"

Dawson shook his head as Niner continued to channel Sir Mix-a-Lot, shaking his own ass as he repeatedly smacked Atlas'.

"On that note…"

"Status?"

Leroux looked at his boss, Leif Morrison, as he entered the operations center. "Chief, we've got over one hundred possibles and we keep finding more as we access additional cameras. One came up as stolen so the FBI is chasing that one down."

"To the exclusion of all else," muttered Sherrie. "No way would pros use a stolen vehicle."

"Maybe they're not pros?" suggested Randy Child, one of the team's newer, and youngest, members. A whiz kid on computers, even by CIA standards, he had proven to be a welcome addition. He just had to work on his brain-mouth barrier a little better.

Leroux shook his head. "Amateurs aren't on two continents, coordinating an armed robbery of a university in Italy, killing six people including four police officers, and kidnapping senior citizens here. These are definitely pros, which means that vehicle is going to be squeaky clean."

"So what are we looking for?" asked Morrison as he eyed the large list of vehicles on one of the displays.

"We need to narrow it down to no more than a handful so Kane can run them down on his own."

Sherrie raised her hand slightly. "I'm doing nothing, maybe I can help?"

Morrison nodded, Leroux's heart leaping as he realized she was about to head out into danger. "Do it."

Sherrie bounced, grinning in delight. She loved her job, that much was obvious to Leroux, and she always jumped at the opportunity to go out on assignment. He just preferred those assignments be black boxes, not ones he would be monitoring.

Flashbacks of watching her being tortured during the coup attempt had his stomach doing flips.

She kissed him on the cheek, patting the other. "Love you."

He smiled weakly. "Love you too."

"Oooh," said Child, his youth shining brightly.

Sherrie winked at him. "Jealous of your boss?"

"Insanely!" Child's eyes suddenly widened and his jaw dropped as he looked at Leroux. "Umm, sorry, boss. I mean, well, umm"—his shoulders slumped in defeat and he stared at his keyboard—"just sorry."

Leroux said nothing, instead exchanging a glance with a smiling Morrison. He waved a final goodbye to his girlfriend as she left the ops center, keeping his expression neutral while his insides leapt with pride at the fact she was *his* girlfriend and other guys found her attractive.

He caught Sonya Tong glaring at the door Sherrie had just left through, then glancing at him, her eyes immediately averted as she realized she had been caught.

I don't think I've ever had two girls interested in me. Ever.

He let a slight smile slip.

Hell, I never had one *until Sherrie.*

Morrison cleared his throat, yanking Leroux out of his self-congratulatory fantasy.

"Sorry, sir," he muttered. "Okay, let's reduce this list. Eliminate all those with local plates. These guys will be from out of town."

"Yes, sir," mumbled Sonya, her fingers flying over the keyboard. Dozens of the list on the display began to turn red from green, the possibles quickly dwindling into more manageable numbers.

Getting there!

185

Maggie Harris Residence, Lake in the Pines Apartments, Fayetteville, North Carolina

Dawson held Maggie tight, neither of them saying anything. It was a scene repeated all too often in his job, and it was a scene repeated across America every day. The difference between a husband or wife going on a business trip and a soldier heading into combat was you were pretty much guaranteed your spouse was coming back unscathed from that business trip.

The soldier, you never knew.

Yet it never stopped them from leaving.

No matter how hard it was.

He let her go and she wiped some tears from her eyes. "Hey, I'll be okay."

"I know, you're Teflon."

"I'd prefer to be Kevlar."

She laughed, swatting him. "You know what I mean."

"I know, I know."

She yawned. "Sorry."

"Overdid it a little today?"

She nodded. "I think so, but it felt so good to be out." She ran her fingers through her hair, over her scar. "And nobody was staring at my head, so I guess that was good. Gave me some of my confidence back."

"That *is* good. If all the kids were able to ignore it, then you know there's nothing to worry about."

"You're right, kids can be so cruel. It drives me nuts when I see kids pointing at someone who's different and their parents doing nothing about it."

"What drives *me* nuts is when you're at a restaurant and they don't control their kids. Did I ever tell you about the time my sister and brother – in-law took my niece to Denny's?"

Maggie shook her head.

Dawson checked his watch. "Long story short, they were eating breakfast, quietly talking, and there was another couple with a kid, same age as Jenny—about five at the time. The kid was screaming and banging things and running around and the parents did nothing, just kept eating. And get this, they were feeding him some of their hash browns. On the table."

"Huh?"

"They'd take handfuls and drop it on the bare table for him to eat. No plate, no paper placemat. Then he'd eat it with his hands, then jump up and go running around again. Apparently everyone was getting pissed off. An elderly couple got up, came over to my sister's table and said, quite loudly, '*You've* got an extremely well behaved child', then left. Sylvia said she was so proud that day. She realized just how blessed they were that they had taught Jenny how to behave from an early age."

"She's a sweet kid."

Dawson looked at his watch. "Okay, enough stories, I really gotta go. What are you going to do?"

"Oh, Shirley's coming over with some wedding catalogues."

"Uh huh."

"Second thoughts?"

"Nope. You're the colonel on this one. Just tell me when to show up, what to do, and I'll try not to kill anyone or blow anything up."

"Good. I doubt we'd get our deposit back if you did."

Dawson grinned and gave her a peck, opening the door to her apartment before turning back toward her and winking.

"But I make no promises about the guys, especially Niner."

Two blocks from Acton Residence, Germantown, Maryland

Kane browsed the feed from Langley, the number of possible vehicles reduced dramatically, the one flashing orange on his tablet eliciting a headshake.

Idiots.

He had tried to convince the Agent in Charge that it was a waste of time, but apparently someone at the Field Office had ordered him to devote his entire team to running it down. After everyone had peeled away from the Actons' curb, it had occurred to him that the stolen SUV might be a genuine red herring, the kidnappers perhaps stealing a decoy vehicle just to throw the hounds off the scent.

A car pulled in behind him and he glanced in his rearview mirror then smiled, pressing the button to unlock the doors. He glanced in his side view mirror, giving Sherrie White the once over, appreciating her sleek form, thanking God that his buddy had found her first. No matter how much he loved sleeping with women, especially women as gorgeous as Sherrie, he'd give it all up—okay, maybe not all. A month or two?—to see his buddy happy.

And Sherrie definitely made his friend happy.

He's one lucky sonofabitch. If he weren't my best friend, I'd be trying to tap that hard.

He shook his head.

Do I really sound like Barney Stinson?

One of his favorite shows was How I Met Your Mother, and he loved the juxtaposition of an openly gay actor playing a serial womanizer.

I wonder if it would have worked as well if Neil Patrick Harris were actually straight.

He had a feeling it wouldn't have.

Sherrie climbed into the passenger seat, leaning over and giving him a peck on the cheek. "Hey, Dylan, good to see you."

"You too. Glad you could make it."

She shrugged. "Not like I'm doing anything. Chris is holed up in an op center and not allowed to leave until the Chief is convinced he's safe, and I'm not scheduled for another op 'til the end of the week."

"So you're bored."

She grinned. "Yup. Chief agreed I could help."

"You can. We need to figure out which, if any, of these vehicles might be our kidnappers'."

Sherrie scanned the list on the tablet, still several dozen vehicles on it. "I'd eliminate any that weren't leaving the city."

Kane smiled slightly. Sherrie was new to the business, at least compared to him, and he always liked to see how junior agent's minds worked—it gave him an insight into how they might perform later in their career. The ones who could think logically were always more successful.

Time to shine, Padawan.

"Why?" he asked, challenging her to explain her logic.

"They wouldn't stay local, they'd risk questions from nosy neighbors in a small town like this."

"Agreed, just like the tip that sent us here in the first place."

"Exactly. They'll want to be heading for an urban center so they can lose themselves in a crowd. I'd eliminate anyone that was heading into the town center, rather than leaving."

"Okay." Kane took the tablet and added some filter criteria to the list. "That leaves ten vehicles, much better. And one of those is the stolen one the FBI is running down."

Sherrie shook her head. "No, the vehicle would be clean."

"Very good, young Padawan."

She grinned. "Learned from the best."

"They do know what they're doing on the Farm." He pointed at the tablet, a grid of nine vehicles showing. "Okay, which ones do you think we can eliminate."

She pointed at one of the vehicles, the rear shot showing large custom exhaust. "Those would be loud and attract too much attention. No way they'd use it."

"Agreed." He tapped the display, eliminating it from the grid.

She pointed at another one. "Kid in the passenger seat."

Kane eliminated it.

"And that one." She pointed again. "And that one."

"Five left."

"That one has only the driver, that one too."

"And then there were three."

Sherrie looked at him, smiling. "Much more manageable."

"And there's three of us."

Sherrie's eyes narrowed. "Who's the third?"

He pointed toward a vehicle as it drove by, parking in front of them. The engine turned off and the door opened, the lithe form of Lee Fang stepping out.

Sherrie's jaw dropped. "Is that who I think it is?"

Kane smiled. "Yup."

Somewhere over the Atlantic

"Man, I could get used to this."

Dawson nodded in agreement at Jimmy's comment. The Gulf V jet that Laura arranged for them was opulent compared to the back of a Herc.

Niner sighed. "I knew I should have married her when I had the chance."

Sergeant Eugene "Jagger" Thomas snorted. "Right. I'm not sure she even knows you exist."

"Oh, we shared a moment."

"Was she there for this moment?"

Niner gave Jagger a look. "Her exact position on the globe is of no importance in my fantasy life."

"Hey, that's another man's wife you're talking about," rumbled Atlas. "And besides, I do believe it was me who first commented on how fine she was, which means I have first dibs if it doesn't work out with the doc."

Niner pointed a finger at him. "Hey, you're so close to being married you shouldn't even be thinking that way."

Atlas' eyes flared slightly. "Yeah, well, let's not rush things."

"Ooh, I do think someone's afraid of commitment."

"Hey, who said anything about commitment?"

The comm system beeped and everyone became quiet as Dawson put it on speaker. "Go head."

"Hey, it's Dylan."

"Hey buddy, you're on speaker with me, Niner, Atlas, Jimmy, Spock and Jagger."

191

"Hey guys. I'll cut to the chase, we're on a deadline. We're trying to trace the vehicle that was spotted leaving the Acton residence, but there's not much to go on. We've got it narrowed down to I think three possibilities, but the FBI disagrees. They're off chasing down a stolen car."

Niner shook his head. "Pros use clean vehicles."

"That's the consensus at this end as well."

Dawson leaned forward. "What can you tell us about this castle in Italy?"

"I've had Leroux send you floor plans and everything else we've got, but the plans are almost seventy years out of date so we have no way of knowing if the owner has made any modifications."

"Who's the owner?"

"It looks like it was bought by a Swiss national named Hermann Kaufer in 1946, just after the war. Apparently he promised to restore it, which he did. He got approval from city council to later amend the agreement turning it into a completely private residence, all previously allowed public tours cancelled."

"Going in as tourists would have made things easier," said Jagger.

"Off the table, unfortunately. But get this. We're monitoring heavy Internet traffic in and out of the place, a lot of heat signatures, dozens of vehicles and what looks like armed patrols."

"They definitely value their privacy. Any idea how many hostiles?"

"Hard to tell, but Langley is thinking it could be as high as two hundred."

"Jesus," muttered Jimmy, making an exaggerated count of the team. "I think we're outnumbered a little."

"Who owns it now?" asked Dawson. "1946 is a long time ago."

"It looks like the original owner died and left it to his son who's listed as the current owner."

Dawson nodded. "Okay, we're going to need to know every way in and out of that place. I mean sewers, drains, tunnels, anything you can get us. Also, monitor those patrols. I want to know if there are any patterns."

"Langley's on it."

"What kind of support can we expect?"

"Nada on the ground, unfortunately."

"We're used to that," said Niner.

"I've got gear waiting for when you arrive."

Dawson looked at a tablet computer, an update coming in from Langley. "And when we get there, what's the mission?"

"Right now we're trying to find the doc's parents and rescue them. The key to finding them may be inside that castle."

Dawson frowned. "If these people were willing to kidnap them once, and apparently keep them for an extended period, they won't hesitate to try again, or take someone else important to the professor to keep him quiet."

Niner leaned forward. "It sounds to me like this castle is important to them, otherwise they'd just pull up stakes and move."

"Agreed," replied Kane. "That's what I'm thinking too. They must have too much invested in there to leave, so they want everyone's silence guaranteed."

Dawson pinched his chin. "Sounds to me like the only way to put an end to this is to end their ties to that castle. Force them out somehow, then the doc doesn't know anything of value."

"Agreed. Any ideas?"

"We could always blow it up," offered Niner.

"You want to blow everything up," said Atlas.

"Hey, a man has to have a hobby."

Kane chuckled. "I don't think you'll have enough C4 for that."

Dawson nodded, pursing his lips as he flipped through the plans for the castle. "I think we need to start thinking in terms of less is more."

"You've got an idea?"

"I think so."

CIA Safe House, Rome, Italy

"Please stay away from the windows, Professor."

Acton growled at Dylan's contact, Mr. Verde, without looking at him. They had been cooped up in the safe house for hours and he couldn't stand it. He was a man of action, not one to sit idly by while others did all the heavy lifting. And what was most frustrating was at the moment, it felt as if nobody was doing any lifting.

Yes, Delta was on its way, but they were hours out, and Kane was doing everything he could back home. The problem was he couldn't see any of it, all he could picture was the most gruesome images of his parents being tortured for something he had impulsively done.

He wanted to be doing something. He wanted to kick the shit out of whoever had taken them, tear the throat out of the man who seemed to be the ringleader.

Yet he couldn't be the leader.

The leader wouldn't go on the heist, not in an organization that big. And he was assuming it was big if they were able to kidnap his parents half a world away so quickly. It meant they had people probably across the globe, able to project their will on command.

Christ, they're like the Triarii.

He shivered at the thought of the ancient organization obsessed with the crystal skulls. It had been his accidental discovery of a skull that had led to the events that pulled them all together several years ago, Bravo Team trying to kill him due to false intel, he fleeing to find Laura, the world's foremost expert on the skulls, and Reading trying to arrest him because he thought he had committed a murder.

195

All because of the Triarii, an apparently benevolent order that had split, resulting in a civil war, for lack of a better term.

Air burst from his lips and he sat down, grabbing the laptop to review the intel Kane had sent.

"They wouldn't be there."

Reading looked up at him. "Who?"

"My parents."

"No."

"We need leverage over them."

Laura shifted in her seat. "What do you mean?"

"Well, they obviously want the portrait. What if we stole it back?"

Reading's eyebrows rose. "Umm, Kane's report suggests possibly two hundred people facing us. It would be suicide."

Laura leaned over and took his hand. "Sweetheart, BD and the guys will be here by the morning. Let's just get some sleep and let them deal with it, okay?"

"No, I can't." Acton leapt to his feet. "It's my parents." He spun toward the CIA agent who was reading a local paper in the far corner of the room. "Can you get me a weapon?"

He shrugged. "Sure. But I won't."

"Why not?"

"I have my orders and they're to keep you here."

"So we're prisoners?"

"Of course not, you're free to die at any time."

Acton frowned. "Funny."

Verde shrugged. "I don't make the rules."

Acton dropped back into his chair, frustrated. Laura rose and stepped behind him, kneading his shoulders. "They'll be okay. As long as we follow their demands."

Acton closed his eyes, her ministrations feeling wonderful. "Yeah, but how do we know what their demands are? We don't have our phones anymore, so we have no way of knowing if they're calling."

"Not true." Acton looked at Verde. "Your phones have been cloned and all calls are being routed through Langley. They'll know if anyone calls."

Acton shook his head.

"Yeah, but they can't answer."

Rocca d'Angera Castle, Angera, Italy

"What do you mean you don't think they're in the hotel room?"

Obersturmbannführer Hofmeister glared at his tech, Karl. He had been roused from the first sleep he'd managed to get in days, caffeine and uppers keeping him going until he had finally crashed. The report from Rome had been that the Actons and their friend had returned to the hotel room by the time their operative had returned, their excursion apparently a prearranged meeting with a contact of Giasson's, at least according to the overheard conversation upon their return.

It seemed plausible. They would all know they were most likely being followed, their phones being tracked. It didn't necessarily mean they had contacted the authorities. He knew from his contacts in the United States that the authorities were involved there thanks to a neighbor of Acton's parents. He wasn't about to kill them over actions Acton had no control over. If he did, then he'd lose the leverage he had over the man.

Though if what Karl had just said were true, it changed everything. He dropped into a chair, exhausted.

"Well, our man lost them at the Vatican when they got into another car, so it was clearly planned. Then he had a flat tire, which I think is too big a coincidence, so that delayed his return to the hotel. By the time he got there, they were already back, which meant their ride essentially just picked them up and drove them back."

"You woke me for that?" Hofmeister leapt to his feet, heading for the door. "I know all that." He grabbed his throbbing forehead. "Please, for your sake, tell me you have more."

Karl gulped. "Well, our bug suggests they went to sleep immediately, and they're all still asleep. I mean, nobody has even got up to go to the bathroom. So I checked Professor Palmer's phone and found it had never left the hotel room, even when they left."

"So? They knew we were probably tracking it."

"Yes, but, sir, if your parents were kidnapped, and you were waiting for a phone call from the kidnappers, would you ever let that phone out of your sight?"

Hofmeister frowned, pursed his lips, then nodded.

"Have our man check the room."

Near Acton Residence, Germantown, Maryland

Kane turned to face the back seat as Fang climbed in. He had forgotten how beautiful she was, in a minimalist sort of way. He had a serious thing for Asian women, and she was a prime specimen, the thought of making a move on her exhilarating, especially knowing she'd have a better than most chance of actually killing him.

Focus, Barney!

"You made good time."

Fang shrugged. "I drove efficiently."

Sherrie extended her hand. "Hi Fang, not sure if you remember me. Sherrie White."

Fang shook the hand. "Yes, I remember. How are you?"

"Good, you?"

Fang shrugged. "Okay, I guess."

Kane looked at her, detecting a note of melancholy in her voice.

I'll have to talk to her when this is all over.

"Okay, here's the situation. We've got three possibles so far and little time." He handed the tablet back to Fang so she could see the images of the SUVs that met the narrowed criteria. "We'll each take one, but surveillance only. You look, assess, then we make a best guess. Do *not* attempt contact, understood?"

Sherrie nodded. "Yup."

Fang nodded, handing back the tablet.

Kane pointed at the first vehicle. "I'll take number one, Sherrie number two, and Fang, you take the third. Your two are close to each other, mine's about half an hour in the opposite direction." His fingers worked the display, sending the data to each of their phones. Sherrie looked at hers.

"This looks like a corporate vehicle."

Kane nodded. "Yeah, the guy was probably here on business. The other two are personal so we're probably rolling up on houses." He looked from Sherrie to Fang. "Good luck, ladies, and be careful. We don't know who we're dealing with."

"You don't think it's the Assembly?"

"The what?"

Kane glanced at Fang, Sherrie's eyes widening slightly at her faux pas. "You didn't hear that, and no, I'm confident it's not." He could tell from Fang's expression that her curiosity had been piqued. Whose wouldn't be? He'd have to make sure he talked to her later to make certain she didn't try to seek out more information, otherwise she might add herself to the Assembly's hit list.

And she had no leverage over them.

Outside the Ambasciatori Palace Hotel, Rome, Italy

Joachim Freitag's eyes bulged. "Yes, sir, I'll check right away." He ended the call and climbed out of his car, rushing across the street and into the luxury hotel, it far nicer than anything he had ever been fortunate enough to stay in. He had grown up in the castle, he a direct descendent of one of the founding fathers. Life was good there though sparse, a loyal subject of the future Reich expected to live a rather Spartan existence, luxuries merely a waste. He had noted, however, that those limitations didn't seem to be forced upon the officers.

But he was merely a foot soldier, like his father before him. Like his grandfather had explained to him before he died, not everyone could be officers. Officers needed reliable soldiers under their command to actually carry out the orders, and the Fourth Reich would need millions of them, millions that would be provided by the research they were conducting, and the new recruits who would flock to their cause when the world hit its low point.

Just like the Third Reich did in Germany during the Great Depression, the Fourth would arise from the ashes of today's chaotic world.

With a little help.

The elevator chimed, the doors opening on one of the top floors, everything a large suite here. He had read the files on his subjects and noted that apparently the woman was extremely rich. As he walked through the opulent hallway, it made him wonder what life must be like never having to lift a finger, never having to answer to anyone.

He frowned at the thought.

Germans are not indulgent.

At least not the foot soldiers.

He put an ear to their door and heard nothing. Knocking gently, he continued to listen, and still heard nothing.

Harder this time.

Nothing.

The sound of dishes rattling at the end of the hall caught his attention just in time and he bent over, pretending to pick something up, then began walking past the hotel employee with a room service cart. Nods were exchanged then Freitag spun around, pistol whipping the man.

He crumpled to the floor.

Freitag grabbed him under the armpits and dragged him toward a utility closet, unlocking the door with the man's pass. He pulled off the employee's jacket and put it on, yanking at it, the front refusing to stretch enough to button.

How small is this guy?

It didn't matter. He left the room, grabbed the cart and quickly pushed it to the Actons' door, knocking loudly. "Room service!"

As expected, there was no answer. He swiped the pass and the light went green, the lock clicking. He pushed open the door with his gun hand and listened. Gentle snoring, nothing more. He stepped inside, carefully closing the door behind him then searched the wall for the light switch.

He flicked it on.

Light immediately bathed the room, and he found no one.

His eyes narrowed.

The cop should be on the couch.

He stepped farther inside, the bedroom doors both closed, two cellphones sitting on the table.

And a third sitting on the couch, the sound of snoring coming from the speaker.

His heart sank.

He's going to kill me.

Irvington Avenue, Bethesda, Maryland

Kane pulled up to the side of the road, immediately comparing the license plate of the navy blue SUV in the driveway to the one pulled by Langley. It was a match. He surveyed the area, by all outward appearances this an upscale family oriented neighborhood, kids playing, couples walking their dogs, driveways filled with minivans, crossovers and SUVs.

Nothing out of place.

Two kids burst from the front door of the residence in question, a man stepping out onto the porch a few moments later. Kane examined the DMV photo.

That's him.

"Be back by nine!"

Shouts of acknowledgements from the kids were heard as Kane exited his vehicle, walking toward the driveway. He held up a fake FBI ID as the man turned to go back inside. "Excuse me, sir, FBI."

The man stopped and stared at him, the concern and slight fear he was used to seeing in the innocent immediately displayed. "Yes? Is there a problem?"

Kane motioned toward the SUV. "Your car matches the description of a vehicle seen near an incident earlier today. Can you tell me why you were in Germantown today?"

The man's eyes popped wide then he stepped out onto the porch, closing the door behind him.

Uh oh, adulterer?

"I was visiting a shop there, getting this." He reached into his pocket, pulling out a small ring box. He flipped it open.

Kane whistled. "Nice."

The man beamed with pride, the fear of a moment ago forgotten. "Yeah, it's our tenth wedding anniversary tomorrow. I couldn't risk getting anything in the area. My wife works in the business and they all talk to each other."

Kane chuckled. "I guess not." He nodded toward the house. "Do you mind if I take a quick look around? It's a rather serious matter."

The man nodded. "Of course." He opened the door and Kane entered, the husband explaining to his wife what was going on as Kane showed his badge. It was a quick search, he already quite certain these people weren't involved, yet it was still necessary, suburban families sometimes much more than what they appeared on the outside.

He bowed slightly to the couple as he walked out the door. "Sorry to disturb your evening. You two have a good night."

"Thank you, officer."

Kane returned to his vehicle, firing off a text to Leroux and the others.

Bethesda a bust.

BMB Biomedical, Baltimore, Maryland

Sherrie rolled up to BMB Biomedical, some sort of medical equipment supplier, the parking lot nearly empty, it well past normal working hours. She pulled into a visitor parking spot and exited her vehicle, walking toward the doors. She tried them. Locked. She knocked on the glass and a security guard inside looked up from whatever he was watching under his desk.

She pressed her fake FBI badge against the glass and the man quickly stood, perhaps not recognizing the badge, though definitely recognizing that only law enforcement would do such a thing.

The doors were quickly unlocked and she held up her badge again. "Special Agent Brown. I'm looking for the driver of a black 2014 Cadillac Escalade registered to BMB Biomedical."

The guard's eyes narrowed slightly. "I think there's a few of those around here. Lotta money, you know." He snapped his fingers. "I've got a list, in case the lot's full. We tow the ones that aren't registered. Just a second." He rushed back to his desk and tapped at his computer. "What's the plate?"

She gave it to him.

"Here it is. Mr. Gervin. He's the CEO." He tapped on his chin. "I think he's out of town though."

Sherrie felt her heart tick a few beats quicker. "Are you sure?"

"Just a second." More tapping. "Yeah, thought so. There's an email here from admin letting us know that his office was going to be renovated starting three days ago while he was in London for business. It has the approved list of contractors that should be given access, you know—"

Sherrie raised a hand, cutting off the rationalization. "He's out of town. Where's his vehicle?"

The guard shrugged. "I dunno. Not here, I can tell you that."

"Do you have an address for him?"

He hesitated. "Um, do I need to give you that?"

She nodded, it a lie, but then she wasn't FBI. "Yes."

More key taps and a printer hummed.

"Here you go."

She waved the sheet of paper. "Thanks, you've been a big help."

She headed for her car, her heart racing. Kane's location was already a bust, and this vehicle now fit the profile. Owner out of town so it wouldn't be reported stolen, and judging by the address, this Gervin lived on the 21st floor of a condo or apartment building.

No nosy neighbors once you were inside.

She started the engine and fired a text message with the address to Kane, Fang and Langley.

Please don't let this be another dead end!

Operations Center 3, CIA Headquarters, Langley, Virginia

"Sir, there's a call coming into Professor Palmer's phone."

Leroux leapt from his seat, heading for Child's station. "Source?"

"Looks like the same as before. It's the kidnappers."

"Shit, they're early. Send it to voicemail." He snapped his fingers, pointing up. "Let's hear it."

The professor could be heard giving a generic greeting followed by a beep, then the voice of someone who didn't sound impressed came on, their words clipped, the tone as if he were containing his anger.

"Professor Acton, you must not love your parents very much. You are not at your hotel room, and you were seen getting into a car that wasn't yours. You were told not to contact the authorities, and you obviously have. You have forfeited your mother's life. Contact us within ten minutes, otherwise you will lose your father as well."

The call ended and Leroux cursed. He snapped his fingers again. "Get me Rome, now! We need to have the professor call him back immediately."

Child's fingers flew as Leroux jacked into his terminal with his head set.

"What about the mother?" asked Sonya, turning in her chair. "It doesn't sound like she's dead yet."

Leroux froze for a moment, then committed to an order he hoped he wouldn't regret later.

"Contact Agent White. Have her make all haste. Contact Kane and Lee as well as the FBI. Have them all converge on that address."

He pointed at Marc Therrien, another one of his analysts. "And get me eyes on that location!"

Giasson Residence, Via Nicolò III, Rome, Italy

Giasson flipped through the files of his staff, shaking his head as he realized any one of them could be his suspect. He yawned, covering his mouth.

I need sleep.

He sighed.

I need answers more.

He pulled his hands back from the laptop and took a deep breath. There were too many possibilities. He had to narrow the list, otherwise he was just wasting time. Somebody had talked, that much was obvious. If he was to assume it was one of his people, then they had to have access to the information.

Which meant they had to have had the ability to be exposed to it.

He brought up the list and quickly eliminated anyone on leave.

Eleven fewer people.

Not much help. But progress.

It had to be someone inside his security office, not one of the guards. None of them would have had an opportunity to overhear something, or be one of the few actually exposed to the information.

Assuming Father Rinaldi made no mention of it.

He had to assume the Father was telling the truth, after all, he was a priest.

Less than twenty names.

Better.

"Now to eliminate those who weren't on duty that evening or overnight."

His wife moaned beside him.

"Sorry, hon, go to sleep."

The theft had taken place in the morning, after the morning shift had already come on duty, but it took time to coordinate an operation like this, hours at least, so the exposure had to have happened before that.

And I didn't tell anyone until after I had reached Hugh!

He frowned, remembering Father Rinaldi had already made the arrangements at the university.

When was that?

He thought back of the events of that day. The shootings, the discovery of the drawing, the collection of evidence including the drawing, it being eventually shown to Father Rinaldi, his subsequent research into what it might be, and his excited visit to his office, requesting permission to call in the Professors.

He chewed his lip, trying to remember when that was. It was late, but when?

After the day shift had left!

He was certain of it. And with there not enough time for the graveyard shift to have acted on this, it had to be someone there that evening. His fingers flew over the keyboard, adrenaline pumping as his fatigue was forgotten.

Twelve.

It was more than usual, but there *had* been four deaths.

He read through the list, every one of them someone he could have sworn only yesterday that he could trust.

If one betrayed us, they were obviously working for someone.

There were two groups at play. The Keepers of the One Truth were definitely involved, the two tattooed victims proof of that. And a second, unknown group, who had murdered six to this point. He found it hard to believe that any one of his staff could be working for them. This was a

211

chance event, a fluke. There was no way this second group could have anyone planted inside just in case by some miracle they'd be needed someday.

No, whoever it is, is working for the Keepers.

That made him feel a little better, and it also made the list a little smaller.

They're all men.

He shook his head.

You don't know that.

It made sense that the Keepers might have infiltrated the Church. In fact, he'd be stunned if they hadn't.

He smiled.

He knew a way he might be able to narrow the list down even further.

And he'd begin with his most likely candidate.

A candidate he hoped wasn't involved.

Prayed wasn't involved.

His good friend, his second-in-command, Gerard Boileau.

He pulled up the man's Facebook page, the two friends online for years.

So he had full access to his photos.

He began flipping through them, searching for anything that might reveal what he was looking for, but the man seemed always to be wearing a suit or button up shirt.

He smiled.

Vacation photos, Sardinia.

Shot after shot of the man's wife and kids, then finally what he was looking for.

Boileau in a shirt, a few buttons undone.

What is that?

It wasn't a tattoo, but there was something. A discoloration of some sort.

A scar?

It almost appeared to be, yet it was hard to tell. There was definitely something, though. He pulled up Boileau's file, skimming through it. There were no references to any chest issues, no leave for heart surgery, and he had known the man long enough to know that if he had gone through anything serious while they were working together, he'd be the first to know.

Whatever it was, predated their knowing each other, so it was easily a decade old.

His eyes closed as he realized it had to be what he feared.

And his heart sank.

CIA Safe House, Rome, Italy

Acton grunted then bolted awake, Mr. Verde shaking his shoulder. A wave of guilt at finally giving into sleep swept over him. "What?"

Verde handed him a phone. "You've got to take this call. The kidnappers called your wife's phone and left a message. They know you left the hotel. We had a recording set up to make it sound like you guys had returned and were sleeping, but that's been found out."

"Our room was bugged?" asked Laura, waking beside him.

"Yes. They say they're going to kill your mother and if you don't call back within the next few minutes, your father as well."

Acton's heart slammed in his chest and bile filled his mouth as the blood rushed through his ears, everything losing focus.

Mom!

Laura grabbed him, squeezing him tight as he fought for control. It was his fault, all his fault. If he had just left well enough alone, his parents would be safe at home, his mother would be alive.

You have to save Dad.

He blinked away the tears, sucking in a deep breath as he took the outstretched phone.

"It's Langley, they're going to route the call so they can trace it."

"Won't they know that it can't be Laura's phone? If they know we're not in the hotel room, they know the phones were left there as well."

Verde shook his head. "No, just say you checked the voicemail. Tell them that Giasson arranged the pickup and that you were taken to a house, you don't know the address, because he was concerned for your safety. Stress that no authorities were contacted, and that you thought the phone had been forwarded but it must not have been set up properly. Tell them that you just found out about the recording, and that it was made by Giasson. You had nothing to do with it."

He nodded, hoping that laying all the blame at their friend's feet wasn't going to cause more problems for him.

"Now keep calm, you need to be able to think."

He inhaled deeply and put the phone to his ear. "Hello?"

"One moment, Professor Acton, while we route your call."

There was a click then the phone rang. It was immediately answered. "Hello?"

"It's me, Jim Acton."

"Professor Acton. You didn't follow our instructions."

Acton tried to remember everything Verde had told him, but he was drawing a blank. Everyone stared at him, their eyes bulging as if they were all trying to urge him to say something.

"Yes, I did." His heart nearly stopped as the words came out.

"You deceived us."

"Of course. You've killed six people. I wasn't about to risk you killing my wife, so we went into hiding."

"You broke your word."

Acton felt his mouth dry and he motioned for water, Laura jumping up to get it from the kitchen. "No, I did no such thing. You said I wasn't allowed to contact the authorities, and that I was to remain silent as to where my phone ended up. You said nothing about having to remain where I was, or to remain in constant contact."

"Your deception has cost you your mother's life."

Acton felt a rage build inside him, his lip curling into a sneer. His voice lowered to almost a growl. "If you kill her, I will tell the world where you are."

There was a chuckle. "Don't threaten me, Professor, when I am holding all the cards. As you said before, we most likely are no longer where you think we are."

Acton took a sip of the water Laura held out to him, handing it back. "If that were true, then I doubt you would be going to such trouble." There was no reply. *Got you!* "If you want your precious secret kept, then don't you dare touch my mother."

"Professor Acton, you seem to think you are in a position to bargain. You mother's fate is sealed due to your actions. Don't let your father's be as well."

The call ended with a click, and Acton jumped to his feet, whipping the phone across the room.

"No!"

West Pratt Street, Baltimore, Maryland

Sherrie stared up at the tall condo building, Mr. Gervin apparently occupying the penthouse. She popped her trunk and began to suit up as Fang's vehicle rushed up behind her. The Asian woman climbed out and nodded toward the building.

"Is that it?"

Sherrie nodded.

"Wow! Is he a member of the ruling class?"

"Wrong country."

Fang shrugged. "I watch the news, they're all the same."

Sherrie handed her a vest, an array of weapons in a hidden compartment in the floor of the trunk. She selected two Glocks, several mags, a suppressor, a knife, three small explosive charges, and night vision goggles. Fitting an earpiece in place, she activated her comm, handing a second unit to Fang as she too began to gear up.

"Control, Freebird-Zero-Two, comm check, over."

"Freebird-Zero-Two, reading you five by five, over."

"Roger that, Control. Do you have eyes on us?"

"Negative, Freebird, we should have target acquisition in less than sixty seconds."

Sherrie flipped up another panel in the trunk and removed a small drone. She handed it to Fang whose eyes widened slightly in surprise.

"It's light."

Sherrie grinned. "But awesome." She activated the app on her phone and the blades spun up, it lifting out of Fang's outstretched hands. Directing it to the penthouse of the complex across the street, she watched the camera view on her display. Within moments, it was in position and she set it to hover, its numerous cameras filming every angle, transmitting regular spectrum and infrared.

"Langley, are you getting this?"

"Confirmed, Freebird. We're showing eight heat signatures. Two appear to be in a hallway near an elevator, four are in the condo unit with two others in an adjacent room. It appears the two separate signatures are your targets, visual indicates they are tied to chairs, over."

Sherrie gave a thumbs up to Fang, happy her hunch had been correct. "What are your instructions, Control?"

"Freebird, this is Control-Actual." Sherrie smiled and her heart skipped as she recognized her boyfriend's voice. "We've just received confirmation that they intend to kill Mrs. Acton. Be prepared to make entry, but hold until backup arrives."

"ETA?"

"Fifteen minutes."

Sherrie looked at Fang who shook her head. "She'll be dead by then," whispered the Chinese exile.

Sherrie nodded in agreement. A hostage was going to die, and she wasn't about to let it happen. "Negative, Control. We're going in."

"Negative, Freebird, you're outnumbered three to one."

Fang help up a finger. "Control, Freebird-Zero-Three. We acknowledge the count, but they're six men and we're two women. It's not a problem, out."

Sherrie grinned. "I think you and I are going to get along just fine."

Operations Center 3, CIA Headquarters, Langley, Virginia

Leroux yanked his headset off, looking at Sonya. "Did they just shut off their comms?"

Sonya stifled a smile, nodding. "Comms are down. Maybe there's a problem?" she suggested, Leroux giving her a look, pointing at the display showing the drone footage. "Umm, sorry, boss. I guess she doesn't want to talk to you."

Morrison entered before Leroux had a chance to respond, though he wasn't sure what he would say, the young woman clearly taking delight in his domestic issues.

"Report."

Leroux looked at him, part of him fuming at what had just happened, not because he was truly angry at an order being disobeyed, but because his girlfriend was about to put herself in grave danger.

Would you feel the same way if it were any other agent?

He had to admit to himself that he probably wouldn't. In fact, he'd probably applaud them for being so brave, for putting their lives at risk to save an innocent civilian against such odds.

Yet things *were* different. It was his girlfriend, the woman he loved, the only woman he had ever completely opened up to.

He couldn't lose her.

And now he knew why he wasn't supposed to be directing ops with her, why nobody was supposed to have a personal relationship with someone whose life may one day be in their hands.

He sucked in a deep breath. "Sherrie—I mean Agent White—has found the hostages. She and Lee Fang are effecting an entrance."

219

"Backup?"

"Kane is ten minutes out, FBI fifteen."

"How many hostiles?"

"Six. Four inside the apartment, two in the hallway by the elevator."

"How are they getting in?"

Leroux shook his head. "Comm problems. I don't know."

"Sir, we've got a visual."

Leroux turned to Child. "Put it up."

A display flickered and a satellite image appeared, Child zooming into the condo building, nothing distinguishable.

"Just a second."

The image changed, a hazy bluish green replacing everything. Leroux caught something out of the corner of his eye. "Pan right."

The image shifted and he smacked his forehead.

"Is that them?"

Morrison put a hand on Leroux's shoulder. "If I know Agent White, I'd have to say yes."

Leroux closed his eyes.

Why did I have to fall in love with a woman with a death wish?

West Pratt Street, Baltimore, Maryland

Sherrie looked at Fang. "Ready?"

Fang nodded and Sherrie took aim, pulling the trigger. The grappling gun fired, the coiled spring sounded almost cartoonish, the rope piled on the ground beside her rapidly playing out as it sailed from the top of the building they were on to the condo unit across from them.

The end slammed into the concrete rooftop, embedding itself firmly. She pulled the rope tight, tying it off then hooking herself on. "See you on the other side."

She stepped off and enjoyed the ride, it the quickest and safest way into the building. Her vehicle was fully equipped, she choosing it from the motor pool specifically for that fact, knowing full well they might have to rescue the hostages on their own. Entering the condo was risky because they didn't know if the doorman could be trusted, and they couldn't ride the elevator to the top, it guarded. That would have meant stairs and time.

But a flash of her FBI badge in the building across the street had them heading swiftly for the roof, and now sliding across to their target building.

Less than five minutes.

Her boots hit the concrete and she squeezed the brake hard, killing her momentum then disconnecting herself. She glanced back and waved, Fang already leaping off the other building.

No fear.

Sherrie held the line until Fang cleared the edge of the roof then headed for the door.

Locked.

She planted a small charge as Fang joined her.

"I get the impression you've done that before."

Fang nodded. "Standard training in the People's Liberation Army Special Forces."

Sherrie guided Fang away from the door. "Remind me not to underestimate them."

"You'd be wise not to."

Sherrie triggered the device, the lock shredded an instant later.

She reactivated her comm.

"Control, Freebird. Any indication our hostiles just heard that?"

"Freebird, Control Actual. Good to hear comms are working again." Sherrie gave Fang a "busted" look, her boyfriend's response dripping with sarcasm. "Negative on any movement, you're clear, over."

"Entering the building now. Can you kill the power?"

There was a pause. "Affirmative, let us know when."

"Stand by."

Fang pulled open the door and Sherrie took point, her Glock drawn. There was a small landing then another door, it unlocked. She pulled it open, a set of stairs revealed. She glanced over the railing and could see no one. She paused to listen.

Nothing.

She took the steps two at a time, stopping at the penthouse level door.

"Freebird, Control Actual. We've got movement. One of the hostiles is heading for the bedroom with a weapon drawn, over."

"Shit!" Sherrie glanced at Fang as she screwed a suppressor in place. "Ready?" Fang nodded, twisting her own onto the end of her Glock. "Control, stand by on those lights."

"Roger that, standing by."

She yanked open the door and Fang burst through, Sherrie directly behind her, weapon raised as Fang took the right side, she the left. Two pops sounded from Fang's weapon then she shifted aim slightly, following it up with two more quick shots.

The hallway targets were down, Sherrie not having fired a shot.

I'm glad she's on my side.

They continued to rush forward in silence. Fang covered them as Sherrie checked the downed men's vitals.

Both dead.

She activated her comm as she tossed a charge to Fang who immediately began to set it on the door to the Penthouse suite. "Control, ready on those lights?"

"Affirmative."

"Kill the lights, now."

The hallway went dark, emergency lights kicking in as Fang activated the explosive device, blasting the lock, the door swinging open. Sherrie flipped her night vision goggles down and swiftly entered the room, three targets plainly visible. She took the first target in her arc, eliminating him with a double-tap to the chest.

"Kill them!" shouted one of the targets, clearly shouting instructions to the other room with the hostages. Two shots fired to her left, one of the targets going down by Fang's hand as she fired two more into the third.

"Langley, have the hostages moved?"

"Negative."

She visualized the image from the drone as she raised her weapon, advancing on the closed bedroom door.

A woman screamed.

A man shouted.

And Sherrie prayed.

She squeezed the trigger, firing round after round in an arc from left to right, all at shoulder height. Holes tore through the drywall separating the rooms, another scream from a woman, then a thump of something hitting the floor. She grabbed the doorknob and pushed against the door, something blocking it. She stuck her weapon then head inside and looked down at the floor, breathing a sigh of relief.

It was the fourth hostile, bleeding from a hole in his neck.

He groaned, then tried to raise his weapon. She pulled her second Glock and pumped three rounds into him, shoving hard against the door. Sweeping the room, Fang watching the door, she looked at the two clearly terrified hostages, and remembered they could see nothing.

"Control, turn the power back on, over."

She flipped up the goggles, Fang doing the same, just as the overhead light flickered on. The panicked woman stared at her then Fang, clearly still terrified. Fang cut them loose and Sherrie knelt in front of them.

"Take it easy, you've probably been sitting awhile; let's get the circulation going first."

"Who are you people?" asked the husband.

Sherrie smiled. "Your son sent us."

Operations Center 3, CIA Headquarters, Langley, Virginia

Leroux exchanged fist bumps with the team, offering up one to Morrison who shook his head then chuckled, granting his underling some skin. To say Leroux was relieved was an understatement. His girlfriend going up against six hostiles was not how he had thought his day would play out, but it was over. Acton's parents were safe, and Sherrie could come back in, perfectly secure while the Italian portion of the operation wound up.

Marc Therrien cleared his throat. "Sir, I think I've figured out why they were using that apartment."

The jubilation immediately ceased, everyone turning to the analyst.

"Go ahead."

"It's listed on SimplyStay, it's like an Airbnb type place. You know, you list your house or apartment for rent. It looks like he does it every time he's out of town on business."

Sonya spun in her chair. "Why would someone so rich do that? It's not like he needs the cash."

"I checked him out. He's the CEO of that biomedical firm, but he's an angel investor in a lot of other companies, including this one."

Leroux pursed his lips. "So he's testing his own product."

"Yup."

"What can you tell us?"

"The listing went up last week and it's now showing as unavailable, so it was obviously rented."

"Can you trace the transaction?"

"Should be able to, give me a few minutes."

Leroux nodded, turning to Child.

"How about we let Professor Acton know his parents are safe."

CIA Safe House, Rome, Italy

"You're sure you're okay?"

"Yes, dear, we're fine."

Just the sound of his mother's voice had Acton collapsing on the couch, the adrenaline he'd been running on done with, his exhaustion already taking over. He closed his eyes, tears rolling down his cheeks as Laura hugged him, Reading on his feet exchanging a handshake with Mr. Verde.

Everyone was elated.

Though none obviously more than him.

"I'm sorry I got you involved," he managed, his voice cracking. "I'm so sorry. I was stupid."

"What's this all about? Why did they take us?"

Acton inhaled, holding it for a moment. "I got mixed up in something in Italy, but you're safe now."

"Who are these people?"

"I'll explain everything later. You're with my friends, they'll get you to safety."

"Interesting friends you have. We're definitely going to have a talk when you get home."

Acton smiled, enjoying the scolding. "Yes, Mom. Where are you now?"

"We're just getting on the elevator. They're taking us somewhere safe, I guess." There was a strange sound on the other end of the line. "Wait a minute, what was that? Oh my God, no!"

"Mom! Mom! What is it? What's happening?"

He heard screams and loud bursts of static, then nothing.

"Mom!" He stared at the phone, the call ended, then looked at Laura. "Something's happened!"

West Pratt Street, Baltimore, Maryland

Kane pulled up outside the condo, parking behind Sherrie's vehicle. He had been pissed when he heard they had gone in without backup, though knew he would have done no different.

And it had all worked out.

He climbed out of the vehicle and headed for the front entrance when he felt the ground shake and a screeching sound tear through the air above him. He looked and a massive fireball erupted from the top of the building. He rushed forward, toward the awning covering the entrance as glass and debris rained down around him.

His phone was already in his hand, dialing Sherrie's number, his comm active in his ear. "Control, Freebird-Zero-One, there's been an explosion here. Call it in, we're going to need police, fire and paramedics."

"Roger that, contacting local authorities now."

"Zero-One, this is Control Actual. We've lost comms with our personnel. Do you have eyes on them, over?"

Kane immediately recognized Leroux's voice and the panic came through the digital equipment loud and clear. He pointed at the security guard behind the front desk who was still half-ducking, half-staring up at the ceiling. "Do you have an evacuation procedure?"

The man nodded.

"Then do it!"

Kane headed for the stairwell, rushing up the steps as fast as he could as Sherrie's phone continued to ring, unanswered, then going to voicemail. He switched, trying Fang's, before he realized his friend was repeating his question.

"Negative, Control, I'm attempting to access the site now. Stand by."

The fire alarm sounded but the stairwell was already starting to fill, panicked residents evacuating, there no ignoring what had happened at the top of the building. As he continued his climb, the numbers surged then dwindled and he was soon at the penthouse level, the door blown off its hinges.

He shoved it aside and stepped out into what could only be described as a war zone. One entire side of the floor, where the hostiles and hostages had been, was gone, the studded walls mere remnants of themselves, giving him a clear view of the apartment, the devastation inside, total. The windows were blown out, the wind whipping around the debris, there few flames, the explosion mostly extinguishing itself as it had rapidly chewed through its oxygen supply.

It was as if it had been designed only to take out this one penthouse unit.

A failsafe?

It made sense, though it meant that they were dealing with a brutal organization willing to kill its own should it become necessary.

And send a message while doing it.

"Control, Zero-One. The entire penthouse level has been taken out. Looks like explosives. Some sort of failsafe."

"Is—is there anyone alive? Can you contact Zero-Two or Three?"

Leroux's voice was cracking and it tore at Kane's heart, his best friend going through something that no one should have to experience.

Morrison should never have let her help.

He shook his head as he made his way deeper down what was once the hallway.

It's nobody's fault. No one expected this.

He spotted what appeared to be charred remains farther ahead, two bodies slammed against the wall containing the elevators, the flesh burned crisp. He knelt down beside them then stood back up.

There was just no way to tell.

"Stand by, we're getting a call from Professor Acton." There was a pause as Kane continued into the apartment, stepping through an opening that was once a wall. Remnants of furniture littered the room, an open concept kitchen to his left charred almost beyond recognition except for the stainless steel appliances, strangely still shining. His comm squawked. "Check the elevator! Acton said they were in the elevator when the explosion happened!"

Kane whipped around and jumped back into the hallway, grabbing the seam of the elevator doors and prying them open. Inside he was greeted with cables, several loose, cut in the explosion. He leaned in and saw the elevator car far below him, the second shaft clear, that car looking like it was already at the bottom.

He stepped out, wrapping his sleeved arms then his legs around the cables, sliding down quickly, ignoring the friction. He came to rest on the top of the car, it protesting loudly at the shift in weight. Still holding onto the cable with one hand, he reached over and yanked the damaged hatch open then peered inside.

"Oh no!"

Operations Center 3, CIA Headquarters, Langley, Virginia

"What did he just say?"

Leroux was in a panic, not sure what to do. It wasn't right. It wasn't fair. A hand gripped his shoulder and spun him around. Morrison snapped his fingers, motioning for the headset. Leroux gave it to him and Morrison fit it in place. He pointed at a chair. "Sit."

Leroux nodded, dropping into the chair and grabbing his head as he squeezed his eyes shut and tried to get control. He felt a gentle hand on his back and he looked up to see Sonya Tong standing in front of him, her eyes filled with tears.

Not now!

She leaned over and gave him a hug. "Don't lose hope," she whispered, then let him go, returning to her station.

"Sir, phone call coming in on Professor Palmer's phone."

Morrison snapped his fingers. "Let our agent know then route it through. Pipe the audio through the speakers."

"Yes, sir."

Leroux sucked in slow, deep breaths, trying to remember what Kane had taught him about combat breathing—or something like that. Tactical? He couldn't remember, but it was starting to work. He glanced over at Sonya, working away at her station, and said a silent apology to her. Yes, she was sweet on him, that he knew, though never did he think she would truly wish any ill will toward Sherrie. She was just concerned about him.

And she was right.

Don't lose hope.

The heads-up was given to the agent, then the phone rang.

"Hello?"

"Professor Acton, your friends have failed and your parents are dead."

"So are you, you son of a bitch. I'm going to find you and kill you if it's the last thing I ever do."

There was a chuckle. "Professor Acton, you will do no such thing. You are going to return home, attend your parents' funeral, and maintain your silence."

"Go to hell."

"Professor, I think you are missing the big picture. Your parents are dead because you know something you shouldn't. You still know something you shouldn't. Killing you isn't an option, because I don't know who you've told. Even if I killed your wife and your friends, Interpol Agent Hugh Reading, and Inspector General Mario Giasson, I could never be sure I got everyone. But if they know your friends and family will die if they speak, I know they will maintain their silence." There was a momentary pause and Leroux rose, wiping his cheeks clear of tears. "To illustrate my point, your friend, Gregory Milton, has a child, does he not? It will be hard for him to save her with that back of his. Perhaps we will pay him a visit."

The call ended, leaving Leroux in shock for a moment.

Then he snapped his fingers.

"Find this Gregory Milton, now!"

Milton Residence, St. Paul, Maryland

Greg Milton moaned in exquisite agony as his wife straddled him, working her thumbs into the small of his back. It was aching from a long day at work, though it was a pain he would never trade for the alternative he had been facing.

Total paralysis from the waist down.

He had been shot in the back and left for dead a few years ago. He was lucky to be alive, and a lifetime in a wheelchair had been a horrible prospect, though one he was willing to live with if it meant spending it with his wife and young daughter.

But the doctors' longshot had paid off, their "most likely" wrong, their "slim chance" a winner. And the recovery had begun. A long, slow, painful recovery, but he was now walking again, able to go most of the day at his job as Dean of St. Paul's University, though if he overdid it, like he had today standing at a podium, delivering a speech, he would pay the price later.

He no longer worried about losing the ability to walk. The doctors had confirmed that was behind him. The question was now whether or not he'd stage a full recovery, or forever experience the pain.

He was determined to see the former win out.

Sandra expertly worked his muscles, she having enrolled in some courses to learn how properly to do this, and she had turned out to be a godsend. She never complained, never asked for a night off, she just did it.

"You have no idea how good that feels, hon."

"Is it working?"

"Oh yeah. I don't know what I'd do without you."

"Hang around in your underwear watching television and eating Cheezies?"

He chuckled. "You're probably right." He glanced back at her. "That doesn't sound half-bad."

She smacked his ass and he reveled in the fact he could feel it.

"Don't start something you're not willing to finish."

She leaned over and kissed him between the shoulder blades. "You know what they say is good for the back."

He grinned, closing his eyes as she continued to rain gentle kisses on him.

Something stirred.

And his phone vibrated on the nightstand.

Sandra leaned over and grabbed it, handing it to him. He looked at it and shook his head. "Don't recognize the number. Let it go to voicemail then get back to that new massage technique you were trying out there."

The phone was returned to the nightstand, the kisses continuing, full mast achieved.

The phone vibrated again.

Sandra sighed, Milton groaned, and the phone demanded attention. She grabbed it again. "Same number."

"Okay, I better take it." She handed him the phone and he swiped his thumb. "Hello?"

"Greg, it's me, Jim. Get Sandra and Niskha out of the house, now! Get to the nearest police station and stay there. Do you hear me?"

Milton's heart raced and he began to roll over, Sandra climbing off him, their fun over. "What's wrong? What's going on?"

"There's no time to explain. Trust no one, not even the police or the FBI. I'll send Dylan to get you."

"Why? Jim, tell me something!"

"My parents are dead. Just move, now!"

CIA Safe House, Rome, Italy

Mr. Verde shook his head, shaking his phone in defeat. "We don't know yet. There was an explosion and they can't reach the agents that rescued your parents. There's another agent on-site trying to confirm what happened."

Acton gripped his hair as he bent forward, pulling hard, Laura leaning against him, her cheek resting on his back as she gently stroked him, trying to comfort him.

It wasn't working.

"They're dead." He sucked in a breath. "And it's my fault."

Reading continued to pace in front of the window they weren't allowed to open. "This won't end," he said, suddenly stopping and whirling toward the group. "This will never end until they're taken out."

Laura lifted her head. "But who is *they*?"

"I don't know, but there's one way to find out."

Acton lifted his head, staring up at his friend. "How?"

"Pay them a bloody visit and get our hands on one of them."

Laura sat up. "Is that even legal?"

Reading shrugged. "No, but we're long past that now. And something tells me they're not going to go crying to the police if we do take one of them."

Acton leapt to his feet, filling his lungs with false courage, his need to do something outweighing his need to act carefully. "Then let's go. I'm done sitting around."

Verde stepped forward. "I can't let you leave."

Acton walked toward the man and stopped inches from his face.

"Just try to stop me."

He felt Laura's hand on his shoulder.

"Try to stop *us.*"

West Pratt Street, Baltimore, Maryland

Kane gently rolled Sherrie over onto her back, the elevator creaking with the shift in mass.

She moaned.

Oh, thank God!

"Are you okay?"

She moaned again and he quickly began an inspection for broken bones or wounds.

Nothing.

She coughed, a burst of pulverized drywall dust erupting from her mouth.

She opened her eyes. "What happened?"

"An explosion took out the penthouse level. Just stay still, this whole thing could drop at any moment."

Fang coughed then rolled over, wiping a hand over her face. He reached over and took her hand. "Just stay still. Let me check you over." He quickly did an assessment and found her clear as well.

He looked at where his partners had been lying and his admiration of them grew. They had thrown themselves over the elderly Actons, shielding them from falling debris.

Incredible.

Fang pushed herself up to a sitting position as Kane rolled Mrs. Acton onto her back, her breathing shallow but steady.

She must have fainted.

He checked Acton's father for a pulse then frowned.

Nothing.

He searched again then held his hand to the man's face.

Again nothing.

"He's not breathing. I've got to start CPR. Hang on."

He rolled the man over and the elevator creaked in protest then slipped, knocking him off his knees.

"Christ, we've got to get out of here." He motioned toward the doors. "See if you can get those open."

He began chest compressions, each pump seeming to piss the elevator off more, as the others pulled at the doors. Suddenly Dorothy Acton gasped, sitting upright. "What happened?" Then she saw Kane working on her husband and cried out. "Oh my God! Eli! Are you okay?" She climbed to her knees and the elevator slipped again. She screamed, Kane reaching over and grabbing her by the shoulder.

"Stay perfectly still."

She nodded, instead clasping her hands together and beginning to pray silently, her eyes glued on her husband's unresponsive face.

As he continued compressions, he glanced behind him to see the inner doors open, a piece of debris wedged into the frame to keep them in place. He turned back to his patient. "What do you see?"

"We're about halfway between levels. I'm going to try and climb up."

"No, if this slips you'll be cut in half."

Sherrie pounded on the bottom of the outer doors. "Help us! We're in the elevator!" She pounded again then stopped, everyone listening.

There were shouts then pounding on the other side. "Anyone in there?"

"Yes, yes we're in here! We need help. Someone's had a heart attack!"

"Just a second!" called the muffled voice and Kane looked over his shoulder to see the outer doors opening.

"Let me take a look," said a second voice, sticking his head in, "I'm a doctor." He saw Kane continuing chest compressions. "Okay, I'm coming in."

Kane held up a hand, stopping him. "No, it's too dangerous. The whole thing could fall with the extra weight."

The man nodded, pulling his head out. "Are you trained?"

"Yes."

"Okay, keep doing what you're doing. The fire department just arrived, I'll get a portable defibrillator down to you."

Kane continued, Fang checking for a pulse and shaking her head.

The elevator shook, everything rattling like an earthquake, then there was a snapping sound overhead and they dropped several more feet, the outer doors disappearing. Kane glanced up through the hatch and couldn't see any cables holding them.

It must be just the brakes now.

He continued his compressions, alternating with mouth-to-mouth.

But if they were damaged…

Shouts from above had him looking again and he breathed a sigh of relief as he saw a firefighter being lowered, a portable defibrillator strapped to his chest. He came to rest just above the elevator and lowered the kit inside. Sherrie reached up and grabbed it, quickly unpacking it as Kane continued his work.

"Do you know how to use that?" asked the firefighter.

Kane glanced up and nodded. "Yes." He ripped his patient's shirt open and he and Sherrie, also trained, stuck the pads into position as the machine powered up. It beeped and Kane removed his hands.

"Clear!"

Sherrie pressed the button and Ellsworth shook. Kane checked the machine.

241

Still a flat line.

"Hit him again."

The machine beeped its readiness, and again he was shocked, his body flopping like a fish on the dock.

And nothing.

Kane closed his eyes, not willing to give up, though knowing there was no point in continuing. But the doc wouldn't want him to stop. "Again," he whispered, Sherrie nodding.

"Clear."

A zap and again, nothing.

Then there was a beep.

Kane leaned over and looked at the machine. Another beep. And then another, the display beginning to show a heartbeat, the rate quickly climbing from five beats, to twenty to sixty, the rhythm steady.

"We've got a heartbeat!" he shouted. Sherrie hugged him and Dorothy collapsed on top of her husband, hugging him and kissing him, her sobs of relief shaking the entire car.

"Okay, we're going to secure you from above. Try to keep still!"

Ellsworth's eyes flickered open and he inhaled deeply.

"Get off me, woman."

Dorothy lifted herself up, the joy in her face obvious as she put her hand on his cheek. "Y-you gave us quite the sc-scare."

He returned the caress. "It's okay, I'm fine. No kidnappers or exploding buildings or collapsing elevators are going to kill me." Dorothy laughed, sniffing. "It'll be all those damned apple pies you keep baking. Do you see any apple pies?"

Dorothy gently slapped his cheek. "No."

"Then I'm not going to die, am I?"

Kane smiled, turning away to give the old married couple as much privacy as was possible, leaving him to wonder what it would be like to have someone is his life that cared about him that much. He found himself staring at Fang as she watched the couple, a slight smile on her face, her mouth open slightly. She caught him and her smile broadened.

Then she looked quickly away.

Maybe one day?

Operations Center 3, CIA Headquarters, Langley, Virginia

Leroux paced in front of the displays, no one daring stare, no one wanting to say anything to him, status reports being provided to Morrison who had wisely stepped in to take over. Nobody would blame him for losing it. It wasn't a failure to care about someone. His reaction was exactly why he was never supposed to have been put in that situation in the first place.

Yet it had happened, and now everyone was waiting for word from Kane, there nothing for almost ten minutes.

The longest ten minutes in his life.

"Sir!"

Sonya looked at Leroux then Morrison, then back at Leroux. "It's Agent White!"

Leroux bounded toward her station, his hand extended. She handed him her headset and he fit it around his ears. "Hon, are you okay?"

"Hey, baby, we're fine, we're all fine."

Leroux collapsed to his knees, turning around and sitting on the floor. "Oh thank God! We all thought you were dead."

"I'm not, so you can stop your worrying."

He smiled, the tears of joy rolling down his cheeks suddenly reminding him that he wasn't the only one hanging on by a thread. "Are Professor Acton's parents okay?"

"Yes. Mr. Acton had a heart attack but Dylan got his heart going again. He's being taken to the hospital now."

Leroux pushed himself to his feet, snapping his fingers at Child. "Get word to Professor Acton that his parents are okay."

Child nodded and Leroux looked at Morrison, his boss giving him a nod and removing his headset.

Control had been returned.

Leroux smiled at him slightly and Morrison left the room, the exact message Leroux needed to be sent at this moment.

You have his confidence.

"Okay, hon, I've got to let you go. Call me when you're secure."

"I will. Love you."

"Love you too."

He hit the button, killing the call and turned to Therrien. "What's the status on our other situation?"

"Retrieval team is inbound, ETA less than ten minutes." Therrien pointed at the screen. "We just got eyes on target."

Leroux looked at the display, a quiet suburban street with little activity.

Except one car sitting with a hot engine and two occupants, almost directly in front of their target's house.

Leroux shook his head.

Either it's an awkward teenage post-date moment, or someone is up to no good.

Milton Residence, St. Paul, Maryland

"Daddy, no!"

Milton picked up his daughter, there no longer time to deal with her childish protests at having been woken. He grabbed her green Froggie and stuck it in her hands, she immediately hugging it tight. His back spasmed and he leaned back with a hiss, grasping at it with his free hand.

"Let me take her." His wife took Niskha and grabbed the overnight bag she had packed, heading for the garage.

"You drive, my back's too sore. I don't think I'd be able to do any quick maneuvers if I had to."

He set the alarm, the chirp the signal for Sandra to open the door. She stepped into the garage, hitting the opener button and the garage door rumbled up. He glanced outside as he rounded the rear of their van and saw no one, though he suspected pros wouldn't be so obvious as to be standing across the street, smoking a cigarette in a trench coat.

Sandra got Niskha situated and climbed into the driver's seat, he getting into the passenger side. She started the van and began to pull out slowly. "Do you really think someone's going to follow us?"

"I don't know. Jim sounded scared. Really scared. And he said his parents were dead. Whatever's going on is serious, and for some reason he thinks our lives are in danger."

Sandra put the car in drive and pulled away from the house. Milton scrunched in his seat, peering out the side view mirror and his heart leapt as he saw headlights turn on, a vehicle pulling away from the curb, just one house down from theirs.

"Shit!"

"Daddy said a bad word!"

"What is it?"

Milton looked again. "I think someone's following us."

"Are you sure?"

He shook his head. "No, just keep going. Let's get to a busy street quickly."

Sandra pulled up to the stop sign at the end of the street, coming to a complete stop and looking in all directions, despite there almost never being any traffic here. She carefully made a right hand turn, Milton's nails digging into his palms as he tried to bite his tongue.

He failed.

"Hon, please, just forget the traffic laws for now. We need to get to the police station quickly."

Sandra began to shake, both hands gripping the steering wheel, the van barely moving forward. "I'm sorry, I'm nervous."

Milton took a breath and tried to sound as calm and sympathetic as possible. "I know you are, hon, so am I, but you've got to accelerate."

"I-I can't seem to press any harder, I'm t-too terrified."

He reached over and put his hand on the wheel. "Just take a deep breath and close your eyes."

"But I'm driving!"

"I know, I'll steer. Just take a deep breath, close your eyes, and press down with your right foot a little harder."

"O-okay." She closed her eyes then immediately opened them. She glanced at him, then nodded, closing her eyes again as she inhaled slowly.

And they began to accelerate, Milton keeping them straight.

"Okay, that's great. Now open your eyes."

She did and adjusted their trajectory slightly, but kept their now reasonable speed. She checked her rearview mirror. "Is that them?"

He glanced in his mirror. "Yes."

"Then they *are* following us."

He frowned. "I don't know. They could be just heading in the same direction."

They rolled up to another stop sign, this time Sandra checking in both directions but continuing through, accelerating immediately.

"You're doing great, hon. Just keep doing that, we'll be there in no time."

She lifted a finger from the steering wheel, pointing ahead. "He's in a hurry."

Milton's heart leapt into his throat as a large SUV raced toward them then cut across their lane, shuddering to a halt as all four doors were thrown open. Sandra slammed on her brakes and screamed as four men leapt out, weapons raised. Milton reached for a wailing Niskha but was jerked back by his seatbelt as the men rushed toward them.

Then straight by.

He turned to watch them and gunfire erupted causing Sandra to scream again, Niskha crying out in fear along with her mother. All four tires of the vehicle behind them were flattened, the engine block filled with lead, those inside hauled out and thrown to the ground. Milton's heart nearly stopped as he saw the men were armed, their weapons kicked away.

They were *following us.*

One of the new arrivals turned, walking back toward their van. He knocked on the window and Milton pressed the button, lowering it. The man leaned over and smiled.

And Milton breathed a sigh of relief, immediately recognizing him as one of the Delta Operators that Acton had so much involvement with.

"Dean Milton, ma'am, Dylan Kane sent us. Sorry we're late."

Approaching Rome, Italy

"Change of plans," said Kane's voice over the speaker. "The doc is heading north to the castle."

Dawson frowned. "That doesn't sound smart."

"Nope, but he's determined to take action himself."

Niner shook his head. "That's just the type of thing that's going to get him killed."

"Well, in his defense he did think his parents were dead when he left and that they were going after his friends. Red has the Miltons secured. Can you think of anyone else they might go after?"

Dawson pursed his lips, thinking. He knew the professors' files, but couldn't think of anyone close besides his students. "Students are about all I can think of."

"Nothing we can really do about them, there's too many. They were definitely watching Milton though, which makes me wonder how they were able to put together a file on Acton so quickly."

Dawson's head bobbed. "Me too. They seem to know everything about him. Parents, friends. You think they've been watching them for a while?"

"We've got no evidence of that, though the Assembly definitely has been."

"Perhaps they're working together?"

"Anything's possible, but they seem to have gone to ground since we named a few of them. I'd be surprised if they'd risk our current state of détente."

Niner huffed. "The doc has pissed off a lot of people over the years. Maybe it's finally caught up to him."

Kane laughed. "He has that, hasn't he? He doesn't have the luxury of anonymity like we do. Makes for a dangerous life."

Niner grinned. "Lucky he's a nice guy and we're willing to interrupt our time off."

Atlas leaned forward. "Karma, baby, karma. If he was an asshole he'd probably be dead by now."

Dawson had to agree. If the man were a prick, none of them would probably be here by now. Fortunately, he was anything but. And his desire to take action was completely understandable, if unwise. "So what's the new plan?"

"Have your pilot divert north. I've already got your supplies rolling in a charter so they'll be there when you arrive. Hopefully you'll be able to get ahead of the professor. One of my guys is driving them."

"And then?"

"Do whatever is necessary to end the threat."

Niner elbowed Jimmy. "Sounds like my typical weekend."

"What, ending the threat of disappointed girlfriends?"

"Hey, they've all been satisfied customers until they met my friends."

"You mean until they met real men," rumbled Atlas.

"Ouch."

Jimmy laughed. "You kind of walked into that one."

Niner gripped his chest, feigning tears. "It's just, well, I never though a friend would ever say something so hurtful."

Atlas rose, extending his arms. "Little lady need a hug?"

Kane laughed over the speaker. "Sometimes I miss working with a team."

Dawson shook his head as Niner's fist darted for Atlas' balls.

"If you were here you wouldn't."

Northbound E80, Italy

Reading turned back in his seat, looking at Acton and Laura, Mr. Verde driving. "Now that we know your parents are safe, what's the plan?"

Acton frowned. He'd been thinking about that. The phone call he had received had been a massive relief, though the news his father had suffered a heart attack was still worrisome. But they were alive and safe. Now he was worried about his best friend and his family. He hadn't heard anything since he had phoned him, so he probably hadn't reached the police station yet.

He checked his watch.

But they should be there by now.

He looked at Reading. "Sit tight for now, gather intel?"

Reading nodded. "Good thinking." He motioned toward Laura's laptop. "You found a hotel that's right across the street from the entrance?"

She nodded, spinning it around. "Already reserved three rooms, but only one has a view of the road."

"One's enough," said Reading. "We'll start photographing who goes in and out, grab license plates, and I'll run everything through Interpol. If we're lucky, there might be some outstanding warrants on one or more of them, and we just call in the authorities."

Laura snapped her laptop shut. "But what if the leak is with the Italians? Wouldn't they just warn them?"

Reading drew in a slow breath, frowning. "They might, but at this point, we don't have much choice."

Acton pursed his lips, shaking his head. Reading was right. They didn't have a lot of options beyond the Delta team going in and stirring up shit. But they were six guys facing a couple of hundred. Now that his parents

251

were safe, he could never ask them to face those odds. "Precision guided bomb dropped from a Raptor might be better."

Reading grinned. "We could always ask."

Verde's phone rang and he took the call, Acton instinctively watching the road, hating it when people used their cellphones while driving. Verde handed it back to Acton. "For you."

"Hello?"

"We're safe!"

Acton breathed a sigh of relief at the sound of his best friend's voice, his eyes closing as the last major stress lifted from his shoulders. "Thank God! I was starting to get worried."

"Yeah, some of the Delta guys somehow got here in time."

"Really?" Acton said a silent prayer of thanks to the men they owed so much to, then mouthed who it was to the others, Laura clasping both hands to her chest in relief.

"Yeah, apparently Kane had a feeling we might be a target if your parents were rescued so he asked BD to send some men. They were almost here when the specific threat was made."

Acton put an arm around Laura, squeezing her against him. "Lucky he was thinking ahead."

"Yeah. Listen, I'm so sorry about your parents."

Acton suddenly realized his friend hadn't heard the news. "They're alive! I just got a call a few minutes ago."

"Thank God! What happened?"

"Some sort of explosion, but they're okay. My dad had a heart attack but Dylan got his heart going again. They're all going to be fine."

"That's great news, Jim. What's going to happen now?"

"We're heading to Angera in northern Italy to try and put an end to this, once and for all."

"Be careful."

Acton smiled. "Aren't I always?"

"Hi, my name is Greg Milton, and you are?"

Acton's smile turned into a grin. "Ha ha. So you know me too well." He became serious. "If we don't remove the leverage problem, this will never end."

"But your parents are safe. So are we."

"That's not the leverage I'm talking about."

Giasson Residence, Via Nicolò III, Rome, Italy

Mario sipped on a coffee, adrenaline no longer enough to keep him awake, his attempts at rest merely tortured excuses. He had to know who had betrayed him. As he cycled through the photos of his staff, of those involved in the two incidents so far, and of everyone involved in the kidnapping of the Pope several years ago, he realized there was no way to know.

The Keepers had a way into the Vatican that had been cut off, though that was only the one he knew about. There could be others. In fact, nothing stopped them from merely taking a job there. The Vatican employed thousands. Who knew how many might be Keepers inside the massive walls? The organization was apparently created by St. Peter himself to protect the Church from outside dangers. They had targeted the new Pope because he was Triarii, but what could they possibly want with a painting by da Vinci? How could it possibly be a threat to the Church?

He looked again at the vacation photo of his second-in-command, Gerard Boileau, the discoloration on his chest in the same location as the tattoos found on the two victims of the Vatican shooting and the other Keepers' bodies they had found after the rescue of the Pope.

Could it be him? A man I have trusted for years?

He sighed, reaching for his phone.

There's only one way to find out.

Northbound E80, Italy

"Goodbye, Dad, you take it easy."

"Your mother isn't letting me lift a finger, so there's no worry about that. I feel fine, just weak, but they said that's normal. Don't worry about me, just take care of yourself and that wife of yours."

"You know I will. Can you put Dylan back on?"

"Sure thing."

There was some rustling from the speaker, the conversation now routed through the car's Bluetooth.

"Hiya, Doc."

"Hey Dylan, are they secure?"

"Yup. I won't be leaving their side and I've got two trained people with me. They're perfectly safe and so are the Miltons."

"Thank you, Dylan. I don't know what I would have done if they had been killed. And thank you—" He paused, his voice cracking, tears filling his eyes as he drew in a deep breath, struggling to regain control. Laura squeezed his arm and he looked at her, nodding. "Thank you for saving my Dad's life."

"Nothin' doing, Doc. You can stop worrying. Now, we've got the two who were following Greg in custody, but they're not talking, and outside of dropping them in Guantanamo, we're probably not going to get anything out of them legally."

"Have you checked their chests?"

"Huh?"

"Check if they have a tattoo of a cross on their chest. If they do, then they're part of the Keepers of the One Truth, if they don't, then they probably aren't."

"Just a second, I'm sending a text." There was some noise then Kane returned. "No tattoos."

Acton nodded, not expecting there to be. "I've been thinking about how they knew so much about me. The Keepers would have had a few years to gather intel on me after our first encounter. Two of their members were killed with the portrait, then it was stolen by this other group. Could they be working together?"

"Doesn't sound like it to me," replied Kane. "If they were, then they'd just hand it over. Why kill them?"

"Maybe they aren't working together, but there's a mole inside the Keepers."

"Now that's possible. Your thieves manage to infiltrate the Keepers, then when the portrait they're after surfaces, the mole lets them know, and then there's a takedown that goes bad. That same mole could have provided your Führer lovers any intel they had gathered on you."

Acton's head nodded slowly, his mind racing with the possibilities. It was all conjecture. Pure conjecture. These two organizations were clearly working at cross-purposes. One wouldn't kill the other if they were cooperating. And for the thieves to know where and when the drawing was going to be at the Vatican, they must have an inside source.

He caught his breath as his mind caught up with something Kane had said. "I want you to stop interrogating the prisoners."

"Why?"

"The reason we got into this is because we found out something we weren't supposed to. Our entire goal here is to end this. We have no idea who these people are or how big their organization is. Even if we had everyone in the castle arrested, there could be dozens or hundreds more around the world."

Reading nodded. "True."

"The only thing we know about them is where they are. If we can nullify that piece of knowledge, then our leverage over them ends."

"And so does the threat," said Kane. "That's smart thinking, Doc, you'd make a good spy."

"Ha! I'll leave that to the youngsters."

"More than happy to oblige. Now, BD and the crew are going to meet you when you arrive. I understand you've got some hotel rooms arranged with a good view?"

"Yes."

"Excellent. They'll set up surveillance there and come up with a game plan."

"Sounds good."

"Okay, just one more thing."

"Yes?"

"Laura, take his cellphone away, just in case he gets tempted to stuff it down the pants of one of them when they try to run away."

Giasson Residence, Via Nicolò III, Rome, Italy

"I have the files you asked for, my friend. But why the urgency?"

Giasson said nothing as Chief Inspector Riva entered his bedroom, a tired Marie-Claude closing the door behind her as she left to prepare more coffee.

You'll have to make it up to her when you're better.

"Show me your chest."

"Huh?"

"Unbutton your shirt. Now."

Riva frowned. "Fine." He unbuttoned about halfway, pulling the shirt open, revealing a hairy chest and a good starter set of man boobs. "Satisfied?"

Giasson nodded, motioning for him to button up. "I am. I'm sorry, but someone betrayed us, though I don't think it was you."

Riva gave him a look, clearly offended. "I can't believe after everything we've been through that you could think it was me."

Giasson sighed, raising a hand. "I know, I know. But I'm going to trust you now, so please take that as assurance I no longer have doubts."

Riva pursed his lips, raising his chin slightly. "But you still do."

Giasson smiled. "You know me too well."

Riva slapped his knee, laughing. "We both do!" He held up a file. "So now that you *are* trusting me, I assume you think it's him?"

"I pray it isn't but I fear it could be. What can you tell me?"

Riva flipped open the file, scanning it with his finger as he gave the highlights. "He has a completely clean record, of course. He's Swiss by birth, but his mother was Italian. His father left his mother when he was young, but young Gerard seemed to keep out of trouble. His father had no record, nor does his mother. There's nothing of interest on his paternal grandparents, but his maternal grandfather is a little more interesting. He was a devout member of the National Fascist Party, rabid apparently. After the liberation, he was hung by a meat hook in the market square in Bologna. That's when the family moved to Switzerland."

Giasson's head was bobbing through the entire summary, his lips pursed. "Interesting, but we can hardly condemn a man for the actions of his grandfather."

"No." Riva's eyes narrowed. "Wait, why did you want to see my chest?"

"I was looking for a tattoo."

"What, like the one on the two victims?"

Giasson nodded.

"Hold on!" Riva flipped through the file and pulled out an old black and white photo, holding it up. "This is a photo of his grandfather after he was executed." He rose and gave Giasson the photo. "Tell me what you see."

Giasson took the photo and examined the grisly scene.

Then gasped.

For the bare chested man, hung like a piece of meat, had a large tattoo that matched those of the victims.

Approaching Malpensa International Airport, Italy

"What are these massive heat signatures?"

Dawson and the others were examining satellite images of their target, sent to them by Langley. A senior analyst they had dealt with on several occasions, Leroux, was briefing them on the latest. "We think they're extremely powerful computers. This facility is a medieval castle in outward appearances only. Inside it's state of the art. They have their own generators plus a massive tap into the local grid, large data pipes plus satellite uplinks, along with quarters for several hundred, most of which appear to be occupied."

Dawson frowned, exchanging glances with the others. "That's what I was afraid of."

"As near as we can determine a significant proportion appear to be working at desks, so might not be trained in combat."

"Uh huh, somehow that doesn't make me feel any better." Dawson leaned back in his chair, pointing at the laptop. "This basically makes my idea a necessity."

"You're a genius, BD!" cried Jimmy.

"Tell the world!" shouted Niner.

"What's your plan?" asked Leroux.

"I intend to use a scalpel rather than a sword." He looked at the large heat signatures occupying almost half the structures within the castle walls. "Do we have any idea what these computers are doing?"

"No, but we've been tracing shipments to the area and they've had an incredible amount of medical equipment shipped in over the years. Whatever it is, it's probably biomedical in nature."

"Really?" asked Niner. "Then what the hell would they want an old painting for?"

"We're not sure, but my guess is this costs a fortune to run, and we can't find any source of funding for whoever they are."

"So they're financing it through art thefts?" Dawson pushed his lips out, drawing in a deep breath through his nose. "Possible, but I've got a feeling there's more going on here than just art thefts."

"It's the only thing we've been able to come up with. The owner is a mystery. It's as if the man has never left the castle. His father is even more of a mystery. We can't find any record of him before the end of the war. He paid for the castle with cash and he too was never seen since. All we know is he was apparently a German, based on his last name and a record scanned into the archives of a meeting between him and the town council at the time of purchase. It described a man who spoke near perfect Italian, with a Bavarian accent."

Dawson's head bounced. "Uh huh, the birthplace of the Nazi Party. So what we're probably dealing with is a man who was a Nazi, escaped with a new identity, well-funded, and is now doing something biomedical."

"His son."

"Right. A dynasty."

Niner shook his head. "That usually means zealots."

Spock sighed. "Which usually means a fanatical willingness to die for one's cause."

Dawson frowned. "Lovely, that's all we need."

Giasson Residence, Via Nicolò III, Rome, Italy

Giasson sat upright in his bed. He had sent Marie-Claude and the children to the neighbor's, just in case something went terribly wrong. Both groups he was dealing with were capable of killing, and what he was about to do could backfire horribly.

The doorbell rang.

Chief Inspector Riva rose from his chair at the foot of the bed. "That must be him. Ready?"

Giasson nodded.

Riva went swiftly to the front door, opening it, the alarm panel in the bedroom chirping.

"Oh, hello, Chief Inspector, I wasn't expecting to see you."

Giasson could barely hear his friend of many years, but enough carried for him to follow what was being said.

"There's been a break in the case. The Inspector General wanted to bring you up to date since he's out of commission for a few days and you'll be taking over."

"Of course, of course!"

Mario swung his legs from his bed, pushing himself to his feet, his shoulder protesting slightly, though not much. He straightened himself and forced a smile on his face as the footsteps echoed through the halls and into the bedroom.

His second-in-command, Gerard Boileau, appeared in the doorway, his face immediately one of surprise and concern, this the first time he had seen Giasson since the shooting.

"Sir! How are you feeling?" He stepped forward and shook Giasson's hand. "I took a moment to say a prayer for you last night. All of us did." He looked at his boss, then the shoulder. "Should you be up?"

Giasson smiled. "I appreciate that." He stepped forward and tore open Boileau's shirt. The man jumped back, shocked, his eyes wide, his jaw dropped.

"What the hell is this?"

Giasson jabbed a finger at the man's chest, the discoloration obvious, the shape circular with four segments that jutted out, it obvious to him it was the scars from the Keepers' tattoo being removed with a laser. "Explain that."

Boileau flushed, grabbing both sides of his shirt as he began to button it up. "A youthful indiscretion. I had it removed before I took the job with you."

"What was it?"

"A cross. I was very religious. I *am* very religious. I thought I was going into the seminary but much to my mother's disappointment, I liked girls too much."

Giasson held out his hand and Riva handed him the photo of one of the victims. "It wouldn't happen to match this."

Boileau's eyes narrowed as he leaned in to examine the photo. "Only in that it was a cross."

"Interesting." Riva handed him the photo of the grandfather. He held it up. "And your grandfather?"

Boileau paled noticeably.

Giasson shook the photo in front of Boileau's face. "We know it was you. We want to know why you did it, and who they are?"

Boileau took a step back, looking about the room. Riva's hand was resting on his gun. He tapped the grip. Boileau's shoulders collapsed and he

263

dropped into a chair, grabbing his head as he stared at the floor. He looked up at Giasson. "I'm sorry, Mario, I never thought I'd have to betray you, but they insisted."

"You could have said no."

Boileau shook his head. "No, I swore an oath to them long before I ever met you."

"The Keepers of the One Truth."

Boileau nodded.

"And what do they want with the portrait?"

"Nothing." Boileau sat up, his eyes wide as if he were desperate to be believed. "The portrait was put under our protection during the Second World War. We thought it had been returned in 1998, but it turns out one of our members, the older victim, switched it out with a forgery that had been made as a decoy. He was dying of cancer so we assume was handing it off to a protégé he could trust."

"Why would he hide it from your organization?"

Boileau shrugged. "I don't know, I haven't been made aware of everything. I just know that when they were killed, I received an emergency communique."

"Where you betrayed me. I was shot!"

Boileau shook his head emphatically. "No, that wasn't my fault. You have no idea how sorry I am for that, but nobody was supposed to get hurt. In fact, I don't think any Keeper knew what was going to happen. You see, we had no plan for this. No one knew the portrait existed until that day."

"Somebody obviously had different plans."

Boileau nodded, his eyes returning to his shoes. "I know. All I did was tell my contact where the portrait was going to be taken, and when. That's all I know. Remember, there was some doubt as to whether or not it was even real, and if it were, then why would we care? We thought we had returned it years ago. If that wasn't the case, then it didn't matter if you had it, since it meant it would eventually end up in the proper hands and we'd be done with it." He looked back up at Giasson. "Sir, Mario, we had *no* reason to try and steal it back!"

Giasson sat on the bed, his energy spent. What Boileau was saying made sense. Too much sense. So much sense it seemed to him that there was no way the Keepers were responsible for the theft and murders at the university.

But Boileau was clearly the source of the leak.

Which meant only one thing.

"You've got a mole within the Keepers."

Boileau's eyes popped wide, his jaw dropping. "It—it would appear so."

Giasson drew in a breath, squaring his shoulders as he tried to appear as intimidating as he could from his seated position. "I want a meeting."

Boileau's eyes narrowed. "With who?"

"Your leader."

Boileau paled by several shades. "I—I don't think that's possible."

Giasson's head dipped as he glared at Boileau.

"Tell him I insist."

Hotel Dei Tigli, Angera, Italy

Mr. Verde's phone was sitting on the coffee table in the much smaller hotel room than Acton had become accustomed to since meeting Laura, it on speaker, Kane providing them with an update. Several duffel bags of supplies had been in the room facing the castle when they arrived, Acton continually impressed with how efficient Kane and his people were.

Sometimes it is like the movies.

Reading was already setting up a camera in the window with a view of the road that led up to the castle and Laura was in one of the other rooms, getting some much-needed rest.

"Bravo Team is on the ground and on route. They should be there any minute. Do you see the black Dacia Duster across the street?"

Verde went to the window. "Yes."

"That's yours, keys should be on the counter."

Acton stepped over to the counter and picked them up, shaking them so Kane could hear. "Got them. Can you get word to Mario so he's not worried about us?"

"Already done. One of our people delivered a message this morning to him after he tried to call Laura's phone."

"What did you tell him?"

"That you are secure and will be in touch."

"He's not going to believe that. Not with what's going on."

"It will have to do."

Acton exchanged a glance with Reading, who didn't look pleased.

"Is *he* secure?" asked Reading.

"Yes, there's several state police at his residence."

Acton frowned. "We don't know if we can trust them."

"He requested them, so he must feel confident."

Acton's eyes narrowed, Reading turning away from the camera, staring at the phone. "That's odd."

Acton nodded in agreement. "I wonder if he's figured something out."

Verde interrupted. "Are those your guys?"

Reading stepped over to the window, Verde pointing at the street below. Reading nodded. "Looks like three of Bravo Team just got here."

"Okay, guys, you're in good hands. I'll let you go. Keep me posted."

Acton leaned toward the phone. "Will do, Dylan. Thanks for everything."

There was a knock at the door as the call ended, and Acton opened it, smiling broadly as Dawson, Niner and Jimmy entered the room. Handshakes were exchanged and introductions made, most using an alias it seemed.

Yet it didn't matter.

The cavalry had arrived, and for the first time since this had all began, Acton felt hopeful they might actually succeed in ending this.

"I thought six of you were coming," said Acton as everyone tried to find a place to sit in the cramped room.

"I sent Atlas, Spock and Jagger to recon the perimeter. They're playing tourist."

Niner grinned. "I picked up some pretty things for them to wear at the airport gift shop."

Jimmy chuckled. "I still can't believe Atlas agreed to wear that hat."

Acton grinned. "Can't wait to see it."

"No need, Doc." Niner reached into a plastic bag and pulled out a boater hat, tossing it over, the colors of the Italian flag proudly encircling the top. "Got one for you."

Acton shook his head then tossed it on the table with a grin. "I'd pay good money to see Atlas in that."

Niner held up his phone, showing a picture of the big man in the hat, appearing none too pleased. "I'll be charging five bucks a copy when the mission is over."

"Put me down for one," said Jimmy.

There was a knock at the door, gentle, and Acton knew immediately it was Laura. Verde opened the door and let her in, her smile brightening the room, everyone getting to their feet.

"I thought I heard a ruckus."

Dawson smiled, extending a hand. "Hey, Professor, how are you?"

Laura pushed it away and gave him a hug. "I think enough bullets have flown past both of us that we can be a little less formal." Dawson awkwardly returned the hug and she moved to Jimmy, he a little more comfortable.

Niner jumped to his feet, arms outstretched, an Ed Grimley pose awaiting her. "Lay it on me, Doc!"

Laura laughed, giving Niner a hug, it returned enthusiastically. He glanced over at Acton and winked. "Never ever let her go, Doc, or I'm calling."

Laura leaned back and slapped him on the chest. "You're too much." She took a seat and everyone else got comfortable. "So where do we stand?"

"Well, first, you need to know one thing about BD."

Laura looked at Niner. "What?"

Dawson smacked his forehead.

"He's engaged!"

Laura cried out in delight, jumping to her feet and giving the big man another hug, this time with a kiss on the cheek. "Maggie must be excited!"

Dawson smiled awkwardly, it clear to Acton that Niner and Jimmy were thrilled with their comrade's discomfort, and equally happy *for* him. Laura returned to her seat and Dawson held up a hand, his head bobbing, his eyes closed. "Okay, okay, we've got a job to do." He opened his eyes, the boisterous Niner silenced. "In talking with Dylan I get the impression you and I are on the same page. Talk to me."

Acton jerked a thumb at the castle out the window. "It seems to me we need to eliminate the leverage we have over them."

"The fact you know where they are."

"Exactly. And short of erasing our memories, we need to make it so that we *don't* know where they are."

"By forcing them to move."

"We *are* on the same page."

Dawson smiled. "Great minds think alike."

"He's a professor, fool, don't be getting cocky."

Dawson gave Niner a look then ran his finger across his throat.

Jimmy slugged the wisecracker.

Acton laughed, Laura giggling. "I've missed you guys," she said.

Niner was about to say something probably totally inappropriate when Dawson leaned over and slapped a hand over the man's mouth. "So we need to make the castle no longer attractive for them to stay in."

Acton nodded. "Right. If they're forced to leave, then we no longer know anything about them."

Dawson removed his hand from Niner's mouth. "That's exactly what I was thinking." Niner's mouth opened and Dawson aimed a finger at it. It snapped shut. He pulled out a laptop, handing it to Jimmy who booted it up. "We've come up with a plan that could work."

"Could?"

"Could. It partially depends on how much the layout has changed since the last survey was done during the war."

"How accurate do you think they were?" asked Laura.

"Very, at the time. The Germans had it surveyed as a potential regional command headquarters, so the plans are very detailed, but it's been over seventy years."

"And if they've changed too much?"

Dawson's eyebrows rose, cocking his head to the side momentarily. "Then the plan might fail miserably."

"Is it risky?"

Dawson nodded. "There's over two hundred people inside that complex, so I'm thinking, yes."

Acton shook his head. "I can't ask you do to this. There has to be another way."

Dawson smiled. "Hey, we're here."

"And I'm already bored," added Niner.

Dawson leaned forward. "Look, if it goes smooth, they'll never know we were there until it's too late."

Acton checked his watch. "I assume you're planning on going in tonight?"

Dawson shook his head. "No, for this to work, it has to be done in broad daylight."

Laura sat upright. "Really?"

"Yes. The more eyes the better."

Rocca d'Angera Castle, Angera, Italy

Atlas stared up at the morning sun, the blue sky overhead unmarred by even a wisp of cloud, the only spoiler of the near perfect canvas a contrail high above, a jetliner heading north. It was a beautiful day in a beautiful location.

Vanessa would love this.

Things with Vanessa were getting serious. Very serious. They had done the weekend getaways successfully, and were now talking something a little more risky.

An actual vacation together.

That meant plane tickets, a hotel room, and no way to escape each other should things go wrong. In the past, he had found it could help decide whether or not a relationship had a future. Couples who didn't travel well together, didn't last.

And this vacation was long overdue.

Between his job—which she knew nothing about—and her culinary classes, finding an actual week to go anywhere together had proven difficult.

She had a two-week break coming up and he had already had it cleared with the Colonel.

He was off.

He just hadn't told her yet because things could change so quickly in his line of work.

Her time off was set in stone, and he was going to surprise her with tickets at the last minute—purchased with trip cancellation insurance just in case—and if all went well, they'd be jetting somewhere semi-exotic. His job

271

meant a lot of the truly exotic was off limits unless parachuting in from the back of a military transport.

"Italy might be a good place to take Vanessa."

Spock cocked an eyebrow. "Care to include us in the first part of that conversation you've been having with yourself?"

"Sorry." He nodded toward the castle wall, a security camera visible. "How about a photo, boys."

Spock and Jagger lined up in front of the wall, striking a pose any eighties hair band would have been proud of, and Atlas snapped the photo.

"Good one!" he laughed, handing the camera over to Spock who switched places. Another photo snapped, a different angle, a process they had been repeating all around the massive structure, each photo automatically uploaded to Langley.

They continued their stroll up the path that ringed the outer fence set about twenty feet from the ancient castle walls themselves. Apparently, the thick walls weren't enough privacy. To Atlas' trained eye, it appeared the occupants wanted a buffer between the walls so their cameras could catch anything that might stray too close.

And provide a kill zone should it become necessary.

They had spotted two entrances so far. The main gate and a rear entrance that didn't appear to be used much, the path leading to it covered in thick grass.

Yet just because there were only two *official* entrances didn't mean there weren't other ways in. They had found several drainage ditches leading to large pipes at the foot of the walls, all with bars preventing entry. But bars were no problem for his team.

"You and Vanessa thinking of going away together?" asked Jagger.

"Yeah, hopefully in a couple of weeks if the world doesn't throw a monkey wrench into the works." He nodded ahead, the path coming to an abrupt end, the castle built into the side of a hill, a sheer rock cliff blocking the rest of the way. He tapped his earpiece casually. "Zero-One, Zero-Seven, we're heading back, over."

"Roger that, Zero-Seven. That first drainage pipe you sent us seems to be the most promising candidate and matches the plans we have."

Atlas nodded as they passed the rear gate, the other two carrying on a conversation to disguise his own. "Agreed. It's got excellent brush cover but there are two cameras that have a good angle on it."

"Any sign of guards?"

"Negative, we haven't seen any, not even at the front gate. They seem to be relying on cameras. I'm thinking they aren't expecting anyone so are keeping a low profile, trying not to look like a Bond villain's lair."

"Okay, get back to the hotel. We've got an op to plan."

Giasson Residence, Via Nicolò III, Rome, Italy

"He has agreed to meet you."

Giasson had to admit he was a little surprised. For the leader of the Keepers of the One Truth to agree to meet must mean he too thought it was important to air their grievances. He was pretty certain it was because of who he was that he was granted an audience. He was after all the head of Vatican security, and these men were apparently sworn to protect the Church, as he was.

Yet they found themselves at cross-purposes.

A meeting was definitely warranted.

"Where?"

"At the final confessional on the right hand side at Santa Maria delle Concezione de Cappuccini Church."

Mario's eyes widened slightly. "Really? In a confessional?"

Boileau nodded. "You must understand that it is essential he remain anonymous. Frankly, it's incredible that he's actually agreed to meet you."

"Have you met him?"

Boileau shook his head emphatically. "No, never."

"Then how will I know it's him?"

Boileau smiled. "He is a man of God. He would not lie."

Giasson wasn't so sure he would agree with that relationship being solid enough to accept on blind faith. "When?"

"I'm to take you there now. No police."

Giasson pursed his lips, looking at Boileau, then nodded, he having no choice.

"Then let's go."

Hotel Dei Tigli, Angera, Italy

Dawson gave two quick raps on the door then entered, closing it quickly behind him. He was greeted with grins.

"Don't you look colorful," said Acton, stepping away from the window. "Is that the new army approved camo?"

Dawson looked down at his bright blue track pants and white sneakers, his windbreaker in Italian colors with Italia emblazoned across the back, and a tri-colored ball cap to match.

"It's urban chic."

Laura giggled.

"We're hiding in plain sight. Anybody monitoring the perimeter is going to see a group of tourists and hopefully dismiss us entirely, or not pay very close attention. We're tooling around town, seeing the sites, and have just discovered a castle that we're going to walk around and take photos of."

Acton tilted his head, raising his eyebrows. "Well, let's hope it works. If it doesn't?"

"Then we fallback and come up with Plan B." He looked at Acton. "You know your part?"

"Yes."

"Good, it's the most crucial part if this is going to work."

Reading's phone beeped and he checked the message. "First batch is coming in."

Dawson stepped over to the laptop as Reading brought up the first files from Interpol, fruits of their surveillance on the castle entrance.

"Christ!"

Dawson turned to Reading. "What?"

"Everyone one of these people are German citizens."

"Living in an Italian city?"

Reading nodded. "From these reports, it looks like they're completely self-contained. None of them appears to be employed, none have ever collected any state benefits. Beyond birth certificates, driver's licenses and passports, they seem to have no involvement outside of that castle."

"Completely self-contained, with all the proper paperwork to safely travel outside when required." Dawson exhaled loudly, nodding at the images as Reading flipped through them. "Notice anything else?"

Reading kept flipping then stopped, leaning back in his chair, he apparently noticing what Dawson had.

Every photo showed a man with blonde hair and chiseled features.

"Bloody hell. It's the Master Race."

Mercy Medical Center, Baltimore, Maryland

Kane sat in the corner of Ellsworth Acton's hospital room, Fang sitting kitty-corner to him, it Sherrie's turn at the door. A computer on Kane's lap showed six dots superimposed over a map, each representing a member of Bravo Team as they made their way to the castle.

He glanced over at Fang, picking absentmindedly at the bottom of her shoe. Her face was long, her eyes drooping. She seemed sad.

"Something bothering you?"

She looked up at him and shook her head. "No, I'm okay."

She didn't sound like it. He put the laptop on the seat beside him and leaned forward. "Hey, you can talk to me. I'm probably one of the few people you actually *can* talk to."

She looked at him, tears filling her eyes. "That's the problem, isn't it?"

He drew in a breath, frowning. He knew exactly what this was all about. "You miss home."

She nodded. "I miss my family, my friends, my job." She cast her eyes to the floor. "My country."

"I know how you feel."

She stared at him. "How could you possibly know?"

He smiled gently. "I have one friend who I barely see. I almost never get to see my family, and when I do, I have to lie about what I do. My father has no respect for my job and I think resents the fact that I left an honorable job in the military to become my cover job. I spend eleven months of the year outside of my country, living in alien cultures, sometimes in caves with none of the things I grew up with, and I have almost no one I can share my troubles with." His smile expanded slightly.

"So, you see, I *do* understand what you're going through. The only difference, and it's a big one, is that I at least *do* get to see my one friend from time-to-time, my parents every once in a while, and my country. That's forever cut off for you."

He leaned forward, putting his hand on her arm. Her eyes darted down to look at the contact and he began to draw away. She reached out with her other hand and put it on top of his, stopping him.

She was craving physical contact.

The poor woman.

He understood that need, that basic human desire to be touched. It didn't have to be anything sexual, just the touch of a caring hand could do wonders to heal the wounded soul. He squeezed her arm and she smiled slightly, her eyes still averted.

"I'll tell you what," he said. "You need a friend. I think I should probably have a second one. How about I start visiting you when I'm stateside? We can talk about whatever you want, since I know your past. No tiptoeing around things."

She looked up at him, eyes slightly wider, a definite smile on her face. She nodded. "I-I'd like that."

"Good. It's settled. I have a second friend."

She stared down at the floor again, squeezing his hand. "And I have one."

He took her hand in both his and held it up to his lips, giving it a gentle, platonic kiss.

"Sometimes one is all you need."

Rocca d'Angera Castle, Angera, Italy

Dawson shrugged off his backpack, placing it on the edge of the path before sitting on a large rock. The others did the same, creating a circle, everyone stretching and groaning as if they had been walking all morning. He pulled out a bottle of water and some beef jerky. He took a swig and pulled on the teriyaki flavored dried meat, handing the bag around, all the while eyeing their surroundings as innocently as possible, the others doing the same, casual banter about the weather and his upcoming wedding providing the background noise should anyone be trying to listen in.

Niner was sitting to his right, his back directly facing the wall and the two video cameras with a view of the drainage ditch. A small computer in his lap was being worked expertly as it reached out, detecting any signals then tapping into them.

"Church wedding?" asked Spock.

"Ha, I can't wait to get some photos of that with my wireless," said Niner. "Both of them."

Dawson nodded.

Both cameras wireless, not hardwired.

"I dunno. Maggie's handling everything."

Niner's head bobbed. "I should be able to help her when I get about ten seconds."

"I told her to tell me where and when to show up."

Spock handed the empty jerky bag to him. Dawson gave him a look and Spock shrugged. "Hey, you brought it."

"You did," agreed Niner as Atlas swatted a fly. "All I can say is when I'm taking your photo, no sudden movements for about thirty seconds, okay? How about we practice?"

They all sat, slight movements only, Dawson mentally counting down the thirty seconds Niner needed to record the tapped feeds. Once recorded, he'd loop them and they should have a nice blind spot to work in, assuming no one decided to check on them personally, or watched the video too closely.

"Okay, you can move now," said Niner. "The video is looping, but I don't know how long we can rely on that so let's boogie."

Dawson pointed at the fence, Atlas and Spock leaping to their feet, cutters in hand, as they made quick work of the chain link. Dawson activated his comm. "Control, Zero-One. We've tapped the security feed and are going in, over."

"Confirmed Zero-One. Good luck, out."

Dawson trusted Leroux, Control for the mission, though he'd prefer Colonel Clancy. That wasn't an option since this wasn't a sanctioned mission, so he'd have to accept the fact that the people they were relying on might not have their back. He trusted some *individuals* in the CIA, but not the organization. They weren't military, they didn't subscribe to the idea of no man left behind. Not because they didn't value their personnel, but because usually that man or woman was undercover, and admitting that they were an asset could compromise other lives.

Atlas bent back the fence and Dawson grabbed his pack, ducking through then sprinting for the barred opening in the side of the castle, a tiny creek, if it could be called that, running out the side, through a small culvert under the path and off into the distance. The size of the opening suggested much greater volumes than they were seeing today, and he had a feeling if it were raining, entering through this hole might not be much of an option.

According to the plans from World War II, this should take them about thirty feet inside before they'd be at an access node in the top of the pipe. That would in turn give them access to the catacombs under the castle.

Catacombs that if they hadn't changed too much, should provide them exactly what they needed.

Niner stepped back from the barred pipe. "I've overridden the security sensor. Blow it."

Atlas nodded, slapping the small charge in place. They all stepped back and Atlas counted off. "Fire in the hole." He clicked the button and the tiny charge made quick work of the lock, though it wasn't as quiet as one would hope.

Dawson activated his comm as Niner checked to confirm the override to the sensor was still functioning. He gave a thumbs up.

"Control, Zero-One. Any sign they heard that?"

"Negative, Zero-One, you're still clear."

"Roger that, making entry now, out."

He urged the others inside, on their knees, and within moments they were out of sight, flashlights turned on. Niner closed the circular gate behind them, securing it with a Ziptie, the locking mechanism no longer functioning to prevent it from swinging open.

"Found it!" hissed Jagger, who had point. "Looks like a metal plate." Dawson waited with the others as a Broco cutting torch cut through what was clearly a modern addition, the original plans indicating it should be another grate that could be easily blown. "Got it."

Dawson looked ahead to see Jagger lowering the hunk of metal, Spock helping him place it quietly on the floor. Jagger stood, the upper half of his body disappearing, then all of him as he pulled himself up.

"Clear."

The rest of the team quickly exited the cramped quarters, Dawson second from last, breathing a sigh of relief as they found themselves in an ancient tunnel junction, three corridors meeting where they now found themselves.

Exactly as the plans indicated.

"Okay, as planned. Remember, comms might be spotty or completely non-functional down here. This is the rally point in ten. Let's move out."

Jagger and Atlas headed left, Spock and Jimmy right, Dawson and Niner directly ahead. The corridor was damp and narrow, the construction ancient, though it seemed solid. Dawson had to move at a crouch, the shorter Niner merely dipping his head slightly.

"They sure were a lot shorter back when this was built."

"We'd be monsters on the battlefield," agreed Dawson.

"Christ, can you imagine Atlas?"

Dawson chuckled. "Two thousand years ago he'd probably be a gladiator."

"I could see that. I've often wondered what I would have been if I were alive back then."

"Princess?"

Niner punched him in the back. "Don't you start."

Dawson held up his fist, freezing, their conversation ended. He had heard something ahead. What, he wasn't sure. It could have been their own echo, or something else. A good commander would have these corridors patrolled, and he had a feeling they were dealing with good commanders.

Footfalls.

He jerked his thumb over his shoulder and he and Niner quietly fell back as the footsteps approached, a conversation drifting toward them. Niner slapped him on the back and he looked, Niner pointing to an alcove in the tunnel big enough to fit him, Niner already backing into one on the opposite wall.

Dawson wedged himself in as he clicked off his flashlight, pulling his knife, Niner doing the same. He activated his comm, whispering an update. "This is Zero-One. We've got activity here. Out."

The voices drew closer and Dawson immediately recognized the language.

German.

Which made perfect sense of course, it matching what their intel had been telling them. This castle was some sort of German enclave buried in northern Italy. The question was what was its purpose, though if he were honest with himself, that was irrelevant to the mission. They had to force these people to move their operation. If they could make staying here untenable, then the leverage the doc had over them would be gone, and these people would have no reason to harass him any longer, unless they wanted revenge.

And he had a feeling they didn't.

You don't stay hidden for seventy years if you take your revenge on anyone who slighted you.

These people were maintaining a low profile. The operation in Rome had obviously been a screw up, and if Acton hadn't tossed his phone in the crate, the necessary second operation would have been a complete success.

Low profile.

If this group truly was a remnant of the Nazis, then his plan, should it succeed, should result in the doc being able to move on with his life without worrying about these people.

A flashlight beam cut through the darkness, casting a dull glow over everything as the footsteps echoed loudly, the conversation about the woman one of them had been paired with, continuing. It sounded like arranged marriages, or arranged liaisons, were the norm here.

Interesting. Might explain a few things.

He controlled his breathing as the flashlight came into view, the beam it was producing past his position now. A match flared, Niner lit up for a brief moment.

Dawson gripped his knife.

"Was ist—"

Dawson stepped out, plunging his knife into the first man's side as his hand clamped down over the guard's mouth. He twisted the blade as Niner sliced his opponent's throat. Dawson continued to hold his writhing man until he finally sighed his last breath.

He looked at the two bodies, frowning. "Lovely. Let's put them in these alcoves and hope for the best." Niner dropped his and helped Dawson lift the first man, who he'd be copulating with tonight no longer a problem for him. They tucked him into the alcove and stepped back, Dawson holding out both hands, willing him not to fall out.

He didn't.

They repeated the process with the other one and Dawson activated his comm. "Bravo Team, Zero-One. We've taken out two guards. There may be others. Proceed with caution, out."

He glanced at Niner.

"This is going to complicate things."

Command Center, Rocca d'Angera Castle, Angera, Italy

Hofmeister entered the Command Center, he having been assigned to internal security while the Congress executive decided what to do about Professor Acton now that his parents and friends had been rescued. At this point Hofmeister couldn't care less, he was more concerned about what they would decide to do with him.

They'll hang me for sure.

If he was lucky.

Or they might use him as a human test subject for the genetic experiments that took place in Building H. He had been in there only once and it was a terrifying place, an experience he never cared to repeat. The deformed creatures, creatures he had to assume were supposed to be human, the results of failed experiments, had given him nightmares for years.

Yet he had never revealed how he had felt to anyone.

Weakness was never tolerated.

And should he be executed for his failure, he would die with honor, setting an example for others who would inevitably follow him.

No one would ever know the fear he felt inside at the prospect of dying.

He didn't believe in God or religion or life after death. He believed in science and German superiority. Yet these past couple of days, with his own death a very distinct possibility, he found his mind wandering, wondering if there was something after death.

Then worrying that if there were, after the life he had led, he wouldn't be going to the nice side of the tracks.

"Your message said there was a problem?"

285

"Yes, sir," replied Sturmmann Koenig, manning the security station. He pointed at one of the screens. This is from camera number four, southern wall."

Hofmeister stared at the image, half a dozen tourists sitting, taking a break from their hike. It was nothing unusual. This was, after all, a castle. Tourists came here all the time, which was why their security was all electronic, there no guards patrolling the walls. They maintained a low profile and gave the locals and the tourists no reason to be suspicious. Tourists sometimes came to the main gates, but they'd be greeted with closed doors and signs indicating it was private property.

No one came in who wasn't part of the Congress, or who was never leaving again.

He watched the image for a few seconds then looked at the Sturmmann. "So? What of it?"

"Well, they've been like that for almost ten minutes."

"So?" Hofmeister could feel his temper begin to boil.

Control yourself.

"Well, they haven't moved at all."

Hofmeister leaned in a little closer. They were definitely moving, though not much. There was a black man who swatted at a fly, so the image wasn't frozen. "They're moving."

"Yes, but watch the black guy."

Hofmeister watched, the man swatting at the fly again. "See, he swats at something. Now keep watching. It goes for about thirty seconds, then…" Another swat. "See, he did it again."

There was a slight jerk of the picture that he had written off the first time as signal interference, it a wireless signal after all.

"Scheisse!"

The video was on a loop.

"I want eyes on that wall, now!"

Operations Center 3, CIA Headquarters, Langley, Virginia

Leroux and his team watched a satellite image of the castle. The tracking devices on the comms the Delta team was wearing were no longer transmitting, the walls too thick, only the occasional stray signal making it out.

But the two hundred plus heat signatures of the castle occupants were clearly visible above them.

And there was activity.

"Zoom in on grid Delta-Six."

Keys were hit and the image zoomed to show half a dozen heat signatures running toward the southern wall, all armed.

"Sir, I think they've figured out the camera tap."

Leroux nodded, agreeing with Child's assessment. "Try to warn them."

"Sir, the comms aren't working."

"Keep trying, we might get lucky."

"Yes, sir."

If we don't reach them, when they try to leave it could be a blood bath.

Catacombs, Rocca d'Angera Castle, Angera, Italy

Dawson pressed his finger to his ear, trying to make out the transmission. He cursed, glancing back at Niner who had his head buried in a tactical computer, a map of the catacombs displayed.

"Did you get any of that?"

"Nope. But I'm assuming it can't be good since they were supposed to maintain radio silence."

Dawson frowned. Niner was right. He was still getting some choppy updates from the other two teams, there enough reflective surfaces for a stray signal to bounce around, but Langley was another matter, and that signal was so bad, it had to be from them.

Somebody must have missed those two guards we took out.

He sucked in a deep breath.

Or they discovered we're not sitting outside, enjoying the sunshine.

"Let's hurry this up."

Niner nodded, pointing ahead. "Sixty feet that way should be what we're looking for."

Dawson moved forward, flashlight and Glock extended in front of him, covering the distance quickly. If they had been discovered already then they were most likely going to get trapped down here.

And if I'm going out, I'm going out with a bang.

The tunnel opened out into a huge area, the vastness eliciting a smile from Dawson.

"Perfect."

All around them stood large columns stretching to the ceiling high above, each column flared at the bottom, even more so at the top. From what the plans indicated, these areas, and several others like them, were the support structure for the entire castle above them.

Time to use a scalpel.

Jagger rounded a corner and cursed, two guards standing there, smoking cigarettes. He squeezed the trigger on his Taser, sending 50,000 volts into the body of the first one, his buddy getting the same treatment from Atlas, neither getting a chance to say a word, instead just shaking all the way to the ground.

He released the trigger and rushed forward, disarming his man and searching him for any comm equipment. He had a radio strapped to his belt, but nothing more. He zip-tied his man, Atlas doing the same.

"How much farther?" he asked.

Atlas pointed ahead. "Should be just up there."

"Good. That signal we got has me worried. Something's gone wrong."

Atlas nodded. "Agreed. Let's plant these charges and get the hell out of here."

Jimmy rounded the corner and hit a wall.

Literally.

He rubbed his face. "Jesus, that's not supposed to be there."

Spock held his flashlight up to his face to show his grin. "That's what you get for rushing."

"Hey, you heard that signal. Something's wrong."

Spock nodded. "Yup." He glanced at his computer. "This is new."

"Where's the secondary detonation point?"

"Back fifty feet then right instead of left."

"Let's do it."

Spock led the way, both men at a jog, there no longer any time to waste. Something was clearly wrong and they had to accomplish their mission or it was all for not. Jimmy wasn't too worried. They always seemed to find a way out, though not always unscathed. And this time the odds were overwhelming.

Okay, maybe I'm a little worried.

Spock deked down the opposite tunnel and they quickly found themselves in a large area with support columns extending above them. Jimmy removed his backpack and unzipped it.

"Let's get these charges set then get back to the rally point."

"Repeat that?"

Hofmeister pressed the headphone against his ear, praying that he had misheard what was just said.

"I repeat, there's no one here."

Hofmeister looked up at the camera feed, it still showing the six men sitting quietly. He turned to Koenig. "You're sure that's the southern wall?"

Koenig nodded. "Absolutely. They shouldn't be able to miss them."

"Can you reset the cameras?"

"I tried that but it did nothing. If it's tapped, it's advanced software, overriding the signal before the camera even has a chance." He snapped his fingers. "But if I reboot the system entirely, I can reset the IP addresses and then their tap will be pointing at the wrong device. We should see the proper feed, but not without shutting down the entire system."

Hofmeister gripped the back of Koenig's chair, his knuckles turning white as he glared at the computer. "Do it." He inhaled deeply, already knowing the truth they would find. "And sound the alarm."

Dawson placed his final charge, setting the detonator to fifteen minutes.

"Do you hear that?"

He cocked an ear, listening for whatever Niner had heard. His eyes narrowed. "Is that an alarm?"

Niner nodded. "I think so. It's so faint it's hard to tell."

Dawson cursed. "Let's get the hell out of here."

Spock stared up, an eyebrow cocked. "Is that an alarm?"

"Damn right it is," said Jimmy, racing from column to column, placing his charges.

Spock quickly placed his last few charges, keeping a wary eye out for any uninvited guests. The area was huge, and the plans showed multiple points of entry, any one of which could be regurgitating guards at them at any moment.

He planted his last charge. "You done?"

Jimmy was sprinting toward him. "Yup."

"Then let's boogey."

Leroux shook his head as all hell broke loose in front of them. Dozens of people were running, their heat signatures indicating armed guards converging on the southern half of the compound, a group already heading outside the walls and toward the entry point the Delta team had used.

"I'm counting over one hundred that appear to be armed."

Leroux spun toward Therrien. "Are you sure?"

"At least."

They don't stand a chance!

He pointed at Child. "Boost the signal, we have to warn them!"

Dawson sprinted down the corridor, Taser in one hand, Glock in the other, as Niner lit the way with a flashlight, Taser at the ready. It was definitely an alarm going off, so they knew his team was there. What they couldn't be sure of is whether they knew *where* his team actually was.

Gunfire might let them pinpoint the exact location.

He squeezed the trigger on his Taser, the guard that had just rounded the corner shaking from the shock, his friend shouting a warning before Niner had a chance to fire his.

Both men jerked to the ground as Dawson continued to advance, checking around the corner to see if there was anyone for the warning to reach.

There was none.

They quickly stripped the men of their weapons and radios, then zip-tied them.

"I think it's safe to say they know we're here."

Dawson nodded. "Yup, which means they either found the guards we eliminated, or discovered the security tap. Either way they know we're down here."

Footfalls echoed toward them, getting louder.

Dawson holstered his Taser, switching to the Glock. "Time to commit."

Niner switched weapons. "With pleasure."

The footfalls echoed through the narrow corridor, getting louder and louder, whoever it was apparently not concerned they were going to be heard.

A flashlight rounded the corner and Dawson dropped to one knee, aiming his flashlight at where he'd guess the man's face would be.

"Thunder!" he challenged.

"Flash!"

Dawson smiled at Jimmy's voice.

Nothing like going old school.

The four men joined up, weapons lowered. "Report."

293

"All charges planted but in the secondary location. Primary was blocked by a new wall. You?"

"All set at our primary. Did you pick up that transmission?"

Jimmy shook his head. "We've been getting nothing but static. Barely heard anything *you* were sending."

"Did you run into Atlas and Jagger?"

"Negative."

"You lookin' for us?"

Atlas' voice echoed from farther down the corridor, his flashlight beam quickly appearing then the man himself, Jagger behind him.

"Report."

"Charges set. Encountered a couple of hostiles, took them down but not out." He glanced at the two lying nearby. "I see you found a couple too."

"Yeah." Dawson pointed up. "I assume everyone is hearing that, not just me?"

Atlas nodded. "Yup. They know we're here."

Spock looked at his computer. "Which means they probably know how we got in."

Dawson agreed. "We need to find another way out of here." He checked his watch. "Who's up first?"

Everyone glanced at their watches, Spock answering first. "Two minutes for ours."

"Seven for ours," said Atlas.

Dawson nodded. "Good, ours are eleven." He pointed at Spock's computer. "Which way to another drainage pipe?"

Spock pointed from where they had just come.

"Then let's get moving and hope the doc does his part."

Acton opened the window to the hotel room, holding a hand up to his ear. "Do you hear that?"

Reading nodded. "Sounds like an alarm. I think it's coming from the castle." He looked at Acton. "Did you hear any explosions?"

Acton shook his head, turning to Verde who was on the phone. "Any word from Langley."

Verde nodded. "It looks like they've been discovered."

"Shit!"

"Oh no!" cried Laura. "Have they been captured?"

Verde shook his head. "They don't know. If they have, their signals are still out of range."

"Any sign of detonations?" asked Reading, Verde relaying the question then shaking his head.

"Negative."

"Then they've failed." Acton's shoulders slumped. "What the hell do we do now? If they've been captured, we need to tell someone, someone has to rescue them."

Reading jabbed a finger at him. "It's *not* going to be you."

Acton gave him half a smile. "Yeah, yeah, I know. We better get in touch with Red. He'll know what to—"

The floor vibrated, glasses shaking on the table, it all over in a few seconds.

"Did you feel that?" asked Acton, standing, his hands held out to his sides.

"The dead felt that," said Reading. He suddenly pointed out the window. "Look!"

Dust was rising from the direction of the castle. There was no fire or smoke, just dust, and he recognized immediately what it was.

Something made of heavy stone had collapsed.

Verde handed him the phone. "That's your cue."

Acton smiled, dialing.

Hofmeister grabbed his phone, the call display indicating a blocked number, though he had a feeling who it was. "Hello?"

"Did you get my message?"

He immediately recognized the voice, and the words sent a pulse of rage through his body as he realized Acton was responsible for whatever had just shook the entire complex.

But how?

"What the hell is going on?"

"You have five minutes to evacuate before the next detonation. I highly recommend you move. Now."

The call ended and Hofmeister slipped the phone into his pocket, his jaw dropping in shock as he stared at the footage, the security cameras just completing their reboot. The entire north side of the castle lay in ruins, walls collapsed, dust everywhere, obscuring the view.

"Casualty report?"

Koenig shook his head. "We don't know yet, but it should be low. They picked the emptiest part of the castle for this time of day. It's like they knew where we weren't."

Hofmeister nodded. "They're sending a message." He pointed at the alarm panel. "Sound the evacuation alarm."

Koenig's eyes shot open wide as he stared at Hofmeister. "Are you sure?"

"Do it! Now!" He turned to the rest of the room. "Make sure the executive is evacuated immediately, initiate total destruction of all paper and digital. Have everyone report to their evacuation rally points and await further instructions."

He left the room, there no time to waste, there no way to tell what building the next detonation might bring down.

How could a lowly professor do all this?

Dawson stared up at the ceiling, a cloud of dust slowly settling.

"Tough old broad, but we're going to need to get out of here. That first one was just a warning. The next two are going to take us out with them."

Spock waved the tablet. "There's no way we'll make the secondary exit point before the next detonation."

"Any suggestions?" asked Niner.

Dawson pointed up. "We go topside."

Niner grinned. "That's just crazy enough to work."

Dawson turned to Spock. "Where's the nearest access point?"

"We spotted one on the way to our detonation point."

Niner looked at him. "You mean you want us to go *toward* the next explosion."

Spock shrugged. "It's the only way I can guarantee we get out of here. Any other location is just a guess."

Dawson pointed. "Then let's move!"

Leroux snapped his fingers. "Okay, people, you know what to do. Start flooding the news wires. Terrorist attack in Angera, Italy." He turned to Therrien. "Do we have the footage from Professor Acton yet?"

"Yes, sir." He pointed at a display showing a cloud of dust or smoke rising above the castle. "Good, I want footage hitting YouTube and LiveLeak now. Get this thing trending. Once we've got some traction, hit the conspiracy sites with the ownership history." He turned to Sonya. "Notify the Italian police that this is where the stolen painting is." He turned to watch the displays. "We want a media circus, people."

Hofmeister sprinted down the hallway, shoving people out of his way as he tried to reach the offices of the executive. Over the PA system the evacuation announcement was playing, a recording made years ago, one its creator was probably certain would never be needed. In the offices he ran past, he could hear papers being shredded and keyboards being tapped away at as evacuation protocols were implemented.

But there wasn't enough haste.

He was the only one who truly knew what was going on, and he was concerned that the Doctor might not be out in time, and he couldn't risk that. The Doctor was their leader, and if he were to die because a lowly professor had somehow tricked them, it could demoralize them all.

The Congress must survive.

He shoved through the doors and out into the courtyard, organized chaos greeting him as vehicle upon vehicle lined up from the motor pool, people climbing into their designated ride, boxes of materials tossed in the back of several transport trucks.

He sighed with relief when he saw the research staff rushing from their building and loaded into a truck, it roaring away with a gnashing of gears. The research would continue, just at a different location. He spotted the doctor getting into the back of a large Mercedes and he raced across the courtyard, dodging vehicles, reaching him just as his son, and the current head of their research, arrived.

The elder Mengele asked the question Hofmeister was dying to ask. "What's the status on the lab?"

"All data is being wiped. We keep nothing printed so there will be nothing left. All data is backed up nightly offsite so all we lose is time."

"And the test subjects?"

"Sanitation procedures have already been executed. No one will know what was happening here."

Mengele smiled. "Good. And the artifacts?"

His son shook his head. "We've got some, but there won't be time for all."

"No matter, we'll simply reacquire them." He motioned for his son to join him. "Get in."

The younger man climbed in and Hofmeister stepped up to the door, Mengele waving him off. "This is *your* doing. Get your own ride." He pointed a finger at him. "And don't even consider not showing up at the rendezvous point."

Hofmeister gulped, jerking out a nod, then stepping back as the door slammed shut and the tires chirped, the two most important people in the Congress escaping.

Our mission will continue.

He looked about for a moment, then began to sprint toward his designated vehicle when there was an incredible rumble, the ground quaking beneath his feet, several times worse than the first, his feet swinging out from under him. He hit the cobblestone hard, his elbow screaming out in pain as he rolled to his side and gasped in horror, the entire medical research facility dropping into the ground, as if Mother Earth herself had swallowed it whole.

"Here they come!" shouted Acton as the first vehicle raced down the road that wound its way up to the castle. A second explosion rocked the room, Acton grabbing onto the windowsill until things settled down, a massive dust cloud, many orders of magnitude bigger than the first, filled the skyline.

"They did it!" Laura squeezed him tight as they watched vehicle after vehicle pour from the castle, an evacuation definitely underway. And judging from the size of the explosions, Dawson's team must have succeeded brilliantly, his plan to take out the structural supports in the catacombs inspired. If it worked—and it certainly appeared it had—then the structures above them would drop into the massive empty spaces of the catacombs below them.

Rebuilding would take years and untold monies.

And a lot of outside help.

Their secret lair was no longer a secret.

"I can hear the locals," said Reading, cocking an ear.

Acton nodded as he heard the first of what he was sure would be many sirens.

"Now let's just hope Langley can do their part," said Verde, joining them at the window, taking another video.

And hope BD and the team get out alive.

Dawson tried the door at the top of the narrow stone staircase. It was locked. He motioned for Niner to give him a charge and it was handed up the line. Dawson quickly put it in place and everyone hustled down a dozen steps and covered their ears, squeezing their eyes shut.

The tiny explosion was deafening in the tight quarters, though if anyone on the other side noticed, there wasn't any indication yet. Dawson climbed back up the stairs, pulling the door open slightly and peering out.

It was chaos.

People were screaming, running in all directions, there clearly a civilian contingent here that lacked discipline. Soldiers in plain black uniforms with no insignia were trying to direct things, he impressed that they seemed to be holding it together, he finding it hard to believe they had ever been able to be properly trained. Then again, there were enough private security companies now to do the job, so anything was possible.

You no longer needed military service to experience boot camp or live fire exercises.

He stepped back inside, glancing at his brightly colored team. "Fashion show's over, boys."

He reached down and pulled his track pants off revealing black fatigues. Tossing the ball cap to the side, he removed his jacket, the black t-shirt underneath more appropriate for the situation. Reaching into his backpack, he stuffed three mags in his pockets, his phone, and a knife. He pointed at Niner. "Make sure you take a couple of charges. Give one to Atlas."

Niner nodded, handing a charge to the big man who pocketed it.

"Ready?"

The team nodded.

"Then let's do this."

"I've got signals again!"

Leroux looked up at the display, Child's announcement turning all heads as six signals suddenly appeared, clustered together with no other heat signatures in their immediate vicinity.

"They're alive!" cheered Sonya, her elation shared by Leroux who had been they were caught in one of the explosions or shot deep in the underbelly of the castle.

He pointed at Child. "Notify Acton."

"What the hell are they doing?"

Leroux stared at the screen. "What?"

Child pointed at the screen. "They're a couple of hundred feet, tops, from the main gate, but they're heading deeper into the complex."

Leroux took in the display, there still over one hundred targets displayed, mostly clustered around the main gate and in the courtyard. The numbers dwindled however in the direction the team was heading. He pointed. "They're heading for the rear entrance. That has to be it."

Child leaned back, grabbing at his hair. "They need to get outside those walls. If they stay inside, there's no one that can help them."

"What's the ETA on the locals?"

"Emergency teams are responding," replied Therrien. "ETA two minutes." He snapped his fingers, pointing at one of the displays. "First footage is going live from the locals."

"Push it. I want every dummy Twitter and Facebook account sharing that. I want #italyattack trending before the hour's out."

"Yes, boss." Therrien's fingers were flying over the keyboard as automated routines manipulated social media in ways only governments could. With thousands upon thousands of dummy Twitter accounts at his disposal, each retweeting each other's messages, each followed by thousands of lemmings who accepted and reciprocated every Follow request, the videos would be in the feeds of millions of people within minutes.

And carnage always got retweeted.

The word would be out, which meant the secret would be out.

Sort of.

Who actually occupied the castle, and what they actually were doing there, nobody would probably ever know.

But everyone would know by the end of the day that the castle existed.

And it had been blown up.

By six red pulsing dots, racing along the side of the courtyard.

Hofmeister rushed over to the command car, the military commander of the facility climbing in. Hofmeister tapped on the window and it rolled down. Commandant Richter leaned toward the window, his expression one of stoic resolve, a man resigned to the fact he would probably be executed before the day's end.

"Who is responsible for this?"

Hofmeister hesitated, though for only a moment. "Professor Acton is claiming responsibility."

"I want him dead."

Hofmeister nodded. "I agree, but there are other considerations."

"Such as?"

"If this one man can do this, rescue his parents and stop the kidnapping of his friends, he is far more connected than we ever realized. Killing him may just make him a martyr."

Richter nodded slowly, his gaze taking in the devastation around them. We'll discuss this at the rally point." He glared at Hofmeister. "Untersturmführer." He motioned to the driver and the car peeled away, leaving Hofmeister to stand there as the realization he had just been demoted set in.

He searched for his assigned car and spotted it. Heading for the idling vehicle, he noticed half a dozen men, all in black with bright white sneakers, heading deeper into the courtyard, in the opposite direction of everyone else.

It must be them!

Rage filled his belly and he pulled his weapon.

Blending in wasn't an option. Though they were mostly in black, Dawson knew they would stand out like sore thumbs, and going one at a time simply wasn't an option—half the complex was about to collapse when the third and final set of explosives took out most of where they were standing.

Gunshots behind him, accompanied by shouting, had him lean into his sprint a little harder, taking a beeline for a collapsed wall as bullets tore into the cobblestone next to him.

He dove.

His knee protested as he slammed into rubble on the other side, the rest of the team leaping over, grunts from most of them, the stone unforgiving. Multiple weapons were firing at them now, more shouts as their opposition grew. He popped up and fired several rounds, quickly assessing the situation before dropping back down.

"Dozen hostiles, fifty yards out, no cover. How long before the next detonation?"

"Less than sixty seconds," replied Jagger.

"Are we safe here?" asked Niner as he fired off several rounds, someone crying out in pain.

Jagger shrugged. "Hopefully."

"You should become a motivational speaker if you ever leave the army." Niner emptied his mag. "I know I feel a lot better now."

"Glad I could help. Thirty seconds."

The ground shook, a rumble coming from below them, Dawson immediately not liking the feeling. "Oh shit!"

"Thirty seconds my ass!" shouted Niner as they all jumped up, sprinting for the rear entrance, the bullets no longer their concern.

Hofmeister marched forward, flanked by half a dozen guards on either side, continually firing at the enemy position, paying no attention to the fact his men were in the open being gun down.

So was he.

And it didn't matter.

He would be blamed.

He wouldn't see tomorrow.

And if he was going to die, then so were those responsible.

Acton had proven he was untouchable, he just hoped the executive realized that. Mengele was a genius like his adoptive father, and he was certain he would. Their adversary had played the game brilliantly. He had tricked them into thinking he was an average professor, then proven himself anything but, his resources beyond anything one could imagine.

Yet more importantly, he had understood what was truly going on, and how to remove himself from the game.

Remove the leverage he had over them.

This castle was lost. No member of the Congress would ever set foot inside again. Their cause would go on, just in a different location, a location that had been prepared decades ago, a location already staffed and ready to receive them in just such an event.

By tomorrow, the research would be underway again, and their mission would continue, these events forgotten.

And Professor James Acton would continue on with his life, he no longer knowing where they were.

He no longer a threat.

Well played, Professor. Well, played.

The ground shook beneath him and he stopped, the gunfire from both sides halting as he tried to steady himself. Their enemy rose, turning tail and fleeing like the cowards they were, but he had to wonder why.

They're in the blast radius!

He turned to his left, sprinting toward the few remaining vehicles, his car still waiting for him, no one daring take it. A shockwave rippled through the ground, knocking him off his feet as all the cobblestones around him seemed to lift several centimeters, as if a great stone had been dropped in a pond. He rolled and gasped in horror as the entire residential block collapsed into the ground, taking half the courtyard with it.

Including his men.

Dawson took cover as Niner blasted the lock on the rear entrance, Atlas pulling it open, Spock and Jimmy rushing through, weapons in front as they made sure the other side was clear.

"Clear!" echoed the two men and Dawson slapped Jagger on the back, the operator rushing through after Atlas and Niner.

"Halt!"

Dawson spun toward the sound, firing two quick shots then two more, two guards dropping before they could get off a shot. They had appeared dazed, as if they had been caught in the explosion and not expecting to find anyone, let alone their enemy.

He kept his weapon raised as he retreated backward, Niner with a hand on his back, guiding his blind exit.

Through the door, he swung it shut. The lock was blown but it would at least force anyone to reveal they were coming should it open again. He glanced over his shoulder and saw Spock blasting the padlock off the fence, throwing the gate open.

"Okay, let's get out of here, dump everything."

Sirens sounded all around them as they sprinted along the path behind the castle, coming around the bend that led down the southern side where they had made their entrance. Dawson tossed his backpack, knife and other paraphernalia, leaving his gun until last, just in case they ran into some hostiles.

He motioned for Spock to take point as they reached the road that ran in front of the castle, dozens of onlookers and emergency personnel swarming the area.

Spock rushed up to the first police officer he saw and pointed at the castle, shouting in perfect Italian. "Terrorists are attacking the castle!"

The crowd panicked, turning en masse and running in the opposite direction, joined by six Delta operators, making their clean escape.

Hofmeister hauled the driver out of his car, pointing at one of the remaining transport trucks. "Go with them!" The man stood there for a moment, bug-eyed, then sprinted toward the truck as it began to pull away. Hofmeister put the car in gear and hammered on the gas, dashing ahead of the truck and racing toward the main gates.

Clearing the now unmanned gates, he barreled down the twisting road, coming out to the municipal road where emergency vehicles were still arriving, the police blocking traffic, giving the evacuees a clear path away from the chaos.

And allowing them all to escape, unfettered.

Hofmeister smiled slightly as he drove deeper into the town, heading for the highway that would lead him out of the area and to his designated rendezvous point about three hours away. Their cover had been perfect. Perfect for over seventy years, it never occurring to the Italian authorities who actually lived there what they were actually doing.

And when they were done sifting through the debris, they'd know little more.

Little paperwork was kept, and what was, had been destroyed. All their digital data was wiped, their backups off site. Their equipment was legal and there would be no indication of what had been going on there. Their experiments had been sterilized with extreme heat, nothing but ashes left of anyone—or anything—the outside world wasn't prepared to hear about.

And as for the trappings of Nazism, only two flags were present in the entire complex, those at the head of the table the executive met around, along with a portrait of Adolf Hitler.

And those would have been taken the moment the alarm sounded.

No one would ever know the storied seventy years of history that had occurred right under their noses.

A history about to end for him.

He slowed, making the turn onto the winding mountain road that led to the highway. When he reached the end, he could literally go left or right. Left would take him toward his rendezvous, right to a new life, a life that he might be able to enjoy for decades to come.

As a traitor.

He took a deep breath and shook his head.

No! I'm a soldier of the Fourth Reich. If I must die as an example to others that failure is not to be tolerated, then so be it!

He closed his eyes for a brief second, gripping the steering wheel.

Then I am to die.

"That's him!"

Reading stared at the laptop showing the images of the cars as they exited the castle, their camera still snapping photos. Acton leapt to his feet as Reading enlarged the photo, there no doubt that the man behind the wheel was the man from Rome.

Alive and well, escaping justice.

Acton grabbed the keys from the counter before Verde could stop him.

"We can't let him get away!" Acton rushed out the hotel room door and toward the stairwell.

"James, wait!"

He glanced back to see Laura running after him, Reading and Verde behind her. She wasn't as quick on her feet as she used to be, and he wanted to slow down for her, but there was no time.

"I'll meet you at the car!"

He slammed through the doors to the stairwell and took the steps two at a time, bursting through the doors and into the small lobby, shocked guests staring in his direction. He pushed through the doors and out onto the street, pressing the button on the fob, the Dacia's lights flashing as the doors unlocked. Yanking open the door, he jumped inside and fired up the engine, rolling the window down, urging the others to hurry as they finally emerged from the hotel.

As they piled into the car, he activated the built-in GPS, a map of the city appearing, then floored it when the last door slammed shut. He turned left, there no choice, the police funneling everyone in that direction, which meant the man responsible for all this had the same lone option.

He glanced at Reading.

"Where would he be heading?"

Reading looked at the GPS. "He'd be leaving town." He scrolled the display and pointed. "Keep going straight. I'll tell you when to turn left. That road will take us down to the highway. At that point we have no way of knowing where he went." Reading twisted in his seat, looking at Verde. "Can you see if your guys have any eyes on him?"

Verde nodded, immediately dialing, Acton laying on his horn as he blasted through the quiet town, passing the few vehicles, everyone holding on for dear life as the driving lessons Laura's ex-SAS security team had taught him, paid off. Reading, a seasoned veteran of the police force, was checking right, calling out when it was clear and when it wasn't, Acton paying attention to the left.

They were making incredible time.

"Is that him?" he asked, a car at the bottom of the hill they were on turning left.

Reading nodded. "Same type of car, could be."

Acton hammered on the brakes, cranking the wheel hard, the traction control helping him hold the turn as he steered them onto the same road as the man responsible for so much misery over the past few days. He floored it, the car leaping forward, quickly gaining on the obviously unsuspecting target when he saw the man's brake lights come on, speed quickly being trimmed.

He hit his own brakes, not sure what was coming around the blind curve, and his jaw dropped as he rounded it, pushing the brakes to the floor. Ahead, a row of men on either side of the road, all in dark brown robes, hoods over their heads, were firing on the car ahead of them.

"Jesus Christ!" exclaimed Acton as they came to a halt only inches from the bumper of the car they were pursuing. The car was stopped, all its tires flattened from the bullets, its driver apparently unscathed, his arms raised.

Two of the monks—for that's what they appeared to Acton to be—rushed forward, one smashing the driver side window then unlocking the door. They hauled the blonde man out and onto the pavement, quickly disarming him. The remaining monks redeployed, half moving farther down the road, half moving toward where Acton had just come, bringing traffic to a halt in each direction, just out of sight of the action.

One of the two holding the blonde man motioned for Acton to get out of the car. Acton nodded, opening his door.

"Are you sure?" asked Laura, reaching forward and grabbing his shoulder.

Acton nodded, looking back at her. "This ends here, one way or the other."

She pursed her lips, nodding. "Okay. Be careful."

Reading opened his door and climbed out as Acton did. Acton looked at him, about to tell him to get back inside, when Reading gave him a look. "Don't even think about it."

Acton nodded, walking over to the two men.

"Professor James Acton?"

He nodded.

The man, his face cloaked by the hood of his robe, pointed to their prisoner. "He is yours to do with as you please." He turned to walk away when Acton held out his hand.

"Wait! Who are you?"

The man turned back to face him then reached up, opening his robe at the top, revealing some of the tattoo Acton had come to know far too well.

"Why are you helping us?"

The man shook his head. "Everything will be explained later."

He turned and walked farther down the hill with the other, the blonde man on his knees, looking up at them.

"We meet again."

The man smiled slightly, then pushed himself to his feet. "Yes, Professor, but you have signed your own death warrant. The, shall we say, administrator, of the castle has ordered your death."

Acton smiled. "And you, of course, will convince him otherwise."

The man smiled broadly, as if amused at Acton's statement. "And why should I do this?"

This was his chance, probably his one chance, to put an end to this. His one piece of knowledge was now useless. He had to convince this man of that so he could convince his superiors.

There was no option for failure.

"You know why. You've seen what I've been able to do. Do you think those who helped me will ever stop if you harm me? You brought this on yourselves when you messed with my family and friends. You wanted to ensure my silence, now you have it. I know *nothing* about you. I have no idea who you are or what you were doing. All I know is that the one piece of information I had, your location, is no longer of importance. My contacts have flooded the Internet and news channels with footage of this castle and what happened here today. Before the day is out, everyone in the civilized world will know the town of Angera and what happened here today." He stepped closer to the man, staring in his eyes. "You *know* you can never return, therefore I have no leverage over you."

He stepped back, pointing up the hill toward the castle, partially visible, dust still rising into the sky. "You've seen the resources at my disposal. Should anything happen to me or anyone I care about, they *will* find you, they *will* kill you, and they *will* expose any secrets you may have." Acton pointed a finger at the man's chest. "Do we have an understanding?"

The man simply stared at him, his face emotionless, before he finally spoke. "I will take your message to our leader."

"Good." Acton pointed at their car, Verde and Laura now standing beside it. "Take it and go."

The blonde man nodded, wasting no time in getting in the car and driving away. Acton stepped to the side of the road, the cars that had been stopped moving again. Laura took his arm. "Do you think it's over?"

Acton shrugged.

"Is it ever?"

Santa Maria delle Concezione de Cappuccini Church, Rome, Italy

Giasson stepped out of the car, Chief Inspector Riva having driven. It hadn't taken long to get here, the drive uneventful, though he had to admit he felt exposed. Now that he knew who the traitor was, he still didn't know the extent of the damage, or how far the infiltration into the Church went.

His longtime friend and confidante, Boileau, sat in the backseat, defeated, saying nothing beyond muttered apologies since they had left for the meeting.

And now they were here, and Giasson wasn't even certain why he had wanted the meeting. What did he hope to accomplish? If the Keepers were truly a two thousand year old organization, what could he possibly hope to do? Ask them to disband? Ask them to leave the Church alone?

Foolish notions.

But he did have questions.

Important questions.

He had received word of what had happened in Angera and he was hopeful that the current crisis might be over, but only for Acton and his family.

Not for him.

He had to protect the Church.

So he had to know what he was facing.

He turned to Riva, then nodded at Boileau. "Stay with him."

"Are you sure?"

Giasson nodded, anything but. "I'll be okay."

He headed into the church, it small by the standards of which he had become accustomed, but was surprised to find it completely empty inside.

313

He spotted the confessional and briskly walked toward it as instructed, his shoulder throbbing with his foolishness. Pushing the curtain aside, he took a seat, the screen immediately sliding open, the lattice preventing him from seeing anything on the other side.

"Inspector General Giasson, it is a pleasure to finally meet you."

Giasson frowned. "You know who I am, who are you?"

"Who I am is no concern of yours. Just know that we are not enemies. We exist to protect the Church, as you do."

Giasson grunted. "You kidnapped a Pope and tried to kill him."

"A false Pope, as you are well aware."

"In your opinion."

"Yes, in our opinion, however that is irrelevant now. Just know that we are always watching, always ready to assist should you need us."

Giasson shook his head at the gall this man was displaying. "I don't see myself ever taking you up on that offer."

"Indeed. I too hope it never becomes necessary as well, however should you need our help, simply ask Brother Gerard."

Giasson wasn't sure the man had understood his point. "Monsieur Boileau won't be working at the Vatican before the day is out."

"Is that a wise choice? He is a good man, and until today, a good friend to you. His loyalty is as yours is, to the Church. He never betrayed that trust. You cannot blame him for the actions of others."

And now was Giasson's opportunity hopefully to get an answer to the question that all of them had been dying to know. "Who were these others?"

"Nazis."

Giasson's eyebrows popped, though he wasn't sure he was actually surprised. "Nazis?"

"Yes. They call themselves the Congress. They were created at the end of the Second World War, their mission to create the Fourth Reich."

Giasson shook his head. "Ridiculous."

"Don't be so quick to dismiss their plans. They were able to influence several members of our order to betray their oath and help them in retrieving several religious artifacts."

"For what purpose?"

"Those that betrayed us believe the chaos in the world today can only be solved by ironfisted rule, and when they learned of the existence of the Congress, they reached out to them, believing that the Fourth Reich is the best way to achieve peace. The one I interrogated just this morning told me he felt that only a modern group of Europeans, willing to exterminate entire races and religions, could bring order, and eventually peace."

"That's madness!"

"Indeed. Unfortunately, frustration runs deep in our order, the leaders of Christian nations too often apologists for the enemies of the Church. The Congress offered an alliance to our members, promising to give the Roman Catholic Church exclusive dominion over men's souls in the new Fourth Reich."

"I would think that would go against the very teachings of the Church."

"Of course it does. Unlike one religion one cannot name without being labelled, Christianity has no imperative to rule the world, despite what some of our believers may have preached centuries ago. We simply want to live in peace, and guide those who choose to believe as we do." There was a sigh from the other side of the screen. "Unfortunately, several of our order disagree."

Giasson winced as a jolt of pain raced up his shoulder and into his chest. "And how does this Congress hope to achieve their goals?"

"Using modern medicine, they intend to perfect the genome, to create a true Master Race, then clone an army that will conquer the world."

Giasson laughed. "Ridiculous."

"Actually, not at all. The cloning can be done today, and with recent breakthroughs, modifying the actual genome is now possible."

"Really?"

There was a chuckle from the other side. "Inspector General, you must lift your nose from your security reports sometimes, and see what is going on in the world around you."

Giasson closed his eyes, nodding slightly. His job was so all consuming he was continually reading threat assessments and the bad news of the day, rather than things like medical breakthroughs that could truly affect the world. "Perhaps I should." He twigged on something. "When the portrait was stolen, the man said that it was the property of the Führer. What did he mean?"

"Ahh, that is the most fantastic part of their plan. They have DNA from Hitler himself, carefully preserved. They intend to clone him when the science is perfected."

"What good would that do?"

"I'm not finished. They then intend to use the religious artifacts they've been gathering for almost a century, to bring back his soul to occupy the clone, thus restoring him to life."

Giasson shook his head, laughing. "That is *absolutely* ridiculous."

"I agree, but never doubt someone's capacity to believe when they have faith. The technology exists for them to accomplish at least part of their task. Do I believe for one second that they might achieve what they hope to accomplish in bringing the greatest butcher ever known to man back to life?" A sigh. "I fear I do, for it would truly be the work of Satan, and I and my order have seen enough over our two millennia to know that evil does exist in this world."

Giasson chewed his cheek, contemplating the man's words. "I of course believe in evil, but I also believe in good, and I cannot believe that God would allow such an abomination to take place."

"I too pray that he wouldn't. However, would it matter? Imagine, should they clone him successfully, and teach him everything he needed to know to pass himself off as the reincarnation of Hitler, would it be enough to rally a group of people, with a genetically superior clone army at their side, to take back what they think they have lost, then ensure it is never lost again? What would happen should such a man come to power again, especially when facing weak-willed nations? There was a final solution before. Imagine one that extends far beyond just the Jewish people. Their goal would be the purification of Europe, then the world. Something that must not be allowed to happen."

Giasson's mind was reeling as he listened to the man in the shadows. He knew enough to know that cloning and genetic manipulation was happening, and that everything except for the ridiculous notion of reincarnation was possible. And the man was right. There had been false prophets before, and should a man arrive who looked and sounded and acted like the leader you were expecting to return, he could indeed see him quickly gaining followers.

Hitler had been democratically elected, a fact that so many had forgotten, and it was in a Germany and a world beset by the Great Depression, where people were desperate, their way of life being destroyed. With economies struggling around the world, Western nations being flooded with refugees and immigrants who shared nothing in common with them, could another collapse be far away?

And if it were to pass, could a man rise once again from the ashes, offering a solution to their problems that today they may find abhorrent, but tomorrow the only terrible answer?

"How can we stop them?"

"For the moment, we can't. We have stopped their infiltration into our order for now, but it may happen again. All we can hope is that when the time comes, for it will come, that humanity has learned enough to know that hatred and prejudice is not the way to resolve our differences. I fear, however, that a price will be paid, a heavy price, before the coming war is finally won. I trust, sir, that you will be on our side should the time come."

Giasson merely nodded, not sure of what to say, the entire notion terrifyingly outlandish. Then he thought of what was happening in the Middle East today, a massive swath of territory cut out of it by religious zealots, slaughtering people by the thousands, systematically raping women and little girls, while millions in the West condemned the military attempts to stop them. It made no sense to him, and reminded him of his history. What would have happened if the world had stood idly by and let Hitler have his way? Could he have ever been stopped?

And should there be a modern day Hitler, who was smart enough not to disturb those powers capable of stopping him early on, could he ultimately win?

He exhaled, realizing how easily desperate people could be led. In the Middle East, they were being led through fear and dogma, yet in Russia, the people were embracing their leader.

Much like the Germans did so long ago.

"Why did you have the painting?" he finally asked, the last of his questions he had planned to ask, the revelations of the last few minutes he was sure to prompt many more.

"It was entrusted to us during the war. Our man was supposed to return it in 1998, but unbeknownst to us, he instead switched it with a forgery we had commissioned as a decoy. We were unaware of this until his death and your involvement." There was a pause. "Inspector General, our time is done. I want you to know that we are no threat to you, as long as you do not go against the best interests of the Church. We will not meet again."

The screen slid closed with a snap, and Mario jumped up. "Wait!" He shoved aside the curtain, determined to see who this man was, then froze at the sight that greeted him on the other side.

A row of monks, leading from the confessional to the door, their heads bowed, shrouded by their cloaks, a wall of devout flesh leaving him nowhere to go but outside. He sighed, walking past the monks, pushing the door to the outside open, the sunlight blinding him momentarily.

He stood on the steps and stared at the crowds passing by. White, black, Muslim, Christian, all going about their daily business, some happy, some sad, all oblivious to the threat they might now face. The idea of a clone army or a resurrected Hitler were simply too fantastic for him to even contemplate, though the notion that there were still groups out there with these insane ideas thought lost to the past, sent a chill rushing through him.

If the events happening around the world, from Russia returning to its old ways, to ISIS establishing its own country, were any indication of humanity's future, he wasn't optimistic.

He reached up and clasped his crucifix in his hand, closing his eyes, a bible quote coming to mind. "In the sweat of thy face shalt thou eat bread, till thou return unto the ground; for out of it wast thou taken: for dust thou art, and unto dust shalt thou return."

May history, and its villains, remain the dust they now are.

Leaving Malpensa International Airport, Italy

Acton leaned back in the leather chair, closing his eyes as the seat wrapped itself around him, their jet lifting off from the ground. It was a more boisterous ride this time, Bravo Team joining them for the return. Giasson had already called, filling them in on what had happened with his end of things, and with details on who these people were that they had gone up against.

The seatbelt light chimed and seatbelts were popped off, everyone congregating around two meeting tables, the conversation continuing about what Giasson had told them.

"So, Doc, you're the smart one, what do you think?" asked Niner.

Acton smiled. "Well, cloning has been around for years, but human cloning has been banned. That's not to say there aren't people out there working toward it, or possibly even doing it. That being said, I think it's just a matter of time before you'd be able to take someone's DNA and clone them with no problem."

Niner sighed. "Imagine, a whole bunch of little Niners running around."

"Goddamned nightmarish world, if you ask me," rumbled Atlas.

"Sounds like Star Wars to me," said Jimmy. "Clone armies, I mean."

Acton nodded. "Definitely sounds like science fiction. The thing about science fiction, though, is it has a nasty habit of becoming science fact, whether we like it or not, like their idea of creating the perfect soldier."

"Yeah, I was wondering about that," said Spock, taking a sip from a water bottle. "How would that work?"

"Well, you've all heard of the work being done to cure genetic diseases. Basically, they try to 'fix' the faulty gene through gene therapy techniques, and if they succeed, the person is essentially cured. We're going to see huge numbers of these therapies over the coming years as the techniques are perfected."

"So it *is* possible?" asked Niner. "Not sure I like the sound of that."

"I'm sure there's a few defects in you they could fix," said Jagger. "Like that mouth of yours."

"And your lips."

Jagger shoved his out even farther. "What you talkin' about?"

"Just to get back to what I was saying, that's *fixing* defective genes, which I think most people don't have a problem with. Where it gets dicey is when you try to manipulate the genome to alter it from its original intention. And that's what this Congress is trying to do. To create a perfect soldier, you're not fixing defects, you're changing the very fabric of what it means to be human."

Niner whistled. "Please tell me *that's* not possible."

Acton raised his eyebrows, tilting his head for a moment. "Unfortunately, it is. At least, *now* it is. The Chinese announced just recently that they had broken the germ line. Essentially what that means is they've been able to manipulate the genome to actually change it." He noted the confused looks. "Okay, imagine this. You have a genetic defect, you correct it, so that person now has the genes they were meant to have all along. They have a baby, their DNA goes into the mix and voila, perfectly normal baby pops out with the genome you're expecting. Homo Sapiens. Because you didn't *change* anything from what it was supposed to be.

"But this new breakthrough allows scientists to actually *change* the DNA from what it is *supposed* to be, to something *new*, and when that person passes on their new DNA, their offspring will have it as well. You essentially create a new species, and you have no idea what the end result might be."

"Jesus," muttered Dawson. "They can do that?"

Acton nodded. "It's illegal research in most of the civilized world, but not in China. They've done it, and they're moving forward. For what purpose is anyone's guess."

"And this is public knowledge?" asked Jimmy.

Acton nodded.

"Which means the Congress now knows," said Laura, the fear clear in her voice. She looked at her husband. "Do you really think they could do this?"

Acton shrugged. "Not today, but a year from now, ten years from now? This is definitely going to be a problem, whether it's from nutbars creating clone armies, or parents trying to create the perfect baby, the future is here, and we've got to get ready for it."

The burner phone Reading had bought rang, Acton holding it in his hand. He held up his finger and everyone became quiet.

"Hello?"

"Professor Acton?"

"Yes."

"We have an agreement."

THE END

ACKNOWLEDGEMENTS

The idea for this story came when I stumbled upon an article describing the very science mentioned in this novel. As stated in the Preface, the science is real, though let's hope there isn't some group of crazed zealots out there trying to recreate a madman with a minion army to rule the world.

Yet the very fact that this is now possible, does make one wonder how it may be put to use in the future. Will it be banned, with it only being done in countries like China, Russia and North Korea, or in the back alleys of America's great cities, where parents desperately try to give their future child the best hope for an uncertain world, where they will have to compete with all the other children whose parents did the same thing?

This technology is coming, and society will need to figure out how to deal with it.

A couple of notes. The Denny's story? True, but it was *my* family sitting there eating breakfast, and yes, we felt proud when the old couple said what they did. I mean, feeding your kid hash browns off a dirty table? Are you kidding me? Sometimes it does make you wonder if manipulating the genome might not be such a bad thing.

And Niskha's green Froggie? It was mine when I was a child, and it sits on my desk to this day.

A few people to thank. My Dad for all the research again, Ian Davidson for some motorcycle info, and Angela Lee for giving Reading a home. My wife, daughter, family and friends, I again thank you.

To those who have not already done so, please visit my website at www.jrobertkennedy.com then sign up for the Insider's Club to be notified of new book releases. Your email address will never be shared or sold and you'll only receive the occasional email from me as I don't have time to spam you!

Thank you once again for reading.

ABOUT THE AUTHOR

USA Today bestselling author J. Robert Kennedy has written over twenty international bestsellers including the smash hit James Acton Thrillers series, the first installment of which, The Protocol, has been on the bestsellers list since its release, including a three month run at number one. In addition to the other novels from this series including The Templar's Relic, a USA Today and Barnes & Noble #1 overall bestseller, he writes the bestselling Special Agent Dylan Kane Thrillers, Delta Force Unleashed Thrillers and Detective Shakespeare Mysteries. Robert lives with his wife and daughter and writes full-time.

Visit Robert's website at www.jrobertkennedy.com for the latest news and contact information, and to join the Insider's Club to be notified when new books are released.

Available James Acton Thrillers

The Protocol (Book #1)

For two thousand years the Triarii have protected us, influencing history from the crusades to the discovery of America. Descendent from the Roman Empire, they pervade every level of society, and are now in a race with our own government to retrieve an ancient artifact thought to have been lost forever.

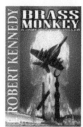

Brass Monkey (Book #2)

A nuclear missile, lost during the Cold War, is now in play--the most public spy swap in history, with a gorgeous agent the center of international attention, triggers the end-game of a corrupt Soviet Colonel's twenty five year plan. Pursued across the globe by the Russian authorities, including a brutal Spetsnaz unit, those involved will stop at nothing to deliver their weapon, and ensure their payday, regardless of the terrifying consequences.

Broken Dove (Book #3)

With the Triarii in control of the Roman Catholic Church, an organization founded by Saint Peter himself takes action, murdering one of the new Pope's operatives. Detective Chaney, called in by the Pope to investigate, disappears, and, to the horror of the Papal staff sent to inform His Holiness, they find him missing too, the only clue a secret chest, presented to each new pope on the eve of their election, since the beginning of the Church.

The Templar's Relic (Book #4)

The Vault must be sealed, but a construction accident leads to a miraculous discovery--an ancient tomb containing four Templar Knights, long forgotten, on the grounds of the Vatican. Not knowing who they can trust, the Vatican requests Professors James Acton and Laura Palmer examine the find, but what they discover, a precious Islamic relic, lost during the Crusades, triggers a set of events that shake the entire world, pitting the two greatest religions against each other. At risk is nothing less than the Vatican itself, and the rock upon which it was built.

Flags of Sin (Book #5)

Archaeology Professor James Acton simply wants to get away from everything, and relax. A trip to China seems just the answer, and he and his fiancée, Professor Laura Palmer, are soon on a flight to Beijing. But while boarding, they bump into an old friend, Delta Force Command Sergeant Major Burt Dawson, who surreptitiously delivers a message that they must meet the next day, for Dawson knows something they don't. China is about to erupt into chaos.

The Arab Fall (Book #6)

An accidental find by a friend of Professor James Acton may lead to the greatest archaeological discovery since the tomb of King Tutankhamen, perhaps even greater. And when news of it spreads, it reaches the ears of a group hell-bent on the destruction of all idols and icons, their mere existence considered blasphemous to Islam.

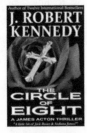

The Circle of Eight (Book #7)

The Bravo Team is targeted by a madman after one of their own intervenes in a rape. Little do they know this internationally well-respected banker is also a senior member of an organization long thought extinct, whose stated goals for a reshaped world are not only terrifying, but with today's globalization, totally achievable.

The Venice Code (Book #8)

A former President's son is kidnapped in a brazen attack on the streets of Potomac by the very ancient organization that murdered his father, convinced he knows the location of an item stolen from them by the late president.

A close friend awakes from a coma with a message for archeology Professor James Acton from the same organization, sending him along with his fiancée Professor Laura Palmer on a quest to find an object only rumored to exist, while trying desperately to keep one step ahead of a foe hell-bent on possessing it.

Pompeii's Ghosts (Book #9)

Two thousand years ago Roman Emperor Vespasian tries to preserve an empire by hiding a massive treasure in the quiet town of Pompeii should someone challenge his throne. Unbeknownst to him nature is about to unleash its wrath upon the Empire during which the best and worst of Rome's citizens will be revealed during a time when duty and honor were more than words, they were ideals worth dying for.

Amazon Burning (Book #10)

Days from any form of modern civilization, archeology Professor James Acton awakes to gunshots. Finding his wife missing, taken by a member of one of the uncontacted tribes, he and his friend INTERPOL Special Agent Hugh Reading try desperately to find her in the dark of the jungle, but quickly realize there is no hope without help. And with help three days away, he knows the longer they wait, the farther away she'll be.

The Riddle (Book #11)

Russia accuses the United States of assassinating their Prime Minister in Hanoi, naming Delta Force member Sergeant Carl "Niner" Sung as the assassin. Professors James Acton and Laura Palmer, witnesses to the murder, know the truth, and as the Russians and Vietnamese attempt to use the situation to their advantage on the international stage, the husband and wife duo attempt to find proof that their friend is innocent.

Blood Relics (Book #12)

A DYING MAN. A DESPERATE SON.
ONLY A MIRACLE CAN SAVE THEM BOTH.

Professor Laura Palmer is shot and kidnapped in front of her husband, archeology Professor James Acton, as they try to prevent the theft of the world's Blood Relics, ancient artifacts thought to contain the blood of Christ, a madman determined to possess them all at any cost.

Sins of the Titanic (Book #13)

THE ASSEMBLY IS ETERNAL.

AND THEY'LL STOP AT NOTHING TO KEEP IT THAT WAY.

When Professor James Acton is contacted about a painting thought to have been lost with the sinking of the Titanic, he is inadvertently drawn into a century old conspiracy an ancient organization known as The Assembly will stop at nothing to keep secret.

Saint Peter's Soldiers (Book #14)

A MISSING DA VINCI.

A TERRIFYING GENETIC BREAKTHROUGH.

A PAST AND FUTURE ABOUT TO COLLIDE!

In World War Two a fabled da Vinci drawing is hidden from the Nazis, those involved fearing Hitler may attempt to steal it for its purported magical powers. It isn't returned for over fifty years.

And today, archeology Professor James Acton and his wife are about to be dragged into the terrible truth of what happened so many years ago, for the truth is never what it seems, and the history we thought was fact, is all lies.

Available Special Agent Dylan Kane Thrillers

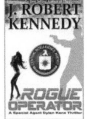

Rogue Operator (Book #1)

Three top secret research scientists are presumed dead in a boating accident, but the kidnapping of their families the same day raises questions the FBI and local police can't answer, leaving them waiting for a ransom demand that will never come. Central Intelligence Agency Analyst Chris Leroux stumbles upon the story, and finds a phone conversation that was never supposed to happen but is told to leave it to the FBI. But he can't let it go. For he knows something the FBI doesn't. One of the scientists is alive.

Containment Failure (Book #2)

New Orleans has been quarantined, an unknown virus sweeping the city, killing one hundred percent of those infected. The Centers for Disease Control, desperate to find a cure, is approached by BioDyne Pharma who reveal a former employee has turned a cutting edge medical treatment capable of targeting specific genetic sequences into a weapon, and released it. The stakes have never been higher as Kane battles to save not only his friends and the country he loves, but all of mankind.

Cold Warriors (Book #3)

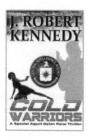

While in Chechnya CIA Special Agent Dylan Kane stumbles upon a meeting between a known Chechen drug lord and a retired General once responsible for the entire Soviet nuclear arsenal. Money is exchanged for a data stick and the resulting transmission begins a race across the globe to discover just what was sold, the only clue a reference to a top secret Soviet weapon called Crimson Rush.

Death to America (Book #4)

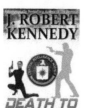

America is in crisis. Dozens of terrorist attacks have killed or injured thousands, and worse, every single attack appears to have been committed by an American citizen in the name of Islam.

A stolen experimental F-35 Lightning II is discovered by CIA Special Agent Dylan Kane in China, delivered by an American soldier reported dead years ago in exchange for a chilling promise.

And Chris Leroux is forced to watch as his girlfriend, Sherrie White, is tortured on camera, under orders to not interfere, her continued suffering providing intel too valuable to sacrifice.

Available Delta Force Unleashed Thrillers

Payback (Book #1)

The daughter of the Vice President is kidnapped from an Ebola clinic, triggering an all-out effort to retrieve her by America's elite Delta Force just hours after a senior government official from Sierra Leone is assassinated in a horrific terrorist attack while visiting the United States. As she battles impossible odds and struggles to prove her worth to her captors who have promised she will die, she's forced to make unthinkable decisions to not only try to save her own life, but those dying from one of the most vicious diseases known to mankind, all in the hopes an unleashed Delta Force can save her before her captors enact their horrific plan on an unsuspecting United States.

Infidels (Book #2)

When the elite Delta Force's Bravo Team is inserted into Yemen to rescue a kidnapped Saudi prince, they find more than they bargained for—a crate containing the Black Stone, stolen from Mecca the day before. Requesting instructions on how to proceed, they find themselves cut off and disavowed, left to survive with nothing but each other to rely upon.

The Lazarus Moment (Book #3)

AIR FORCE ONE IS DOWN

BUT THEIR FIGHT TO SURVIVE HAS ONLY JUST BEGUN!

When Air Force One crashes in the jungles of Africa, it is up to America's elite Delta Force to save the survivors not only from rebels hell-bent on capturing the President, but Mother Nature herself.

Available Detective Shakespeare Mysteries

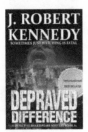

Depraved Difference (Book #1)

SOMETIMES JUST WATCHING IS FATAL

When a young woman is brutally assaulted by two men on the subway, her cries for help fall on the deaf ears of onlookers too terrified to get involved, her misery ended with the crushing stomp of a steel-toed boot. A cellphone video of her vicious murder, callously released on the Internet, its popularity a testament to today's depraved society, serves as a trigger, pulled a year later, for a killer.

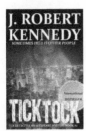

Tick Tock (Book #2)

SOMETIMES HELL IS OTHER PEOPLE

Crime Scene tech Frank Brata digs deep and finds the courage to ask his colleague, Sarah, out for coffee after work. Their good time turns into a nightmare when Frank wakes up the next morning covered in blood, with no recollection of what happened, and Sarah's body floating in the tub.

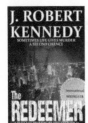

The Redeemer (Book #3)

SOMETIMES LIFE GIVES MURDER A SECOND CHANCE

It was the case that destroyed Detective Justin Shakespeare's career, beginning a downward spiral of self-loathing and self-destruction lasting half a decade. And today things are only going to get worse. The Widow Rapist is free on a technicality, and it is up to Detective Shakespeare and his partner Amber Trace to find the evidence, five years cold, to put him back in prison before he strikes again.

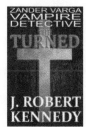

The Turned: Zander Varga, Vampire Detective, Book #1

Zander has relived his wife's death at the hands of vampires every day for almost three hundred years, his perfect memory a curse of becoming one of The Turned—infecting him their final heinous act after her murder.

Nineteen year-old Sydney Winter knows Zander's secret, a secret preserved by the women in her family for four generations. But with her mother in a coma, she's thrust into the front lines, ahead of her time, to fight side-by-side with Zander.

Printed in the USA
CPSIA information can be obtained
at www.ICGtesting.com
LVHW012136290824
789700LV00028B/170